H.C. McNeil

Mufti

H.C. Mcneile

Mufti

1st Edition | ISBN: 978-3-75241-193-5

Place of Publication: Frankfurt am Main, Germany

Year of Publication: 2020

Outlook Verlag GmbH, Germany.

Reproduction of the original.

MUFTI

by

HERMAN CYRIL McNEILE

PROLOGUE

I

The officer lying back in the home-made chair tilted the peak of his cap over his eyes and let his book slip gently to the ground. A few moments later, after various unavailing waves of the hand, he pulled out a handkerchief of striking design and carefully adjusted it over his face. Then, with his hands dug deep in his pockets to remove even a square inch of skin from the ubiquitous fly, he prepared to slumber. And shortly afterwards a gentle rise and fall of the centre bulldog, so wonderfully portrayed on the bandana, announced that he had succeeded.

To anyone fresh from England who desired to see War the scene would have been disappointing. There were no signs of troops swinging down a road, singing blithely, with a cheery smile of confidence on their faces and demanding to be led back forthwith to battle with the Huns. There were no guns belching forth: the grim Panoply of War, whatever it may mean, was conspicuous by its absence. Only a very fat quartermaster-sergeant lay asleep in the sun and snored, while an ancient and dissolute old warrior, near by, was engaged in clearing out a drain as part of his Field Punishment, and had just discovered a dead dog in it. He was not singing blithely: he had no cheery smile of confidence on his face: he was just talking—gently to himself.

The field was on a slight ridge. Above the camp there floated one of a line of sausage balloons, and the cable to which it was attached stretched up taut from some point near the farmhouse behind. A triangular flag, like a burgee, flew straight out in the breeze from half-way up the cable, and the basket, looking absurdly small, hung down like a black dot below the balloon.

Peace was the keynote of the whole situation. In front the country lay stretched out, with its hedges and trees, its fields and farmhouses. In certain places there ran long rows of poles with strips of brown material stretched between them, which a spectator would rightly conclude was camouflage erected to screen the roads. Only from what? Where was the Boche in this atmosphere of sleep and quiet?

Beyond the silent countryside rose a line of hills. They seemed to start and finish abruptly—an excrescence in the all-pervading flatness. On the top of the near end of the line, clear cut against the sky, the tower and spires of a great building; at the far end, on a hill separated—almost isolated—from the main ridge, a line of stumps, gaunt tooth-pick stumps standing stiffly in a row. There was no sign of life on the hills, no sign of movement. They were dead and cold even in the warm glow of the afternoon sun. Especially the isolated one at the far end with its row of sentinel trees. There was something ghostly about it—something furtive.

And then suddenly a great column of yellow smoke rose slowly from its centre and spread like a giant mushroom. Another and another appeared, and the yellow pall rolled down the side twisting and turning, drifting into the air and eddying over the dark, grim slope. Gradually it blotted out that isolated hill, like fog reeking round a mountain top, and as one watched it, fascinated, a series of dull booms came lazily through the air.

"Jerry gettin' it in the neck on Kemmel." Two men passing by were regarding the performance with perfunctory interest, while the purple bulldog still rose and fell, and the dissolute old warrior did not cease talking to himself.

"Derek scooped the bally lot as usual." An officer appeared at the entrance of a tin structure in one corner of the field with a bundle of letters in his hand. "Look at the dirty dog there—sleeping like a hog—in the only decent chair."

He disappeared inside to emerge again in a moment with a badminton racket and a shuttlecock. "On the bulldog—one round rapid fire." He fired and with a loud snort the sleeper awoke.

"You are charged with conduct to the prejudice, etc.," said the marksman severely, "in that you did spread alarm and despondency amongst the troops by disguising yourself as a disease and making noises indicative of pain."

Derek Vane stretched himself and stood up. "We are feeling well, thank you— and require nourishment. Does tea await me, and if not—why not?" He took his mail and glanced through it. "How they love me, dear old boy! What it is to be young and good looking, and charm… ."

There was a loud shout and the deck chair became the centre of a struggling mob. Shortly afterwards a noise of ripping canvas announced that it had acted as deck chairs have acted before when five people sit on them at the same moment.

"Look out, you mugs, you've broken it." Vane's voice came dimly from the ground. "And my face is in an ants' nest."

"Are you good looking and charming?" demanded an inexorable voice.

"No. Get off, Beetle; you've got bones on you like the human skeleton at Barnum's."

3

"What are you like?" pursued the same inexorable voice.

"Horrible," spluttered Vane. "A walking nightmare; a loathly dream."

"It is well—you may arise."

The mass disintegrated, and having plucked the frame of the chair from the body of an officer known to all and sundry as the Tank—for obvious reasons —they moved slowly towards the mess for tea.

In all respects an unwarlike scene, and one which would disappoint the searcher after sensation. Save for the lorries which bumped ceaselessly up and down the long straight road below, and the all-pervading khaki it might have been a scene at home before the war. The yellow fog had cleared away from Kemmel, and over the flat country the heat haze rose, shimmering and dancing in the afternoon sun. In the field next to the camp an ancient Belgian was ploughing, his two big Walloon horses guided by a single cord, while from behind the farm there came the soft thud-thud of a football.

And then it came. In a few seconds the air was filled with the thumping of Archie and the distant crackle of machine-guns.

"By Jove! there he is," cried the Tank. "He's got him too."

The officers halted and stared over the dead town of Poperinghe, where flash after flash of bursting shrapnel proclaimed a Boche aeroplane. They saw him dive at a balloon—falling like a hawk; then suddenly he righted and came on towards the next. From the first sausage two black streaks shot out, to steady after a hundred feet or so, and float down, supported by their white parachutes. But the balloon itself was finished. From one end there glowed for an instant a yellow furnace of fire. Then a flame shot up, followed by clouds of black smoke. Like a stone, the basket crashed down, passing the two white, drifting specks on the way, and leaving behind it a long streak of black.

Rolling from side to side like a drunken man, the aeroplane was coming towards its next quarry. Lewis guns, machine-guns, Archies were now all firing full blast, but the pilot continued on his course. Tracer bullets shot up like lines of light, but so far he had come through untouched. From the balloons the observers dived out until at one moment there were ten in the air. And each balloon in turn followed its owners, a flaming, smoking remnant …

Then came the end—as suddenly as it had begun. A tracer bullet seemed to pass right through the aeroplane. Like a tiny ball of fire the bullet struck it, and then went out. The plane swerved violently, righted and swerved again. Then it spun down, rocking from side to side, while a burst of white flame roared all round it. And, falling a little faster than the plane, two black spots,

4

which did not steady after a hundred feet. They crashed fifty yards from the tin hut, and almost before they reached the ground the officers were on the spot. A little distance away the aeroplane was blazing, and they could feel the heat as they bent over the pilot and his observer. They were both dead, and the pilot was unrecognisable; a bullet had entered the base of his skull from behind. But the observer was not much damaged outwardly. He lay—arms outstretched—looking up at the sky, on the ground that the farmer had just ploughed. He seemed to smile cynically at the hoarse cheering now spreading from field to field, from camp to camp. Perhaps even then he had realised the futility of it all …

For a few seconds Derek Vane looked at him gravely, while close by two excited men from different units argued raucously as to which battalion had brought the aeroplane down.

"I tell yer I saw the ruddy bullet hit the perisher right in the middle," cried one claimant. "It were old Ginger's gun, I tell yer. E's a fair corker is Ginger with a Lewis."

The smile spread till it was almost a grin on the dead man's face. Muscular contraction, of course, but… . With a sudden movement Vane stooped down and covered the face.

"Sergeant-Major." He turned to the N.C.O. beside him. "Armed guard round the plane at once till the Flying Corps arrive. Bring these two bodies into the camp on stretchers."

Five minutes later they sat down to tea and an unopened mail. The farmer had resumed his ploughing—the football enthusiasts their game. Twenty-five Lewis guns and twelve Vickers sections were all composing reports stating that their particular weapon had done the deed, and somebody was putting another fog cloud on Kemmel.

In fact, the only real difference in the scene after those ten short minutes was that by the ruins of a deck chair two German airmen with their faces covered lay very still on stretchers… .

II

Two hours later. Vane handed his steel helmet to his batman and swung himself into the saddle on his old grey mare. There was touch of Arab in her, and she had most enormous feet. But she fulfilled most of the requirements a man looks for in a war horse, which are not of necessity those he requires in a mount with the Grafton. She scorned guns—she repudiated lorries, and he could lay the reins on her neck without her ceasing to function. She frequently fell down when he did so; but—*c'est la guerre*. The shadows were beginning to lengthen as he hacked out of the camp, waving a farewell hand at a badminton four, and headed for Poperinghe.

Poperinghe lay about a mile up the road towards his destination, and Vane had known it at intervals for over three years. He remembered it when it had been shelled in April '15 at the time of the first gas attack, and the inhabitants had fled in all directions. Then gradually it had become normal again, until, after the Passchendaele fighting of 1917, it had excelled itself in gaiety. And now in May 1918 it was dead once more, with every house boarded up and every window shuttered. The big cobbled square; the brooding, silent churches, the single military policeman standing near his sand-bagged sentry-box—and in the distance the rumble of a wagon going past the station—such was Poperinghe as Vane saw it that evening.

A city of ghosts—deserted and empty, and as the old grey mare walked sedately through the square. Vane felt that he understood the dead airman's smile.

Sometimes a random shot would take effect, but the bag was soon removed. That very afternoon a driver with his two horses had been hit direct. The man, or what was left of him, had been removed—only the horses remained, and a red pool coated with grey dust. The mare edged warily around them, and a swarm of flies, bloated, loathsome brutes—buzzed angrily up as she passed.

"It's not fair, old girl," said Vane bending over and patting her neck; "but I s'pose it's only in keeping with everything else these days—it's not fairness that counts; it's just luck—fatuous idiotic luck. It's not even a game; it's a wild-cat gamble all over the world. And may Heaven help us all when the bottom does drop out of the market."

The grey mare ambled placidly on up the main Ypres road undisturbed by his philosophy. The dead of her kind were already forgotten, and the nose-bag on the saddle would be all the better for emptying. On each side of the road were gun positions, and Vane kept a sharp look out as he trotted on. If there was one thing he loathed above all others it was the gunner humorist who, with malice aforethought, deliberately waited to fire his gun until some helpless passer by was about a yard from the muzzle. But at the moment everything seemed quiet. The evening hate was not due yet; and Vane reached Brandhoek cross roads without having his eardrums burst.

On the Decauville track close by stood eight trains, stacked with rows and rows of cylinders, and he contemplated them grimly. Each train was drawn by an ugly-looking petrol electric engine. The whole eight would shortly run at close intervals to the nearest point to the front line. Then Vane, with a large pushing party, could man-handle the trains into the position decided on—a few hundred yards behind the outpost line. And as a method of fighting it struck him as poor.

Whatever may be said about Might and Right, there is an element which must appeal to every normal being in the triumph of strength and hardihood over weakness. It may be wrong; it happens, however, to be natural. But there is nothing whatever to appeal to the average man in the ability of some professor of science, working in his laboratory miles away, to produce a weapon which strikes down alike the strong and the weakling with an agony which makes death a blessed relief. Gas—just a refinement of modern war introduced by the brains of many eminent gentlemen. And it must be in the nature of a personal triumph for them to realise that their exhaustive experiments with guinea pigs and rabbits have caused thousands to fear at first they were going to die, and later to fear still more that they were not.... .

Vane nodded to the gas officer and got on board the little tractor which was to take him to the front trenches.

Chugging along through screen after screen of brown camouflage which hid the little railway line from the watchful gaze of Kemmel, he seemed to be passing through some mysterious land. By day it was hideous enough; but in the dusk the flat dullness of it was transfigured. Each pond with the shadows lying black on its unruffled surface seemed a fairy lake; each gaunt and stunted tree seemed to clothe itself again with rustling leaves. The night was silent; only the rattle of the little train, as it rumbled over bridges which spanned some sluggish brook or with a warning hoot crossed a road—broke the stillness. Great shell-holes filled with rotting debris flashed by, the mouldering ruins of an old château frowned down as they twisted and turned through the grounds where once men had flirted and women had sighed. Now the rose garden was used as a rubbish heap for tins; and by the over-grown sundial, chipped and scarred by a stray shell, two wooden crosses stuck out of the long rank grass. At last they reached the Canal, and the engine stopped near the Lille road.

Close by, the flares lobbed up, green against the night; and a white mist covered the low-lying ground. Across the road lay trees in all directions, while, through the few that remained standing, a cold bright moon threw fantastic shadows. On each side of the road, screened by the embankment from machine-gun fire, sat groups of men waiting for the trains.

At last Vane heard the first one—faintly in the distance. It loomed up suddenly out of the mist and crept across the road. Without a word the men detailed to push it seemed to rise out of the ground. Silently they disappeared with it, like ghouls at some mysterious ceremony. With muffled couplings it made no sound; and in a few minutes it was ready in position, with its leading truck where once the owner of a farm had sat before the fire, after the day's work.

And so they came—eight in all. Any noise—any suspicion on the part of the Boche, a bare quarter of a mile away, and a machine-gun would have swept the ground. But the night was silent, the flares still went peacefully up, and the wind had not changed. It blew gently and steadily towards the German lines. Only there was now just a faint smell of pineapple in the air; one of the cylinders was leaking... .

Figures loomed up unexpectedly out of the mist; occasionally a low curse could be heard as a man stumbled into a shell hole... .

"Everything all right; everybody clear?" The gas expert peered at Vane in the darkness. "Right! well, let her go."

A series of reports sounded deafeningly loud, as the detonators of the cylinders were fired by electricity; a steady, hissing noise as a great wall of white vapour mingled with the mist and rolled forward towards the Germans. The gas attack had begun. To an airman returning from a bombing raid, who circled for a moment above, it looked like a sheet being slowly spread over the country below; a beautiful—an eerie—picture. To those on the ground who watched it, it seemed as a solid wall of dense fog moving relentlessly forward—like the mist that comes creeping over the Downs till those caught in it can scarce see their hand in front of their face. To the Boche it was death... .

Patrols going out the next night found men twisted and blackened with the smell of pineapple still on their swollen lips; in the hospitals behind, men writhed and muttered hoarsely, struggling for breath and struggling in vain. The attack had been successful—and all was as it should be. Undoubtedly the Germans started gas in a country where the prevalent wind was south-west—and it doesn't pay in war to be a fool. ...

Vane wished that one or two German men of science had been occupying the Boche outpost line instead of... . War—modern war!

"It will go clean through their helmets," said the gas expert. "One hour in most cases, and when it gets weaker, twenty-four—or even more. That's the stuff to give 'em."

At last the performance was over, and the trains having delivered the goods returned to their own place.

"Most successful." The gas expert, rubbing his hands together, came up to Vane as he stood on the Lille road. "I think we've got quite a number of the blighters. And not a single casualty!"

"Good," said Vane. "But what a filthy method of fighting."

"The Germans started it," returned the other.

"I know they did," laughed Vane. "That's probably why it's so filthy."

The gas officer looked thoughtful. "I'm not certain that I agree with you, Vane. War is such a filthy business, however you look at it, that one would be a fool not to harness science in every possible way ..."

"Don't you believe it," scoffed Vane. "Science has harnessed us. We've started the bally motor with the gear in, and now we're running after it trying to catch up. Can I give you a lift back on my private stink machine? ..."

They strolled up the road together to where the tractor was waiting.

"Man no longer the master of his destiny, you mean?" said his companion.

"Don't make me laugh too loud," returned Vane, "or the Boche might hear; unless you've killed 'em all ..."

"You're wrong, my friend—utterly wrong." They came to where the railway track crossed the road and he halted to pull out his pipe, before getting on to the little engine.

"I tell you, Vane ..."

And at that moment a flight of cockchafers seemed to sweep down the road. Vane felt the stinging pain in his right shoulder, and then he looked foolishly at the gas expert ...

"You were saying," he began ...

But his late companion had taken a machine-gun bullet through his heart.

CHAPTER I

The beach at Paris Plage is associated in the minds of most people who went there before the war with a certain amount of gaiety. There were bands, and fair ladies, and various other delights generally connected with popular French watering-places. Incidentally the beach is a beach—not a collection of sharp boulders. There is real sand—lots of it; the sort that gets hot and comforting in the sun, and invites people who have eaten too much luncheon to sleep. And during the war, though the bands and other delights have departed, the sand has remained a source of pleasure to hundreds of people in need of a temporary rest cure. They have come from the big hospitals at Etaples; they have come from the officers' rest-house. Some have even come in motor cars from the trenches just for the day, and one and all they have lain on the beach and slept and then departed the better for it.

On a certain afternoon during the height of the German offensive in the spring of 1918 a girl was sitting on the beach staring out to sea. On the horizon a black smudge of smoke stood up against the vivid blue of the sky; while, close in shore, a small sailing boat was barely making headway in the faint breeze.

The girl was a V.A.D., and the large French family which had planted itself close by cast little curious glances at her from time to time. And she was worth looking at, with her fair hair, deep blue eyes and that wonderful complexion which seems to be the exclusive property of the British. Madame remarked on it to Monsieur, glancing at the white faces of her own daughters three, and Monsieur grunted an assent. Personally he was more occupied with the departed glories of Paris Plage than with a mere skin of roses and milk; at least the worthy man may have deemed it desirable to appear so.

"Pauvre petite," went on the kindly matron, "but she looks tired ... so tired." She heaved a deep sigh. "Mais que voulez-vous? c'est la guerre." She watched her offspring preparing to paddle, and once again she sighed. There was no band, no amusement—"Mon Dieu! but it was triste. This accursed war —would it never end?"

Margaret Trent's looks did not lie; she was tired. The rush of work just lately had almost broken her physical endurance, and there seemed but little chance of any slackening in the near future. She felt that all she wanted was rest— utter, complete rest, where such things as bandages and iodine were unknown. And even as the longing came to her she knew that a week of it would be all that she could stand. She could see beyond the craving ache to stop—the well-nigh irresistible cry of her body for rest. She could feel the call of spirit dominating mere bodily weariness. And it drove her on—though every muscle cried a halt.

Before the war she had been in that set which drifted pleasantly through life, and yet she had not been of it. She danced perfectly; she played tennis and golf and went to the proper places at the proper times—but she was different. She had in her a certain idealistic dreaminess, an intense love of the beautiful in life. Sordid things filled her with a kind of horror, and when the war came she tried to banish it from her mind like a dreadful nightmare. But there were stories in the papers, and there were letters from friends telling of losses and unspeakable sufferings. There was war all round her and one day the great unrest got hold of her, and would not be put aside. She felt she had to do something …

And so she became a V.A.D. and in the fulness of time arrived in France. Her friends prophesied that she would last a month—that she would never stand the sight of blood and wounds. Her answer had been two years at Etaples. And to those who know, that is an answer conducive of many things.

At times she tried to recall her outlook on life four years ago. She had enjoyed herself up to a point, but all the time she had been groping towards something she did not possess. She had read carefully and with discrimination, and the reading had only filled her with an added sense of her own futility. She felt that she wanted to do something—but what was there for her to do?

Marriage, naturally, had come into her mental horizon. But there had only been one man who had ever attracted her sufficiently to make it anything but an idle speculation. There had been a time, one season in London, when this man had been her constant companion, and she had been far from disliking it. At times he had seemed to be serious, and as a matter of fact the subtle difference between her and the stock pattern crowd had interested him more than he admitted even to himself. Then one day she discovered that a certain flat and its occupant were very closely connected with his bank account. It was by pure accident that she found it out. A chance remark which she overheard at a dinner party… . And the night before at the Grafton Galleries she had allowed him to kiss her as she had never before allowed a man …

It revolted her; and the man, astonished at first at her sudden change of manner, finally became annoyed, and the episode ceased. They still met; there was no quarrel—but they met only as casual acquaintances.

It was at that stage of her reflections that a shadow fell across her and she looked up. For a moment the coincidence failed to strike her, and then with a surprised little laugh she held out her hand.

"Why, Derek," she said, "I was just thinking of you."

Vane, his right arm tightly bound in a sling, sat down beside her.

"I thought you looked pretty weary," he laughed. "Jove! but it's great seeing you again, Margaret ...! And the peace of it all." He waved his left hand round the deserted beach. "Why, it's like old times—before the world went mad" ... He fumbled with his cigarette case, until she took it out of his hand, and struck a match for him.

"What ward are you in?" she asked, when he had made himself comfortable.

"Number 13; got here yesterday."

"I come on night duty there to-night. What's your trouble?"

"Machine-gun," he answered briefly. "A nice clean one through the shoulder. And the man beside me took the next bullet through his heart." He laughed shortly. "What a gamble—what a dam silly gamble, isn't it?"

She looked thoughtfully out to sea. The train of ideas his sudden appearance had interrupted was still half consciously occupying her mind.

"Four years, isn't it, since we met?" she said after a while.

"Four centuries, you mean. Four wasted centuries. Nothing will ever be the same again."

"Of course it won't. But don't you think it's just as well?" She faced him smilingly. "There was so much that was all wrong, Derek; so much that was rotten."

"And do you think that four years' insanity is going to prove the remedy?" Vane laughed cynically. "Except that there are a few million less men to carry on the rottenness"—

Margaret shook her head. "We wanted something to wake us up; it's been drastic, but we're awake."

"And what most of us want is to go to sleep again. Don't you feel tired, Margaret, sometimes?"

"Yes—I suppose I do. But it's the tiredness that comes with doing—not drifting.... It's we who have got to make the new Heaven and the new Earth, Derek ..."

Again Vane laughed. "Still as idealistic as ever, I see. Six months after peace we shall be scrambling and fighting and snarling again—after jobs and money and work."

Margaret Trent was silent, tracing a pattern in the sand with her finger. "The worry of scrambling after a job is not likely to hit you very hard," she said at length.

"Which is perhaps as well," he returned lightly; "for I'm certainly too weary to take the trouble. I shall go away, if I'm alive to do it, to the South Sea Islands and live on fruit. The only proviso is that it should be sufficiently ripe to drop into my mouth, and save me the trouble of picking it."

The girl turned and looked at him suddenly. "You've got it rather bad, old boy, haven't you?"

"Got what?" he asked slowly.

"Mental jaundice," she answered. "Your world askew."

"Do you wonder?" he returned grimly. "Isn't the world askew?"

"And if it is, someone has got to put it back."

"That's what the little boy said when he pulled the chest of drawers over on top of him and lay struggling under it. But he couldn't do it himself. It's got beyond us, Margaret—and God seems to have forgotten. There is just a blind, malignant Fate running the show."

She looked at him gravely. "You're wrong, Derek—utterly wrong. The game is still in our hands, and we've got to keep it there. What are you smiling at?"

"I was wondering," he answered, "whether the last time I was told I was wrong, the sentence would have been concluded similarly. Unfortunately, the speaker died in the middle, thereby proving his contention."

"Oh! but you're little," she cried, striking her hands together. "Don't you see that you've got to look beyond the individual—that you've got to think Big?"

"We leave that to the newspaper men," he retorted cynically. "Our smiling heroes; our undaunted soldiers! They are heroes, those Tommies; they are undaunted, but it's because they've got to be. They're up against it—and the Juggernaut of Fate knows he's got 'em. And they know he's got 'em. They just eat and drink and are merry for to-morrow they.... Ah! no; that's wrong. We never die out here, Margaret; only the other fellow does that. And if we become the other fellow, it's so deuced unexpected I don't suppose it matters much."

"But, we've got to go through with it, haven't we?" she said quietly.

"Of course we have," he answered with a laugh; "and the knowledge of that fact cuts about as much ice with the men in the mud holes up there as brave little Belgium or suffering little Serbia. I tell you we're all dazed, Margaret— just living in a dream. Some of us take it worse than others, that's all. You want the constitution of an elephant combined with the intelligence of a cow to fight these days."

"And yet," she said with a grave little smile, "under-lying it all, there's the big ideal surely… . If I didn't think that, if I didn't know that, I … I couldn't go on."

"To which particular ideal do you allude?" he asked cynically. "The League of Nations; or the triumph of Democracy, or the War to end War. They all sound so topping, don't they? received with howls of applause by the men who haven't had their boots off for a week." He thumped the sand savagely. "Cut the cackle, my dear girl; cut the cackle. This little performance was started by a few of the puppets who thought they had a winning hand, and the other puppets called a show down. And then the game passed out of their hands. They write books about it, and discover new Gods, and pass new Acts of Parliament—but the thing takes no notice. It just goes on—inexorably. Man has been dabbling with stakes that are too big for him, Margaret. And the trouble is that the cards up in the trenches are getting mighty tattered."

She looked at him curiously. "I'd never have thought it would have taken you like that, Derek … Not quite as badly."

"You formed your opinion in the bad old days, didn't you?" he said lightly. "When we danced and made love at the Grafton Galleries." She flushed a little, but did not lower her eyes. "Such a serious girl you were too, Margaret; I wonder how you ever put up with a brainless sort of ass like me."

"Because I liked you," she answered quietly, and suddenly it struck Vane, almost with a feeling of surprise, that the girl sitting beside him was more than attractive. He wondered why he had let her slip so easily out of his life. And the train of thought once started seemed a not unpleasant one… . "You'll get it back soon, Derek—your sense of proportion. You've got to."

"So that I can help build the new Heaven and the new Earth," he laughed.

"So that you may help build the new Heaven and the new Earth," she repeated gravely rising to her feet. "I must go back or I'll miss my tea."

"Have a cup with me in the village." Vane scrambled up and fell into step beside her. They passed Monsieur still snoring, and Madame nodding peacefully over her knitting, and crossed the deserted promenade. Then in silence they walked up into the main street of the little town in search of a tea shop.

"Do you realise, Margaret," he remarked as they sat down at a small marble-topped table, "that I haven't seen or spoken to a woman for six months? … Heaven help us! Aren't there any cakes?"

"Of course not," laughed Margaret, "nor milk, nor sugar. There's a war on up the road. You want about ten drops of that liquid saccharine." In the sunny street outside, soldiers in various stages of convalescence, strolled aimlessly about. An occasional motor car, containing officers—on duty, of course— slowed down at the corner opposite and disgorged its load. A closer inspection of one of them might have revealed a few suspicious looking gashes in the upholstery and holes in the mud-guards. Of course—shrapnel— but, then shrapnel did not occur by the sea. And on what duty could officers from the shrapnel area be engaged on at Paris Plage? ... However, let us be discreet in all things.

In a few hours that shrapnel scarred car would be carrying its freight back to Boulogne, where a table at the restaurant Mony had already been secured for dinner. Then back through the night, to call at various dilapidated farms and holes in the ground, in the area where shrapnel and crumps are not unknown.... But just for a few brief hours the occupants of the car were going to soak themselves in the Waters of Forgetfulness; they were going to live—even as the tripper from the slums lives his little span at Margate. And they were no whit less excited at the thought ...

They did not show it by an excessive consumption of indigestible fruit, or by bursting into unmelodious song. True, the greatest of all the "Q" men, who had come officially from a Nissen hut near Poperinghe to study the question of salvaged materials at the base, had waved a friendly hand at all the ladies— beautiful and otherwise—whom they met. But then save for salvage he was much as other men. And with that exception they just lay back in the car and thought; while the trees that were green rushed past them, and war was not.

Thus had they come to the sea. To-morrow once more the flat, dusty country with the heat haze shimmering over it and every now and then the dull drone of some bursting crump, or the vicious crack of high explosive. Behind, the same old row of balloons; in front, the same old holes in the ground.... But to-day—peace.... .

Vane thoughtfully stirred the pale straw-coloured concoction reputed to be tea on the table in front of him. The remark Margaret had made to him on the beach was running through his mind—"The new Heaven and the new Earth." Yes, but on what foundations? And would they be allowed to anyway? Reconstruction is work for the politician—not for the soldier.... . Most certainly not.... . The soldier's ignorance on every subject in the world except fighting is complete. And even over that he's not all he might be: he requires quite a lot of help from lawyers, doctors, and successful grocers.... . In fact, the only thing he is allowed to do quite on his own is to die ...

Vane smiled a little bitterly, and Margaret leaned across the table towards him.

"You'll get it back soon, Derek—believe me, old boy."

"That's very possible. But will the people at home? I'm jangled, Margaret, I know it—just for the time.... However, don't let's talk about me. Tell me about yourself...."

The girl shrugged her shoulders slightly. "I don't know that there's much to tell. I've never been so happy in my life as I am at present ..."

"In spite of all that?" He pointed out of the window to two soldiers limping painfully by on sticks.

"Yes—in spite of all that. One gets accustomed to that—and one's doing something. After all, Derek, you get accustomed to death and mutilation up there in front. It doesn't affect you...."

"No, not to the same extent as it did. In a way, I suppose not at all. But you— you were so different." He thoughtfully drained his tea cup, and set it down again, and for a space neither of them spoke.

"I can't help laughing at the comparison," said Margaret suddenly. "Five years ago you and I were sitting in Rumpolmayer's, surrounded by sugar cakes, being smart."

"They're doing that now in London except for the sugar cakes."

"We shouldn't have been silent for a moment, and we should have enjoyed ourselves thoroughly ... I wonder—"

"It was our only standard, wasn't it?"

"And now we can sit over a cup of weak and nasty tea—without milk and not talk for effect.... What's going to happen, Derek, to you and me afterwards? We can never go back to it?"

"No—you can't put back the clock—and we've grown, Margaret, years and years older. So have thousands of others—the boys up yonder, their people at home. But what about the business train to Brighton, and the occupants thereof? ... Have they felt this war, except to make a bit more boodle out of it?"

"They're only a small minority."

"Are they? They're a damned powerful one." He laughed a little bitterly. "And they're artificial—just like we were before the war."

"That's why it's we who have got to do the rebuilding. Even if it's only the rebuilding the house in our own little tiny circle, with simplicity and reality as the keystones.... You see, if you get enough tiny circles sound and good, in time the others may follow...."

"Dear lady, you've become very optimistic." Vane's eyes smiled at her. "Let's hope you're right." He paused and looked at her quietly. "Margaret. I've never asked you before—but you're different now—so different. Incidentally so am I. What was it, that made you alter so suddenly?"

Margaret rose to her feet, and shook her head. "I'll tell you some day, Derek, perhaps. Not just now. I must be getting back to the hospital."

"Will you come out and have tea with me to-morrow?" For a few moments she looked at him as if undecided, and then suddenly she seemed to make up her mind.

"All right," she said with a smile. "I'll come, I want to deal with this jaundice of yours. One must live up to a professional reputation."

CHAPTER II

A hospital is much the same anywhere, and number 13 General at Etaples was no exception. On each side of the big marquee ran a row of beds in perfect dressing. The sheets were turned down on the design so ably portrayed in the War Office Sealed Pattern X.B.451.—"Method of turning down sheets on Beds Hospital." On "Beds Barrack" the method is slightly different and is just as ably shown on Sealed pattern X.B.452. During moments of intense depression one is apt to fear the war-winning properties of X.B.451 and 452 have not been sufficiently appreciated by an unintelligent public.

The period of strain incurred on entrance was over as far as Vane was concerned. For the sixth time since leaving his battalion he had, in a confidential aside, informed a minion of the B.A.M.O. that he was a Wee Free Presbyterian Congregationalist; and for the sixth time the worthy recipient of this news had retired to consult War Office Sealed List of Religions A.F.31 to find out if he was entitled to be anything of the sort. In each case the answer had been in the negative, and Vane had been entered as "Other Denominations" and regarded with suspicion. One stout sergeant had even gone so far as to attempt to convert him to Unitarianism; another showed him the list, and asked him to take his choice.

In the bed next to him was a young Gunner subaltern, with most of his right leg shot away, and they talked spasmodically, in the intervals of trying to read month old magazines.

"Wonderful sight," remarked the Gunner, interrupted for a moment in his story by the eternal thermometer. "Firing at 'em over open sights: shrapnel set at 0. Seemed to cut lanes through 'em; though, God be praised, they came on for a bit, and didn't spoil our shooting."

Vane, sucking a thermometer under his tongue, nodded sympathetically.

"A bit better than sitting in a bally O.P. watchin' other fellows poop at the mud."

"How did you get yours?" he queried, as the Sister passed on.

"Crump almost at my feet, just as I was going into my dug-out.... Mouldy luck, and one splinter smashed the last bottle of whisky." The gunner relapsed into moody silence at the remembrance of the tragedy.

Two beds further along the Padre was playing a game of chess with a Major in the Devons; and on the opposite side of the tent another chaplain, grey haired and clean shaven, was talking and laughing with a boy, whose face and

18

head were swathed in bandages.

The R.C. and the C. of E. exponents hunting in couples as these two always did.... They are not the only two who before the war would have relegated the other to the nethermost depths of the deepest Hell; but whose eyes have been opened to wisdom now.

Vane was no theologian—no more than are the thousands of others across the water. Before the war he had been in the habit of dismissing any religious question by the comforting assertion that if all one's pals are in Hell, one might as well join them. But in the Game of Death the thoughts of many men have probed things they passed over lightly before. It is not doctrine they want; faith and belief in beautiful formulas have become less and less satisfying. They are beginning to think for themselves, which is anathema to the Church. Of old she prevented such a calamity by a policy of terrorising her followers; of later years she has adopted the simpler one of boring them. And yet it is only simplicity they want; the simple creeds of helping on the other fellow and playing the game is what they understand. But they will have to be reminded of it from time to time. One wonders whether the Church will be big enough to seize the opportunity that stares her in the face.

Vane nodded to the grey-haired Roman Catholic as he paused at the foot of his bed.

"Shoulder painful?" The priest held out a lighted match for Vane's cigarette.

"Throbs a bit, Padre; but it might be worse." He smiled and lay back on his pillows. "An arm makes one feel so helpless."

"I think I'd sooner lose an arm than a leg," remarked the Gunner from the next bed. For a while they pursued this debatable point, much as men discuss politics, and incidentally with far less heat.... It was a question of interest, and the fact that the Gunner *had* lost his leg made no difference to the matter at all. An onlooker would have listened in vain for any note of complaint.... .

"Time you were getting to sleep—both of you." Margaret's voice interrupted the conversation, and Vane looked up with a smile. She was shaking an admonitory finger at Father O'Rourke, and with a sudden quickening of the pulse he realised how perfectly charming she looked.

"Sister, dear," said the Gunner, "you're on my side, aren't you? It's better to lose an arm than a leg, isn't it?"

For a moment she affected to consider the point. Then suddenly she smiled, and came between their beds. "Unless you both of you go to sleep at once I'll come and wash you again."

With a groan of horror the Gunner hid himself under the bed-clothes, and Margaret, still smiling, turned to Vane.

"Good night, Derek," she said very low. "Sometimes I just want to sit down and howl... ." And Vane, looking up into her face, saw that her eyes were a little misty... .

Gradually the ward settled down into silence. Right at the other end a man was groaning feebly; while just opposite, looking ghastly in the dim light, a boy was staring round the tent with eyes that did not see. For hours on end he lay unconscious, breathing the rattling breath of the badly gassed; then suddenly he would lift his head, and his eyes, fixed and staring, would slowly turn from bed to bed. He looked as a man looks who is walking in his sleep, and Vane knew he was very near the Great Divide. He had been hit in the chest by a piece of shell, and a bit of his coat impregnated with mustard gas had been driven into his lungs... . Every now and then Margaret passed noiselessly down the centre between the two rows of beds. Once she lent over Vane and he closed his eyes pretending to be asleep. But every time as she came to the boy opposite she stopped and looked at him anxiously. Once she was joined by a doctor, and Vane heard their muttered conversation ...

"I can't get him to take his medicine, Doctor. He doesn't seem able to do anything."

"It doesn't much matter, Nurse," he whispered—why is it that the sick-room whisper seems to travel as far as the voice of the Sergeant-Major on parade? "He won't get through to-night, and I'm afraid we can't do anything."

The doctor turned away, and Margaret went to the end of the tent and sat down at her table. A reading lamp threw a light on her face, and for a while Vane watched her. Then his eyes came back to the boy opposite, and rested on him curiously. He was unconscious once again, and it suddenly struck Vane as strange that whereas, up in front, he had seen death and mutilation in every possible and impossible form—that though he had seen men hit by a shell direct, and one man crushed by a Tank—yet he had never been impressed with the same sense of the utter futility of war as now, in face of this boy dying in the bed opposite. To have come so far and then to pay the big price; it was so hard—so very pitiful; and Vane turned over to shut out the sight. He felt suddenly frightened of the thing that was coming nearer and nearer to the dying boy; furious at the inability of the science which had struck him down to save him... .

Vane closed his eyes and tried to sleep, but sleep was far away that night. Whenever he opened them he saw Margaret writing at her table; and once there came to him an irresistible temptation to speak to her. He felt that he wanted her near him, if only for a moment; he wanted to lean on her—he wanted to be taken in her arms like a little child. Angrily he closed his eyes again. It was ridiculous, absurd, weak… . But there have been times in this war when the strongest man has sobbed like a child in his weakness… .

"Sister!" Vane hardly recognised it as his own voice calling. "Sister!" Margaret came towards him down the ward. "Could you get me something to drink?"

In a moment she had returned with some lemonade. "I thought you were asleep, Derek," she whispered. "Are you feeling feverish?"

She put a cool hand on his forehead, and with a sigh of relief Vane lay back. "I'm frightened, Margaret," he said so low that she scarce could hear him. "Just scared to death … of that boy opposite. Ain't I a damned fool?"

Her only answer was the faintest perceptible pressure on his forehead. Then his hand came up and took hers, and she felt the touch of his lips on it. For a moment she let it rest there, and then gently withdrew it, while with a tired sigh Vane closed his eyes… .

He slept maybe for two hours, and then he found himself wide awake again—every nerve intent, like a man aroused by a sudden noise. Margaret was reading at her table; the man at the other end still groaned feebly in his sleep; the boy was staring dazedly at nothing in particular—but there was something else. He knew it.

Suddenly Margaret put down her book, and half rose from her chair, as if listening; and at the same moment the Gunner woke up. Then they all heard it together—that high pitched, ominous drone which rises and falls in a manner there is no mistaking.

"Boche," said the Gunner, "Boche, for a tanner. And lots of them."

"Damn the swine," muttered Vane. "Can't they even leave a hospital alone?" The next minute any lingering hope was destroyed. Both men heard it—the well-known whistling whooce of the bomb—the vicious crack as it burst; both men felt the ground trembling through their beds. That was the overture … the play was about to commence… .

All around them bombs rained down till the individual bursts merged into one continuous roar. The earth shook and palpitated, and, to make matters worse, the lights suddenly went out. The last thing Vane saw was Margaret as she made her way, calmly and without faltering, to the boy's bed. He had a picture, printed indelibly on his brain, of a girl with a sweet set face, of a gaping boy, stirred into some semblance of remembrance by the familiar noise around him. And then, in the darkness, he made his way towards her.

There was a deafening crash close to him, and a fragment tore through the side of the tent. He could see the blinding flash, and involuntarily he ducked his head. Then, running and stumbling, he reached her. He felt her standing rigid in the darkness, and even at such a moment he felt a sudden rush of joy as her hands come out to meet him.

"Lie down," he shouted, "lie down at once… ."

"The boy," she cried. "Help me with him, Derek."

Together they picked him up, fumbling in the darkness, and laid him on the ground beside his bed. Then Vane took her arm, and shouted in her ear, "Lie down, I tell you, lie down … quite flat." Obediently she lay down, and he stretched himself beside her on the ground. To the crashing of the bombs were now added the shouts and curses of men outside; and once Margaret made an effort to rise.

"The patients, Derek. Let me go."

With his one sound arm he kept her down by force. "You can do nothing," he said roughly. He felt her trembling against him, and a wave of fury against the airmen above took hold of him. He was no novice to bombing; there had been weeks on end when the battalion had been bombed nightly. But then it had been part of the show—what they expected; here it was so different.

A sense of utter impotence filled his mind, coupled with a raging passion at the danger to the girl beside him. And suddenly his lips sought hers.

"It's all right, my dear," he kept on saying, "quite all right. It'll be over soon." And so almost unconscious of what they said or did, they lay and listened to the tornado of Death around them… .

It is on record that one man once said that he thought it was rather amusing to be in a raid. That man was a liar. He was also a fool… . To be bombed is poisonous, rather more poisonous than to be shelled. If there are no dug-outs there is only one thing to be done, and that is what Vane was doing.

To lie flat on the ground minimises the danger except from a direct hit; and a direct hit is remarkably sudden. And so—since every occupant of Number 13 was well aware of this fact, approximately five seconds elapsed after the light went out before all the patients who could move, and most of those who couldn't, were lying on the floor beside their beds.

Gradually the explosions became fewer and fewer; though the earth still shook and throbbed like a living thing, and at last it seemed to Vane that the raid was over. He was lifting himself on his elbow preparatory to going outside and exploring, when an ominous whistling noise seemed to pierce his very brain. He had just time to throw himself on to the girl beside him so that he partially covered her, when the last bomb came. He heard the top of the marquee rip: there was a deafening roar in his ears: a scorching flame enveloped him. He lay stiff and rigid, and the thought flashed through him that this was the end. The next moment he knew he was safe, and that it was merely another close shave such as he had not been unaccustomed to in the past. The bomb had burst in the tent, but the Fate which ordained things had decided it should miss him. It had done so before, and Vane laughed to himself …

"Close, my lady, very close," he whispered—"but not quite close enough." With a quick, savage movement he turned Margaret's face towards him, and kissed her on the lips. For a while she clung to him, and then he felt her relax in his arms. She had fainted, and as he realised this, he felt something pressing down on him. With his sound arm he fumbled above his head, and found it was the canvas of the tent.

Tugging and scrambling, he half dragged, half carried Margaret through the entrance which still remained intact, and laid her down on the grass outside. Men and nurses were moving about in the darkness, stumbling over guy ropes and tent pegs. For the moment every one was too intent on his own affairs to bother over a mere faint, and Vane left her lying against the side of the tent. Then he cautiously felt his way round to investigate the damage. A great crater midway between Number 13 and the next tent showed where the first close one had fallen, but he had no wish to explore that any further. He stumbled round the edge and went on. Then in the faint light given by the moon, he saw what had happened when the last bomb had burst. It was nothing worse than many similar sights he had seen, but Vane as he looked at the wreckage cursed bitterly and fluently. And then of a sudden he stopped cursing, and drew a deep breath… . Staring up at him in the cold white light was what was left of the Gunner subaltern. The bomb had burst at the foot of his bed … A cheery soul … A bitter end …

Opposite, the bed blown in half, the boy who would not have lasted through the night sprawled uncouthly on to the floor. God knows! a merciful release… . A few hours sooner—that's all… . And to both—Kismet.

All around lay fragments and debris. For a few seconds he stood there motionless, while every now and then the canvas heaved where it lay on the ground, and someone crawled out into the open. Then he felt a touch on his arm, and, turning, he saw Margaret. Dry-eyed, she watched with him, while the wounded dragged themselves painfully past the still smoking crater, and the acrid smell of high explosive tainted the air.

In the far distance the drone of aeroplanes was getting fainter and fainter.

Success had crowned the raider's daring exploit; they were entitled to their well-earned rest. And so for a space did Vane and Margaret stand.... It was only when very gently he slipped his arm round her waist that a hard dry sob shook her.

"Oh! the devils," she whispered—"the vile devils."

CHAPTER III

The following afternoon Vane turned his steps once again towards the beach at Paris Plage. The wreckage in the hospital had been cleared away, and there were rows laid side by side in the mortuary. Over everyone there breathed a sense of restless excitement and fierce anger, and Vane wanted to get away by himself. He felt that he had to think.

For suddenly and quite unexpectedly Margaret Trent had become a factor in his life. After long years their paths had touched again, and Vane found that he could not turn away with the same careless indifference as he had in the past. Though she had always attracted him, he had never seriously contemplated the final step; he had had far too good a time as a bachelor. And then when she had so unaccountably cooled towards him, he had shrugged his shoulders and sought distraction elsewhere.

Before the war Derek Vane had been what is generally described as a typical Englishman. That is to say, he regarded his own country—whenever he thought about it at all—as being the supreme country in the world. He didn't force his opinion down anyone's throat; it simply was so. If the other fellow didn't agree, the funeral was his, not Vane's. He had to the full what the uninitiated regard as conceit; on matters connected with literature, or art, or music his knowledge was microscopic. Moreover, he regarded with suspicion anyone who talked intelligently on such subjects. On the other hand, he had been in the eleven at Eton, and was a scratch golfer. He had a fine seat on a horse and rode straight; he could play a passable game of polo, and was a good shot. Possessing as he did sufficient money to prevent the necessity of working, he had not taken the something he was supposed to be doing in the City very seriously. He had put in a periodical appearance at a desk and drawn pictures on the blotting paper; for the remainder of the time he had amused himself. He belonged, in fact, to the Breed; the Breed that has always existed in England, and will always exist till the world's end. You may meet its members in London and in Fiji; in the lands that lie beyond the mountains and at Henley; in the swamps where the stagnant vegetation rots and stinks; in the great deserts where the night air strikes cold. They are always the same, and they are branded with the stamp of the breed. They shake your hand as a man shakes it; they meet your eye as a man meets it. Just now a generation of them lie around Ypres and La Bassée; Neuve Chapelle and Bapaume. The graves are overgrown and the crosses are marked with indelible pencil. Dead—yes; but not the Breed. The Breed never dies.....

We have it on reliable evidence that the breed has its faults; its education is rotten. Men of great learning and understanding have fulminated on the subject; women with their vast experience have looked upon the Breed with great clarity of vision and have written as their eyes have seen; even boys themselves who doubtless must be right, as the question concerns them most, have contributed to current literature one or two damning indictments.

It may well be that hunting butterflies or dissecting rats are more suitable pursuits for young Percival Johnson than doing scram practice up against the playground wall. It may well be that it would be a far, far better thing for mob adoration to be laid at the feet of the composer of the winning Greek Iambic rather than at the cricketing boots of the Captain of the Eleven. It may be so, but, then, most assuredly it may not... .

The system which has turned out hundreds of the Breed, and whose object is to mould all who pass through it on the model of the Breed, is not one to be dismissed lightly. Doubtless it has its faults; a little more latitude both in games and work might be allowed; originality encouraged more. But let us be very certain before we gaily pull the system to pieces that the one we erect in its place will stand the strain, and produce the one great result beside which everything else is as nothing. For if, at the price of team work and playing for the side, we can only buy two or three more years of individualism—at an age when the value of individualism is, at best, a doubtful blessing and, at worst, sheer blatant selfishness—we shall indeed have messed things up. The cranks will be delighted; but the Empire will gnash its teeth.

And now after nearly four years in the fiercest forcing house of character Derek Vane found himself trying to take an inventory of his own stock. And since the material question of money did not come in to cloud the horizon, he felt he could do it impartially. There are many now who, having sacrificed every prospect, find their outlook haunted by the spectre of want; there are many more, formerly engaged in skilled trades such as engineering or mining, who find that they have four years of leeway to make up in their profession—four years of increased knowledge and mechanical improvements—unknown to them, but not to their competitors, who remained behind. But such prospects did not trouble him. The future, as far as money was concerned, was assured.

Vane thoughtfully lit a cigarette. It seemed to him that he had wasted four of the best years of his life, sitting, save for brief intervals, on the same filthy piece of ground, with the sole object of killing complete strangers before they killed him. In this laudable pastime he had succeeded to the extent of two for certain and one doubtful. The only man whom he had really wanted to slaughter—a certain brother subaltern who offended him daily—he had been forced to spare owing to foolish regulations... . And now this youth was at home as a Temporary Lieutenant-Colonel in sole control of an ante-chamber in one of the large hotels, with a staff of four flappers, who presented papers for his signature every other Tuesday from 2.30 to 4.

With a short laugh he got up and shook himself. In the distance some sand dunes beckoned invitingly—sand dunes which reminded him of the width of Westward Ho! and a certain championship meeting there long ago. Slowly he strolled towards them, going down nearer the sea where the sand was finer. And all the time he argued it out with himself. Four years wasted! But had they been wasted? What had he got out of them anyway? Wasn't he twice the man that he had been four years ago? Or had it all been futile and useless? ...

No man who has been through the rapids can find his feet in an hour's self-analysis. It takes time; and during that time much may happen, good or ill, according to the manner of the finder. The great unrest of the world is not felt by the men in the trenches. It seethes and boils outside, and only when a man comes back to so-called peace does he reach the whirlpool, which lies at the end of the rapids. Then, if he be of the type of Vane, is the time of danger. To lose one's sense of proportion in France is dangerous; to lose it in England may be fatal. One has so much more freedom.

At intervals during the War Vane had sampled the whirlpool, while on leave, and the effect it had produced in him had been transitory. The contrast was so immense that it had failed to move him permanently. The time that he had been in its clutches was too short. He retained just a fleeting picture of feverish gaiety which seemed out of perspective; of profound bores who discussed the mistakes of the Higher Command in the arm chairs of the Club; of universal chatter concerning rations and meat coupons. Then he had left, and in a few short hours had been back once more in the mud holes. A good leave? Oh! undoubtedly, just as it should have been, where the one thing necessary was contrast. But even then it had irritated him at times to realise how completely they failed to understand. He would not have had them understand—true. If the alternative had been put to him; if he had been told that it was in his power to make these people see the things that he had seen, and hear the things that he had heard, he would not have done so. They were better as they were—affording the contrast; enabling men to forget.

But leave is one thing, permanence is another. And at the moment Vane was faced with the latter. The doctor had talked airily of three or four months, and after that in all probability a spell of light duty, and to Vane that seemed like a permanency. It is one thing to drug oneself in the waters of Lethe for a fortnight of one's own free will: it is altogether different to be drugged by others for good. And dimly he felt that either he or they would have to go under. Two totally incompatible people cannot sit next one another at dinner for long without letting some course get cold. Unless one of them happens to be dumb... .

But were they totally incompatible? That seemed to be the crux of the whole matter. To the soldiers, pulling together, unselfishness, grinning when the sky is black, that is the new philosophy. One hesitates to call it new. It existed once, we are given to understand—or at any rate it was preached and practised in days gone by. Since then it has become unfashionable... .

And what about *les autres*—who have kept the home fires burning? For a moment Vane stopped and stared in front of him; then he laughed aloud. As has been said, he was jangled—so perhaps he may be forgiven.

It was on the other side of the dunes that he suddenly found Margaret. She had her back towards him as he came over the top, and in the sand his footsteps made no noise. And so she continued her pursuit of throwing stones at a bottle a few yards away, in ignorance of the fact that she had an audience. It is a lazy occupation at the best of times and her rendering of it was no exception to the rule. For whole minutes on end she would sit quite still gazing out to sea; and then, as if suddenly realising her slackness, she would continue the bombardment furiously.

For a while Vane watched her thoughtfully. Was she the answer? To go right away with her somewhere—right away from the crowd and the strife of existence: to be with her always, watching her grow from the wife to the mother, seeing her with his children, feeling that she was his and no one else's. God! but to think of the peace of it... .

He watched the soft tendrils of hair curling under the brim of her hat; the play of her body as she picked up the stones and threw them. Around him the coarse grass bent slightly in the breeze and the murmur of the sea came faintly over the dunes. Away in front of him stretched the sand, golden in the warm sun, the surface broken every now and then by the dark brown wooden groins. Not a soul was in sight, and save for some gulls circling round they two seemed the only living things... . With a sudden smile he stooped down and picked up a stone—several, in fact, and fired a volley. There was a tinkling noise, and the bottle fell. Then he waited for her to look round. For just a little while there was silence, and then she turned towards him with a smile... . And in that moment it seemed to him that he had found the answer he sought. Surely it was just a dream, and in a moment he would wake up and see the dreadful face of the mess waiter appearing down the dug-out steps. It is impossible to stumble over sand dunes and find Margarets in France. These things simply do not happen. One merely stumbles over the cobbles and sees the woman who keeps the estaminet round the corner washing the floor. And her lips do not part in the dawn of a smile—mercifully; her eyes are not big and blue. It was all a dream! last night was all a dream. Just one of those pictures he had seen sometimes in the candle light, when it guttered in the draught, as the big crump burst outside... .

"Derek, that wasn't fair." With an effort he pulled himself together and regarded her gravely. Then he scrambled down the sandy bank to her side.

"Do you mind pinching me?" he remarked, holding out his hand. "Hard—very hard... . I want to make certain I'm not dreaming."

"Why should you be?" Her voice was faintly tremulous. "And why have you got your eyes shut?"

"Pinch me, please, at once." Vane's hand was still held out, and she gave it a gentle nip. "Go on, harder … Ah! that's better. Now promise me you won't disappear if I open my eyes."

"I promise," she answered solemnly, but struggling to withdraw her hand from both of his, where he had caught it… .

"Oh! my dear, my dear," he whispered. "It's just too wonderful to be true. The peace of it, and the glory, and you… . I'll be waking up in a minute, my lady, and find myself crawling round the outpost line."

He laughed gently and triumphantly, and drew her towards him. Only when his arm was round her, did he pause… . And then it was the look in her eyes, as much as her two hands pressed against his chest, that stopped him. "What is it, Margaret, my lady? Aren't you going to kiss me?"

"No, Derek—not yet. Perhaps once before we go… . Please, take your arm away."

For a moment he hesitated. "Even after last night."

She nodded. "Principally because of last night."

With a little lift of his eyebrows Vane did as he was bid. "I knew there was a catch somewhere," he murmured plaintively. "You don't want me to go away and leave you, do you?"

She shook her head and smiled. Then she patted the ground beside her. "Come and sit down; I want to talk to you. No—not too near."

"Don't you trust me?" he demanded half sullenly, as he took a seat somewhat further removed from temptation.

"My dear Derek, it would take more than a mere European war to make some leopards I know of change their spots."

In spite of himself Vane laughed. "Well, dash it, Margaret, there was a distinct flavour of the pre-war about you last night."

She closed her eyes, and her hands clenched. "Oh! don't, Derek; don't, please. As long as I live I shall never forget it. It was too horrible." She turned away from him shuddering.

"Dear—I'm sorry." He leaned forward and took her hand. "I didn't realise quite what it must mean to you. You see it was that poor boy who was dying in the bed opposite mine that made me jumpy … frightened … God knows what! The smash up of the raid itself left me almost cold by comparison… . I suppose it was the other way round with you… . It's just a question of what one is used to—anyway, don't let's talk about it."

For a while they sat in silence, and then Vane spoke again. "You know I'm crossing to-morrow, I suppose?"

"Yes." Margaret nodded. "I didn't think you'd stop long."

"Are you sorry I'm going?"

"Of course I am," she answered simply. "You know that.... But I think perhaps it's just as well."

"Just as well!" repeated Vane. "Why?"

"Because ... oh! because of a lot of things. You'd interfere with my work for one."

"How dreadful," said Vane with mock gravity. "You'd mix the medicines and all that, I suppose." Then he turned to her impulsively. "Margaret, my dear, what does it matter? This work of yours won't go on for ever. And after the War, what then?"

"That's just it," she said slowly. "What then?"

"Well, as a preliminary suggestion—why not marry me?"

She laughed—a low, rippling laugh.

"Do you remember what you said to me in the tea shop yesterday about not having seen a girl for six months?"

"What on earth has that got to do with it?" said Vane frowning. "I'm not a child or a callow boy. Do you suppose at my age I don't know my own mind? Why, my dear girl...." Her eyes met his, and the words died away on his lips.

"Don't, dear, don't. You're insulting both our intelligences." With a slight laugh she leaned over and rested her hand on his. "You know perfectly well what I mean."

Vane grunted non-committally. He undoubtedly did know what she meant, but at that moment it was annoying to find she knew it too....

"Listen, Derek; I want to put things before you as I see them." With her elbows on her knee, and her chin cupped in the palms of her hand, she was staring across the stretch of tumbled, grass-grown hillocks.

"We know one another too well not to be perfectly frank. How much of last night was just—what shall I say—nervous tension? Supposing some other girl had been in my place?"

Impetuously he started to speak, but once again the words died away on his lips as he saw the half-tender, half-humorous look in her eyes.

"Dear," she went on after a moment. "I don't want to hurt you. I know you think you're in love with me to-day; but will you to-morrow? You see, Derek, this war has given a different value to things…. Whether one likes it or not, it's made one more serious. It hasn't destroyed our capacity for pleasure, but it's altered the things we take pleasure in. My idea of a good time, after it's over, will never be the same as it was before."

Vane nodded his head thoughtfully. "I'm not certain, dear, that that's anything to worry about."

"Of course it isn't—I know that. But don't you see, Derek, where that leads us to? One can't afford to fool with things once they have become serious…. And to kiss a man, as I kissed you last night, seems to mean very much more to me than it did once upon a time. That's why I want to make sure… ." She hesitated, and then, seeming to make up her mind, she turned and faced him. "I would find it easier now to live with a man I really loved—if that were the only way—than to be kissed by two or three at a dance whom I didn't care about. Do you understand?"

"My dear, I understand perfectly," answered Vane. "The one is big—the other is petty. And when we live through an age of big things we grow ourselves."

"I gave you that as a sort of example of what I feel, Derek," Margaret continued after a time. "I don't suppose there is anything novel in it, but I want you so frightfully to understand what I am going to say. You have asked me to marry you—to take the biggest step which any woman can take. I tell you quite frankly that I want to say 'Yes.' I think all along that I've loved you, though I've flirted with other men…. I was a fool five years ago… ."

He looked at her quickly. "Tell me; I want to know."

"I found out about that girl you were keeping."

Vane started slightly. "Good Lord! But how?"

"Does it matter, old man?" Margaret turned to him with a smile. "A chance remark by Billy Travers, if you want to know. And then I asked a few questions, and put two and two together. It seemed a deliberate slight to me. It seemed so sordid. You see I didn't understand—then."

"And now? Do you understand now?" He leaned towards her eagerly.

"Should I have said to you what I have if I didn't?" She held out her hand to him, and with a quick movement he put it to his lips. "I've grown, you see … got a little nearer the true value of things. I've passed out of the promiscuous kissing stage, as I told you… . And I think I realise rather more than I did what men are… . One doesn't make them up out of books now. All this has taught one to understand a man's temptations—to forgive him when he fails." Then a little irrelevantly—"They seem so petty, don't they—now?"

Vane gently dropped the hand he was holding, and his face as he looked at her was inscrutable. Into his mind there had flashed Lear's question: "And goes thy *heart* with this?" Then irritably he banished it.... God bless her! She was all heart: of course she was.

"Will you tell me where exactly you have arrived at?" he asked quietly.

"At the certainty that there lies in front of you and me work to be done. I don't know what that work will prove to be—but, Derek, we've got to find out. It may be that we shall do it together. It may be that my work is just to be with you. And it may be that it isn't that you won't want me. Ah! yes, dear," as he made a quick, impatient movement. "There is always the possibility. I want you to go and find out, Derek, and I want you to make sure that you really want me—that it isn't just six months in Flanders. Also," she added after a pause, "I want to be quite sure about myself." For a while Vane stared out to sea in silence.

"Supposing," he said slowly, "the work in front of me is back to Flanders again, as it probably will be. And supposing I'm not so lucky next time. What then?"

She turned and faced him. "Why then, dear, Fate will have decided for us, won't she?"

"A deuced unsatisfactory decision," grumbled Vane. "Margaret, I don't want to worry you; I don't want to force myself on you ... but won't you give me some sort of a promise?"

She shook her head. "I'll give you no promise at all, Derek. You've got to find yourself, and I've got to find myself; and when we've both done that we shall know how we stand to one another. Until then ... well just give it a miss in baulk, old man."

Vane regarded her curiously. "If last night and this afternoon had happened before the war, I wonder what your decision would have been?"

"Does it matter?" she answered gently. "Before the war is just a different age." For a while she was silent; then she drew a deep breath. "Don't you feel it as I feel it?" she whispered. "The bigness of it, the wonder of it. Underneath all the horror, underlying all the vileness—the splendour of it all. The glory of human endurance.... People wondered that I could stand it—I with my idealism. But it seems to me that out of the sordid brutality an ideal has been born which is almost the greatest the world has ever known. Oh! Derek, we've just got to try to keep it alive."

"It's the devil," said Vane whimsically. "Jove! lady dear, isn't the blue of the sky and the sea and the gold of the sand just crying out to be the setting of a lovers' paradise? Aren't we here alone just hidden from the world, while the very gulls themselves are screaming: 'Kiss her, kiss her?' And then the fairy princess, instead of being the fairy princess to the wounded warrior, orders him to go back and look for work. It's cruel. I had hoped for tender love and pity, and behold I have found a Labour Bureau."

Margaret laughed. "You dear! But you understand?" She knelt beside him on the sand, and her face was very tender.

"I understand," answered Vane gravely. "But, oh! my lady, I hope you're not building fairy castles on what's going to happen after the war. I'm afraid my faith in my brother man is a very, very small flame."

"All the more reason why we should keep it alight," she cried fiercely. "Derek, we can't let all this hideous mutilation and death go for nothing afterwards."

"You dear optimist," Vane smiled at her eager, glowing face so close to his own. "Do you suppose that we and others like us will have any say in the matter?"

She beat her hands together. "Derek, I hate you when you talk like that. You've got it in you to do big things—I feel it. You mustn't drift like you did before the war. You've got to fight, and others like you have got to fight, for everything that makes life worth living in our glorious, wonderful England."

"Would the staff be a little more explicit in their Operation Orders, please?" murmured Vane. "Whom do you propose I should engage in mortal combat?" He saw the slight frown on her face and leant forward quickly. "My dear, don't misunderstand me. I don't want to be flippant and cynical. But I'm just a plain, ordinary man—and I'm rather tired. When this show is over I want peace and rest and comfort. And I rather feel that it's up to the damned fools who let us in for it to clear up the mess themselves for a change."

"But you won't later, old boy," said the girl; "not after you've found yourself again. You'll have to be up and doing; it will stifle you to sit still and do nothing." She looked thoughtfully out to sea and then, as he kept silent, she went on slowly, "I guess we all sat still before this war; drifted along the line of least resistance. We've got to cut a new way, Derek, find a new path, which will make for the good of the show. And before we can find the path, we've got to find ourselves."

She turned towards him and for a long minute they looked into one another's eyes, while the gulls circled and screamed above them. Then slowly she bent forward and kissed him on the mouth.... "Go and find yourself, my dear," she whispered. "Go and make good. And when you have, if you still want me, I'll come to you."

* * * * *

At the touch of her lips Vane closed his eyes. It seemed only a few seconds before he opened them again, but Margaret was gone. And then for a while he sat, idly throwing stones at the overturned bottle. Just once he laughed, a short, hard laugh with no humour in it, before he turned to follow her. But when he reached the top of the sand dune, Margaret was almost out of sight in the distance.

Next day he crossed to England in the *Guildford Castle*.

CHAPTER IV

Derek Vane did not remain long in hospital. As soon as the dressings for his shoulder had become quite straightforward, the machine, in the shape of two doctors from Millbank who formed the Board, took him in its clutches once more and deposited him at a convalescent home. Not one of the dreary, routine-like places which have been in the past associated with convalescence, but a large country house, kindly placed at the disposal of the War Office by its owner.

"Rumfold Hall for you, Vane," said the senior of the two doctors. "A charming house; Lady Patterdale—a charming woman."

"Rumfold Hall!" echoed Vane. "Good Heavens! I know it well. Danced there often during the old *régime*."

"The old régime?" The doctor looked puzzled.

"Yes. It used to belong to the Earl of Forres. He couldn't afford to keep it up and his other places as well, so he sold it to Sir John Patterdale.... Made his money in hardware, did Sir John.... Surely you know Patterdale's Patent Plate."

The Board opined that it did not, and departed to the next case. It even seemed to regard such flippancy with a certain amount of suspicion; but then Medical Boards are things of some solemnity....

And so in the course of two or three days Vane drove up to the historic gates of Rumfold Hall in an ambulance. The house, situated in the heart of Surrey, was surrounded by extensive grounds. The view from it was magnificent, stretching away for miles and miles to the south, and terminating in the purple downs: and Vane, as the car waited for the gates to be opened, felt that indefinable thrill of pride that comes to every man when he looks on some glorious stretch of his own country. He noticed that the lodge-keeper had changed since he was there last, and not, it struck him, for the better. How well he remembered old John, with his sweet old wife, and their perfectly kept patch of garden and spotless little kitchen.... He had had two sons, both in the Grenadiers, magnificent, strapping fellows—and Vane wondered what had become of them....

Somehow he couldn't quite imagine old John not touching his hat as the ambulance came in; whereas his successor merely gazed curiously at the occupants, and then slouched back into the lodge.... Of course hat-touching is a relic of feudalism, and, as such, too hideous to contemplate in this age of democracy; but still—like a smile—it costs little and gives much pleasure.

From the condition of the grounds it did not seem that the present owner had been very greatly troubled by the labour shortage. The flower beds were a riot of colour; the grass was short and beautifully kept. And as the ambulance rounded a corner of the drive and the house opened up in front Vane saw that tennis was in full swing on the lawns.

"Say—what sort of a guy is this fellow?" asked a New Zealander opposite him suddenly. "It seems to me to be some house."

Vane looked at him thoughtfully for a moment before replying, and the car was already slowing down before he finally spoke. "He's a substitute for the old order of things. And according to the labels of all substitutes, they are the last word in modern efficiency."

The car pulled up at that moment, and they stepped out to find Lady Patterdale standing on the steps to welcome them.

Let it be said at once that Lady Patterdale was a perfect dear. One lost sight of her incredible vulgarity in view of the charming kindliness of her heart. And, after all, vulgarity is only comparative. In the sanctity of the little shop in Birmingham where Sir John had first laid the foundations of his fortune, aspirates could drop unheeded. What mattered then, as always, was whether the heart was in the right place. With Lady Patterdale it was… .

And because *au fond*, she was such a dear, it made it all the more pathetic to see her in such surroundings. One felt, and one felt that in the bottom of her heart she felt, that she would have been far more happy in the kitchen. Except that in the kitchen her lost aspirates would probably have been handed back to her on a salver, whereas in the drawing-room they were ground into the carpet… . The spread of education has made the kitchen a very dangerous place.

In appearance Lady Patterdale was short and stout; eminently the type of woman who, if clothed according to the dictates of common sense, would be called a "comfortable old party." One could imagine her in a cotton dress, with her sleeves rolled up above her elbows, displaying a pair of plump forearms and wielding a rolling pin in front of a good hot fire. Covered with flour—her face very red—she would have been in her element… . As it was, the dictates of fashion had cast their blight over the proceedings.

The name of her dressmaker is immaterial. Originally Smith & Co. in all probability, it had now become Smythe et Cie, and advertised in all the most exclusive papers. Unfortunately, in the case of Lady Patterdale they did not stop at advertising. They carried out their dreadful threats and clothed her.

The result was incredible. She resembled nothing so much as a bursting melon. Onlookers shuddered at times when they thought of the trust reposed by Providence and Lady Patterdale in a few paltry hooks and eyes. The strain appeared so terrific—the consequences of a disaster so appalling.

As Vane stepped out of the ambulance Lady Patterdale, supported on either side by one of the nursing staff, advanced to meet him. Her jolly old face was wreathed in smiles; cordiality and kindliness oozed from her.

"Welcome, both of you," she cried. "Welcome to Rumfold 'all."

The Sister on her left started as if a serpent had stung her, and Vane decided that he did not like her. Then he turned to the kindly old woman, and smiled.

"Thank you, Lady Patterdale," he said, taking her outstretched hand. "I'm sure it's going to be topping."

"You're just in nice time for luncheon," she continued, as she turned to welcome the New Zealander. "And after that you'll be able to find your way about the 'ouse."

Lunch was the only meal where all the convalescents met, as, generally, some of them had retired before dinner. It was served in the old banqueting hall, which, when Vane remembered it, had been used for dancing. The officers had it to themselves, the nursing staff feeding elsewhere... .

The contrast struck Vane forcibly as he sat down at the long table. The last time he had been in the room he and three or four kindred spirits had emptied a fruit salad into a large wind instrument just before the band played the final gallop... .

"Beer, sir, or cider?" He half turned to answer, when suddenly the voice continued, "Why, but surely, sir, it's Mr. Vane?"

He looked up and saw the same butler who had been at the Hall in the old days.

"Why, Robert," he said delightedly, "you still here? Jove! but I'm glad to see you. I thought Sir John had made a clean sweep of all the staff."

The butler nodded his head sadly. "All except me, sir—me and Mrs. Hickson. She was the housekeeper, if you remember. And she couldn't stand it—that is, she had to leave after a year."

"Ah!" Vane's tone was non-committal. "And what's become of old John—at the Lodge?"

"He went, sir. Sir John found him too slow." Robert poured out a glass of beer. "He's in the village, sir. One of his sons was killed at Noove Chappel."

"I'm sorry about that. I must go and see him."

"He'd be proud, sir, if you'd be so kind. I often goes down there myself for a bit of a chat about the old days." With a sigh the old butler passed on, and Vane returned to his lunch... .

"You seem to know our archaic friend," remarked the officer sitting next him. "He's a dear old thing... ."

"He's one of a dying breed," said Vane shortly. "I would trust old Robert with everything in the world that I possessed... ."

"That so?" returned the other. "Has he been here long?"

"To my certain knowledge for twenty-five years, and I believe longer. It almost broke his heart when he heard that Lord Forres was going to sell the place." Vane continued his lunch in silence, and suddenly a remark from the other side of the table struck his ears.

"I say, old Side-whiskers hasn't given me my fair whack of beer." It was a youngster speaking, and the remark was plainly audible to the old butler two places away. For a moment his face quivered, and then he returned to the speaker.

"I beg your pardon, sir," he remarked quietly. "Let me fill your glass."

"Thanks, old sport. That's a bit better looking." Vane turned to his neighbour with an amused smile.

"Truly the old order changeth," remarked the other thoughtfully. "And one's inclined to wonder if it's changing for the better."

"Unfortunately in any consideration of that sort one is so hopelessly biassed by one's own personal point of view," returned Vane.

"Do you think so?" He crumbled the bread beside him. "Don't you think one can view a little episode like that in an unbiassed way? Isn't it merely in miniature what is going on all over the country? ... The clash of the new spirit with the one that is centuries old."

"And you really regard that youth as being representative of the new spirit?"

"No one man can be. But I regard him as typical of a certain phase of that spirit. In all probability a magnificent platoon commander—there are thousands like him who have come into being with this war. The future of the country lies very largely in their hands. What are they going to make of it?"

The same question—the same ceaseless refrain. Sometimes expressed, more often not. ENGLAND in the melting pot—what was going to happen? Unconsciously Vane's eyes rested on the figure of the old butler standing at the end of the room. There was something noble about the simplicity of the old man, confronted by the crashing of the system in which he and his father, and his father's father had been born. A puzzled look seemed ever in his eyes: the look of a dog parted from a beloved master, in new surroundings amongst strange faces. And officially, at any rate, the crash was entirely for the benefit of him and his kind …. wherein lay the humour.

Vane laughed shortly as he pushed back his chair. "Does anything matter save one's own comfort? Personally I think slavery would be an admirable innovation."

Sir John Patterdale was everything that his wife was not. The unprecedented success of his Patent Plate had enabled him to pay the necessary money to obtain his knighthood and blossom into a county magnate. At one time he had even thought of standing for Parliament as an old and crusted Tory; but up to date the War had prevented the realisation of such a charming idyll. Instead he sat on the bench and dispensed justice.

In appearance he was an exact counterpart of his wife—short and fat; and his favourite attitude was standing with his legs wide apart and his thumbs in the arm-holes of his waistcoat. Strong men had been known to burst into tears on seeing him for the first time arrayed as the sporting squire; but the role was one which he persistently tried to fill, with the help of a yellow hunting waistcoat and check stockings. And when it is said that he invariably bullied the servants, if possible in front of a third person, the picture of Sir John is tolerably complete. He was, in short, a supreme cad, with not a single redeeming feature. Stay—that is wrong. He still retained the love of his wife, which may perhaps—nay, surely shall—be accounted to him for righteousness… .

To her he was never the vain, strutting little bounder, making himself ridiculous and offensive by turn. She never got beyond the picture of him when, as plain John Patterdale, having put up the shutters and locked the door of the shop, he would come through into their little living-room behind for his supper. First he would kiss her, and then taking off his best coat, he would put on the old frayed one that always hung in readiness behind the door. And after supper, they would draw up very close together, and dream wonderful dreams about the future. All sorts of beautiful things danced in the flames; but the most beautiful thing of all was the reality of her John, with his arm round her waist, and his cheek touching hers.

Sometimes now, when the real truth struck her more clearly than usual—for she was a shrewd old woman for all her kindness of heart—sometimes when she saw the sneers of the people who ate his salt and drank his champagne her mind went back with a bitter stab of memory to those early days in

Birmingham. What had they got in exchange for their love and dreams over the kitchen fire—what Dead Sea Fruit had they plucked? If only something could happen; if only he could lose all his money, how willingly, how joyfully would she go back with him to the niche where they both fitted. They might even be happy once again... .

He had needed her in those days: turned to her for comfort when business was bad, taken her out on the burst—just they two alone—when things looked up and there had been a good day's takings. The excitement over choosing her best hat—the one with the bunches of fruit in it... . As long as she lived she would never forget the morning she tried it on, when he deserted the shop and cheered from the bedroom door, thereby losing a prospective customer.

But now, all he cared about was that she should go to the best people and spare no expense.

"We can afford it, my dear," he was wont to remark, "and I want you to keep your end up with the best of 'em. You must remember my position in the county."

Even alone with her he kept up the pretence, and she backed him loyally. Was he not still her man; and if he was happy, what else mattered? And she would call herself a silly old woman... .

But there was just once when he came back to her, and she locked away the remembrance of that night in her secret drawer—the drawer that contained amongst other things a little bunch of artificial grapes which had once adorned the hat... .

There had been a big dinner of the no-expense-spared type; and to it had been invited most of the County. Quite a percentage had accepted, and it was after dinner, just before the guests were going, that the owner of a neighbouring house had inadvertently put his thoughts into words, not knowing that his host was within hearing.

"It makes me positively sick to see that impossible little bounder strutting about round Rumfold."

"Impossible little bounder." It hit the little man like a blow between the eyes, and that night, in bed, a woman with love welling over in her heart comforted her man.

"It wasn't him that had been meant... . Of course not ... . Why the dinner had been a tremendous success... . Lady Sarah Wellerby had told her so herself... . Had asked them over in return... . And had suggested that they should give a dance, to which she and her six unmarried daughters would be delighted to come."

But she didn't tell him that she had overheard Lady Sarah remark to the wife of Admiral Blake that "the atrocious little cook person had better be cultivated, she supposed. One never knows, my dear. The ballroom is wonderful and men will come anywhere for a good supper... ." No, she didn't tell him that: nor mention the misery she had suffered during dinner. She didn't say how terrified she was of the servants—all except old Robert, who looked at her sometimes with his kindly, tired eyes as if he understood. She didn't even take the opportunity of voicing the wish that was dearest to her heart; to give it all up and go right away. She just coaxed him back to self-confidence, and, in the morning, Sir John was Sir John once more—as insufferable as ever. And only a tired old woman knew quite how tired she felt....

One of Sir John's pet weaknesses was having his wife and the staff photographed. Sometimes he appeared in the group himself, but on the whole he preferred impromptu snap-shots of himself chatting with wounded officers in the grounds. For these posed photographs Lady Patterdale arrayed herself in a light grey costume, with large red crosses scattered over it: and as Vane was strolling out into the gardens after lunch, he ran into her in this disguise in the hall.

"We're 'aving a little group taken, Captain Vane," she said as she passed him. "You must come and be in it."

"Why, certainly, Lady Patterdale; I shall be only too delighted. Is that the reason of the war paint?"

She laughed—a jolly, unaffected laugh. "My 'usband always likes me to wear this when we're took. Thinks it looks better in a 'ospital."

As Vane stepped through the door with her he caught a fleeting glimpse of officers disappearing rapidly in all directions. Confronting them was a large camera, and some servants were arranging chairs under the direction of the photographer. Evidently the symptoms were well known, and Vane realised that he had been had.

This proved to be one of the occasions on which Sir John did not appear, and so the deed did not take quite as long as usual. To the staff it was just a matter of drill, and they arranged themselves at once. And since they were what really mattered, and the half-dozen patients merely appeared in the nature of a make weight, in a very short time, to everyone's profound relief, the group had been taken... . Vane, who had been sitting on the ground, with his legs tucked under him to keep them in focus, silently suffering an acute attack of cramp, rose and stretched himself. On the lawn, tennis had started again; and she could see various officers dotted about the ground in basket chairs. He was turning away, with the idea of a stroll—possibly even of seeking out old John in the village, when from just behind his shoulder came a musical laugh.

"Delightful," said a low, silvery voice; "quite delightful."

Vane swung round in time to catch the glint of a mocking smile—a pair of lazy grey eyes—and then, before he could answer, or even make up his mind if it had been he who was addressed, the girl who had spoken moved past him and greeted Lady Patterdale.... .

He waited just long enough to hear that worthy woman's, "My dear Joan, 'ow are you?" and then with a faintly amused smile on his lips turned towards the cool, shady drive. Margaret's remark in the sand dunes at Etaples anent leopards and their spots came back to him; and the seasoned war horse scents the battle from afar.... .

CHAPTER V

It was under the shade of a great rhododendron bush that Vane was first privileged to meet Sir John. The bush was a blaze of scarlet and purple, which showed up vividly against the green of the grass and the darker green of the shrubs around. Through the trees could be seen glimpses of the distant hills, and Vane, as he stumbled unexpectedly into this sudden bit of fairyland, caught his breath with the glory of it. Then with drastic suddenness he recalled that half-forgotten hymn of childhood, of which the last line runs somewhat to the effect that "only man is vile."

Sir John was in full possession, with an unwilling audience of one bored cavalryman. It was one of his most cherished sentiments that nothing aided convalescence so much as a little bright, breezy conversation on subjects of general interest—just to cheer 'em up, and make 'em feel at home.... .

At the moment of Vane's arrival he was discoursing fluently on the problem of education. The point is really immaterial, as Sir John discussed all problems with equal fluency, and the necessity for answering was rare. He had a certain shrewd business-like efficiency, and in most of his harangues there was a good deal of what, for want of a better word, might be termed horse sense. But he was so completely self-opinionated and sure of himself that he generally drove his audience to thoughts of poisons that left no trace or even fire-arms. Especially when he was holding forth on strategy. On that subject he considered himself an expert, and regularly twice a week he emptied the smoking-room at Rumfold by showing—with the aid of small flags—what he would have done had he been in charge of the battle of the Somme in 1916. He was only silenced once, and that was by a pessimistic and saturnine Sapper.

"Extraordinary," he murmured. "I congratulate you, Sir John. The plan you have outlined is exactly in every detail the one which the Commander-in-Chief discussed with me when overlooking the charming little village of Gueudecourt. 'Johnson,' he said, 'that is what we will do,' and he turned to the Chief of Staff and ordered him to make a note of it." The Sapper paused for a moment to relight his pipe. Then he turned impressively to Sir John. "There was no Chief of Staff. The Chief of Staff had gone: only a few bubbles welling out of the mud remained to show his fate. And then, before my very eyes, the C.-in-C. himself commenced to sink. To my fevered brain it seemed to be over in a minute. His last words as he went down for the third time were 'Johnson, carry on.' ... Of course it was kept out of the papers, but if it hadn't been for a Tank going by to get some whisky for the officers' mess, which, owing to its pressure on neighbouring ground squeezed them all out again one by one—you know, just like you squeeze orange pips from your fingers—the affair might have been serious."

"I did hear a rumour about it," said the still small voice of a machine-gunner from behind a paper.

"Of course," continued the Sapper, "the plan had to be given up. The whole of G.H.Q. sat for days in my dug-out with their feet in hot water and mustard.... A most homely spectacle—especially towards the end when, to while away the time, they started sneezing in unison...."

A silence settled on the smoking-room, a silence broken at last by the opening and shutting of the door. Sir John had retired for the night....

At the moment that Vane paused at the entrance to his bit of fairyland Sir John was in full blast.

"What, sir, is the good of educating these people? Stuffing their heads with a lot of useless nonsense. And then talking about land nationalisation. The two don't go together, sir. If you educate a man he's not going to go and sit down on a bare field and look for worms...." He paused in his peroration as he caught sight of Vane.

"Ah! ha!" he cried. "Surely a new arrival. Welcome, sir, to my little home."

Restraining with a great effort his inclination to kick him, Vane shook the proffered hand; and for about ten minutes he suffered a torrent of grandiloquence in silence. At the conclusion of the little man's first remark Vane had a fleeting vision of the cavalry-man slinking hurriedly round two bushes and then, having run like a stag across the open, going to ground in some dense undergrowth on the opposite side. And Vane, to his everlasting credit be it said, did not even smile....

After a while the flood more or less spent itself, and Vane seized the occasion of a pause for breath to ask after old John.

"I see you've got a new lodge-keeper, Sir John. Robert tells me that the old man who was here under Lord Forres is in the village."

"Yes. Had to get rid of him. Too slow. I like efficiency, my boy, efficiency.... That's my motto." Sir John complacently performed three steps of his celebrated strut. "Did you know the Hearl?" Though fairly sound on the matter, in moments of excitement he was apt to counterbalance his wife with the elusive letter....

Vane replied that he did—fairly well.

"A charming man, sir ... typical of all that is best in our old English nobility. I am proud, sir, to have had such a predecessor. I number the Hearl, sir, among my most intimate friends... ."

Vane, who remembered the graphic description given him by Blervie—the Earl's eldest son—at lunch one day, concerning the transaction at the time of the sale, preserved a discreet silence.

"A horrible-looking little man, old bean," that worthy had remarked. "Quite round, and bounces in his chair. The governor saw him once, and had to leave the room. 'I can't stand it,' he said to me outside, 'the dam fellow keeps hopping up and down, and calling me His Grace. He's either unwell, or his trousers are coming off.'" Lord Blervie had helped himself to some more whisky and sighed. "I've had an awful time," he continued after a while. "The governor sat in one room, and Patterdale bounced in the other, and old Podmore ran backwards and forwards between, with papers and things. And if we hadn't kept the little blighter back by force he was going to make a speech to the old man when it was all fixed up... ."

At last Sir John left Vane to himself, and with a sigh of relief he sank into the chair so recently vacated by the cavalryman. In his hand he held a couple of magazines, but, almost unheeded, they slipped out of his fingers on to the grass. He felt supremely and blissfully lazy. The soft thud of tennis balls, and the players' voices calling the score, came faintly through the still air, and Vane half closed his eyes. Then a sudden rustle of a skirt beside him broke into his thoughts, and he looked up into the face of the girl whom Lady Patterdale had greeted as Joan.

"Why it's my bored friend of the photograph!" She stood for a moment looking at him critically, rather as a would-be purchaser looks at a horse. "And have they all run away and left you to play by yourself?" She pulled up another chair and sat down opposite him.

"Yes. Even Sir John has deserted me." As he spoke he was wondering what her age was. Somewhere about twenty-two he decided, and about ten more in experience.

"For which relief much thanks, I suppose?"

"One shouldn't look a gift host in the stockings," returned Vane lightly. "I think it's very charming of him and his wife to have us here."

"Do you? It's hopelessly unfashionable not to do war work of some sort, and this suits them down to the ground... . Why the Queen visited Rumfold the other day and congratulated Lady Patterdale on her magnificent arrangements." There was a mocking glint in her eyes, otherwise her face was perfectly serious.

"You don't say so." Vane gazed at her in amazement. "And did you dress up as a nurse for the occasion?"

"No, I watched from behind a gooseberry bush. You see, I'm a very busy person, and my work can't be interrupted even for a Royal visit."

"Would it be indiscreet," murmured Vane, "to inquire what your work is?"

"Not a bit." The girl looked solemnly at him. "I amuse the poor wounded officers."

"And do you find that very hard?" asked Vane with becoming gravity.

"Frightfully. You see, they either want to make love to me, or else to confide that they love another. My chief difficulty as I wander from bush to bush is to remember to which class the temporary occupant belongs. I mean it's a dreadful thing to assure a man of your own undying devotion, when the day before you were sympathising with him over Jane not having written. It makes one appear of undecided intellect."

"Why don't you institute a little system of labels?" asked Vane. "Blue for those who passionately adore you—red for those who love someone else. People of large heart might wear several."

"I think that's quite wonderful." She leaned back in her chair and regarded Vane with admiration. "And I see that you're only a Captain.... How true it is that the best brains in the Army adorn the lower positions. By the way—I must just make a note of your name." She produced a small pocketbook from her bag and opened it. "My duties are so arduous that I have been compelled to make lists and things."

"Vane," he answered, "Christian—Derek."

She entered both in her book, and then shut it with a snap. "Now I'm ready to begin. Are you going to amuse me, or am I going to amuse you?"

"You have succeeded in doing the latter most thoroughly," Vane assured her.

"No—have I really? I must be in good form to-day. One really never can tell, you know. An opening that is a scream with some people falls as flat as ditch-water with others." She looked at him pensively for a moment or two, tapping her small white teeth with a gold pencil.

Suddenly Vane leaned forward. "May I ask your age, Joan?"

Her eyebrows went up slightly. "Joan!" she said.

"I dislike addressing the unknown," remarked Vane, "and I heard Lady Patterdale call you Joan. But if you prefer it—may I ask your age, Miss Snooks?"

She laughed merrily. "I think I prefer Joan, thank you; though I don't generally allow that until the fourth or fifth performance. You see, if one gets on too quickly it's so difficult to fill in the time at the end if the convalescence is a long one."

"I am honoured," remarked Vane. "But you haven't answered my question."

"I really see no reason why I should. It doesn't come into the rules—at least not my rules.... Besides I was always told that it was rude to ask personal questions."

"I am delighted to think that something you were taught at your mother's knee has produced a lasting effect on your mind," returned Vane. "However, at this stage we won't press it.... I should hate to embarrass you." He looked at her in silence for a while, as if he was trying to answer to his own satisfaction some unspoken question on his mind.

"I think," she said, "that I had better resume my official duties. What do you think of Rumfold Hall?"

"It would be hard in the time at my disposal, my dear young lady, to give a satisfactory answer to that question." Vane lit a cigarette. "I will merely point out to you that it contains a banqueting chamber in which Bloody Mary is reported to have consumed a capon and ordered two more Protestants to be burned—and that the said banqueting hall has been used of recent years by the vulgar for such exercises as the fox trot and the one step. Further, let me draw your attention to the old Elizabethan dormer window from which it is reported that the celebrated Sir Walter Raleigh hung his cloak to dry, after the lady had trodden on it. On the staircase can be seen the identical spot where the dog basket belonging to the aged pug dog of the eighteenth Countess of Forres was nightly placed, to the intense discomfiture of those ill-behaved and rowdy guests who turned the hours of sleep into a time for revolting debauches with soda water syphons and flour. In fact it is commonly thought that the end of the above-mentioned aged pug dog was hastened by the excitable Lord Frederick de Vere Thomson hurling it, in mistake for a footstool, at the head of his still more skittish spouse—the celebrated Tootie Rootles of the Gaiety. This hallowed spot has been roped off, and is shown with becoming pride by the present owner to any unfortunate he can inveigle into listening to him. Finally I would draw your attention...."

"For Heaven's sake, stop," she interrupted weakly. "The answer is adjudged incorrect owing to its length."

"Don't I get the grand piano?" he demanded.

"Not even the bag of nuts," she said firmly. "I want a cigarette.

They're not gaspers, are they?"

"They are not," he said, holding out his case. "I am quite ready for the second question."

She looked at him thoughtfully through a cloud of smoke. "Somehow I don't think I will proceed along the regular lines," she remarked at length. "Your standard seems higher."

"Higher than whose?" Vane asked.

"Than most of the others." Her smile was a trifle enigmatic. "There is a cavalryman here and one or two others—but ... well! you know what I mean."

"I do know what you mean—exactly," he remarked quietly. "And, Joan, it's all wrong."

"It's all natural, anyway. Their ways are not our ways; their thoughts are not our thoughts.... I can't help whether I'm being a poisonous snob or not; it's what I feel. Take Sir John. Why, the man's an offence to the eye. He's a complete outsider. What right has he got to be at Rumfold?"

"The right of having invented a patent plate. And if one looks at it from an unbiassed point of view it seems almost as good a claim as that of the descendant of a really successful brigand chief."

"Are you a Socialist?" she demanded suddenly.

"God knows what I am," he answered cynically. "I'm trying to find out. You see something has happened over the water which alters one's point of view. It hasn't happened over here. And just at the moment I feel rather like a stranger in a strange land." He stared thoughtfully at a thrush which was dealing with a large and fat worm. Then he continued—"You were talking about outsiders. Lord! my dear girl, don't think I don't know what you mean. I had a peerless one in my company—one of the first and purest water— judged by our standards. He was addicted to cleaning his nails, amongst other things, with a prong of his fork at meals.... But one morning down in the Hulluch sector—it was stand to. Dawn was just spreading over the sky—grey and sombre; and lying at the bottom of the trench just where a boyau joined the front line, was this officer. His face was whiter than the chalk around him, but every now and then he grinned feebly. What was left of his body had been covered with his coat: because you see a bit of a flying pig had taken away most of his stomach."

The girl bit her lip—but her eyes did not leave Vane's face.

"He died, still lying in the wet chalky sludge, still grinning, and thanking the stretcher bearers who had carried him." He paused for a moment—his mind back in the Land over the Water. "There are thousands like him," he went on thoughtfully, "and over there, you see, nothing much matters. A man, whether he's a duke or a dustman, is judged on his merits in the regimental family. Everyone is equally happy, or equally unhappy—because everyone's goal is the same."

"And over here," put in the girl, "everyone's goal is different. How could it be otherwise? It's when you get a man trying to kick the ball through the wrong goal—and succeeding—that the trouble comes."

"Quite right," agreed Vane. "Personally I'm trying to find out what my own goal is."

"What was it before the war?"

"Soda water syphons and flour; hunting, cricket and making love."

"And you don't think that would still fill the bill?"

"The Lord knows!" laughed Vane. "In the fulness of time probably I shall too."

"And how do you propose to find out?" persisted the girl.

Once again Vane laughed. "By the simple process of doing nothing," he answered. "I shall—as far as my arduous military duties allow me—carry on... . I believe everyone is carrying on... . It's the phase, isn't it? And in the process, as far as it progresses before I have to return to France—I may get some idea as to whether I am really a pronounced Pacifist or a Last Ditcher."

For a while she looked at him curiously without speaking. "You're somewhat different from most of my patients," she announced at last.

He bowed ironically. "I trust that in spite of that, I may find favour in your sight. It's something, at any rate, not to be labelled G.S., as we say in the Army."

"Frankly and honestly, you despise me a little?"

Vane considered her dispassionately. "Frankly and honestly, I do. And yet ... I don't know. Don't you see, lady, that I'm looking at your life through my spectacles; you look at it through your own. For all I know you may be right, and I may be wrong. In fact," he continued after a short pause, "it's more than likely it is so. You at any rate have not been qualifying for a lunatic asylum during the past four years."

She rose from her chair, and together they strolled towards the lawn. Tennis was still in full swing, and for a time they watched the game in silence.

"Do those men think as you think?" she asked him suddenly. "Are they all asking the why and the wherefore—or is it enough for them to be just out of it?"

"It's enough for us all for the time," he answered gravely. "And then it tugs and it pulls and we go back to it again... . It's made everyone a bit more thoughtful; it's made everyone ask the why and the wherefore, insistently or casually, according to the manner of the brute. But Hell will come if we don't —as a whole—find the same answer... ."

She idly twisted her parasol, and at that moment the cavalryman lounged up. "Thought you'd deserted us, Miss Devereux." He glanced at Vane and grinned. "I appeal to you," he cried, "as an infantry soldier to state publicly whether you have ever seen a more masterly bit of scouting than mine when the old man buttonholed you. Jove! you should have seen it. Purple face caught him by the rhododendron bush, where he'd been inflicting himself on me for a quarter of an hour; and in one minute by the clock I'd got to ground in the parsley bed."

They all laughed, and for a few minutes the two men chatted with her; then Vane disappeared into the house to write letters. It was a slow and laborious process, and, as a rule, he wrote as few as possible. But there was one he had to get off his conscience, though he dreaded doing so. A promise to a dead pal is sacred... .

At length the scrawl was finished, and looking up from the writing table he saw Joan Devereux passing through the hall. He got up and hurried after her. "Would you mind addressing this for me?" He held out the envelope. "I've managed to spoil the paper inside, but I don't want to tax the postman too highly."

With a smile she took the letter from him, and picked up a pen. "Well," she said after a moment, "I'm waiting."

She looked up into his face as he stood beside her at the table, and a glint of mischief came into her eyes as they met his. He was staring at her with a thoughtful expression, and, at any rate for the moment he seemed to find it a pleasant occupation.

"And what may the seeker after truth be thinking of now?" she remarked flippantly. "Condemning me a second time just as I'm trying to be useful as well as ornamental?"

"I was thinking... ." he began slowly, and then he seemed to change his mind. "I don't think it matters exactly what I was thinking," he continued, "except that it concerned you. Indirectly, perhaps—possibly even directly … you and another… ."

"So you belong to the second of my two classes, do you?" said the girl. "Somehow I thought you were in the first… ."

"The class you embrace?" asked Vane drily.

With a quick frown she turned once more to the table. "Supposing you give me the address."

"I beg your pardon," said Vane quietly. "The remark was vulgar, and quite uncalled for. After four years in the Army, one should be able to differentiate between official and unofficial conversation."

"May I ask what on earth you mean?" said the girl coldly.

"I take it that your preliminary remarks to me in the garden were in the nature of official patter—used in your professional capacity… . When off duty, so to speak, you're quite a normal individual… . Possibly even proper to the point of dulness." He was staring idly out of the window. "In the States, you know, they carry it even further… . I believe there one can hire a professional female co-respondent—a woman of unassailable virtue and repulsive aspect—who will keep the man company in compromising circumstances long enough for the wife to establish her case."

The girl sprang up and confronted him with her eyes blazing, but Vane continued dreamily. "There was one I heard of who was the wife of the Dissenting Minister, and did it to bolster up her husband's charities… ."

"I think," she said in a low, furious voice, "that you are the most loathsome man I ever met."

Vane looked at her in surprise. "But I thought we were getting on so nicely. I was just going to ask you to have lunch with me one day in town—in your official capacity, of course… ."

"If you were the last man in the world, and I was starving, I wouldn't lunch with you in any capacity." Her breast was rising and falling stormily.

"At any rate, it's something to know where we stand," said Vane pleasantly.

"If I'd realised that you were merely a cad—and an outsider of the worst type —do you suppose that I would have talked—would have allowed… ." The words died away in her throat, and her shoulders shook. She turned away, biting furiously at her handkerchief with her teeth. "Go away—oh! go away; I hate you."

But Vane did not go away; he merely stood there looking at her with a faint, half-quizzical smile on his lips.

"Joan," he said, after a moment, "I'm thinking I have played the deuce with your general routine. All the earlier performances will be in the nature of an anti-climax after this. But—perhaps, later on, when my abominable remarks are not quite so fresh in your mind, you won't regard them as quite such an insult as you do now. Dreadful outsider though I am—unpardonably caddish though it is to have criticised your war work—especially when I have appreciated it so much—will you try to remember that it would have been far easier and pleasanter to have done the other thing?"

Slowly her eyes came round to his face, and he saw that they were dangerously bright. "What other thing?" she demanded.

"Carried on with the game; the game that both you and I know so well. Hunting, cricket and making love... . Is it not written in 'Who's Who'—unless that interesting publication is temporarily out of print?"

"It strikes me," the girl remarked ominously, "that to your caddishness you add a very sublime conceit."

Vane grinned. "Mother always told me I suffered from swelled head... ." He pointed to the envelope still unaddressed, lying between them on the writing table. "After which slight digression—do you mind?"

She picked up the pen, and sat down once again. "I notice your tone changes when you want me to help you."

Vane made no answer. "The address is Mrs. Vernon, 14, Culman Terrace, Balham," he remarked quietly.

"I trust she is doing war work that pleases you," sneered the girl. She handed him the envelope, and then, as she saw the blaze in his eyes, she caught her breath in a little quick gasp.

"As far as I know," he answered grimly, "Mrs. Vernon is endeavouring to support herself and three children on the large sum of one hundred and fifty pounds a year. Her husband died in my arms while we were consolidating some ground we had won." He took the envelope from her hand. "Thank you; I am sorry to have had to trouble you."

He walked towards the door, and when he got to it, he paused and looked back. Joan Devereux was standing motionless, staring out of the window. Vane dropped his letter into the box in the hall, and went up the stairs to his room.

CHAPTER VI

There was no objection to Vane going to London, it transpired. He had merely to write his name in a book, and he was then issued a half-fare voucher. No one even asked him his religion, which seemed to point to slackness somewhere.

It was with feelings the reverse of pleasant that Vane got into the first-class carriage one morning four days after he had written to Mrs. Vernon. She would be glad to see him, she had written in reply, and she was grateful to him for taking the trouble to come. Thursday afternoon would be most convenient; she was out the other days, and on Sundays she had to look after the children... .

Vane opened the magazine on his knees and stared idly at the pictures. In the far corner of the carriage two expansive looking gentlemen were engaged in an animated conversation, interrupted momentarily by his entrance. In fact they had seemed to regard his intrusion rather in the light of a personal affront. Their general appearance was not prepossessing, and Vane having paused in the doorway, and stared them both in turn out of countenance, had been amply rewarded by hearing himself described as an impertinent young puppy.

He felt in his blackest and most pugilistic mood that morning. As a general rule he was the most peaceful of men; but at times, some strain inherited from a remote ancestor who, if he disliked a man's face hit it hard with a club, resurrected itself in him. There had been the celebrated occasion in the Promenade at the Empire, a few months before the war, when a man standing in front of him had failed to remove his hat during the playing of "The King." It was an opera hat, and Vane removed it for him and shut it up. The owner turned round just in time to see it hit the curtain, whence it fell with a thud into the orchestra... . Quite inexcusable, but the fight that followed was all that man could wish for. The two of them, with a large chucker-out, had finally landed in a heap in Leicester Square—with the hatless gentleman underneath. And Vane—being fleet of foot, had finally had the supreme joy of watching from afar his disloyal opponent being escorted to Vine Street, in a winded condition, by a very big policeman... .

Sometimes he wondered if other people ever felt like that; if they were ever overcome with an irresistible desire to be offensive. It struck him that the war had not cured this failing; if anything it had made it stronger. And the sight of these two fat, oily specimens complacently discussing business, while a woman—in some poky house in Balham—was waiting to hear the last message from her dead, made him gnash his teeth.

Of course it was all quite wrong. No well-brought-up and decorous Englishman had any right to feel so annoyed with another man's face that he longed to hit it with a stick. But Vane was beginning to doubt whether he had been well brought up; he was quite certain that he was not decorous. He was merely far more natural than he had ever been before; he had ceased to worry over the small things.

And surely the two other occupants of the carriage were very small. At least they seemed so to him. For all he knew, or cared, they might each of them be in control of a Government Department; that failed to alter their littleness.

Fragments of their conversation came to him over the rattle of the wheels, and he became more and more irate. The high price of whisky was one source of complaint—it appeared, according to one of them, that it was all going to France, which caused a shortage for those at home. Then the military situation.... Impossible, grotesque.... Somebody ought to be hanged for having allowed such a thing to happen. After four years to be forced back—inexcusable. What was wanted was somebody with a business brain to run the Army.... In the meantime their money was being wasted, squandered, frittered away....

Vane grew rampant in his corner as he listened; his mental language became impossibly lurid. He felt that he would willingly have given a thousand or two to plant them both into that bit of the outpost line, where a month before he had crawled round on his belly at dawn to see his company. Grey-faced and grey-coated with the mud, their eyes had been clear and steady and cheerful, even if their chins were covered with two days' growth. And their pay was round about a shilling a day....

It was just as the train was slowing down to enter Victoria that he felt he could contain himself no longer. The larger and fatter of the two, having concluded an exhaustive harangue on the unprecedented wealth at present being enjoyed by some of the soldiers' wives in the neighbourhood—and unmarried ones, too, mark you!—stood up to get his despatch case.

"It seems a pity, gentlemen, you bother to remain in the country," remarked Vane casually. "You must be suffering dreadfully."

Two gentlemen inferred icily that they would like to know what he meant.

"Why not return to your own?" he continued, still more casually. "Doubtless the Egyptian Expeditionary Force will soon have it swept and garnished for you."

The train stopped; and Vane got out. He was accompanied to the barrier by his two late travelling companions, and from their remarks he gathered that they considered he had insulted them; but it was only when he arrived at the gate that he stopped and spoke. He spoke at some length, and the traffic was unavoidably hung up during the peroration.

"I have listened," said Vane in a clear voice, "to your duologue on the way up, and if I thought there were many like you in the country I'd take to drink. As it is, I am hopeful, as I told you, that Jerusalem will soon be vacant. Good morning... ."

And the fact that two soldiers on leave from France standing close by burst into laughter did not clear the air... .

"Jimmy," said Vane half an hour later, throwing himself into a chair in his club next to an old pal in the smoking-room, "I've just been a thorough paced bounder; a glorious and wonderful cad. And, Jimmy! I feel so much the better for it."

Jimmy regarded him sleepily from the depths of his chair. Then his eyes wandered to the clock, and he sat up with an effort. "Splendid, dear old top," he remarked. "And since it is now one minute past twelve, let's have a spot to celebrate your lapse from virtue."

With the conclusion of lunch, the approaching ordeal at Balham began to loom large on his horizon. In a vain effort to put off the evil hour, he decided that he would first go round to his rooms in Half Moon Street. He had kept them on during the war, only opening them up during his periods of leave. The keys were in the safe possession of Mrs. Green, who, with her husband, looked after him and the other occupants of the house generally. As always, the worthy old lady was delighted to see him... .

"Just cleaned them out two days ago, Mr. Vane, sir," she remarked. New-fangled Army ranks meant nothing to her: Mr. Vane he had started—Mr. Vane he would remain to the end of the chapter.

"And, Binks, Mrs. Green?" But there was no need for her to answer that question. There was a sudden scurry of feet, and a wire-haired fox-terrier was jumping all over him in ecstasy.

"My son, my son," said Vane, picking the dog up. "Are you glad to see your master again? One lick, you little rascal, as it's a special occasion. And incidentally, mind my arm, young fellow-me-lad."

He put Binks down, and turned with a smile to Mrs. Green. "Has he been good, Mrs. Green?"

"Good as good, sir," she answered. "I'm sure he's a dear little dog. Just for the first week after you went—the same as the other times—he'd hardly touch a thing. Just lay outside your door and whined and whined his poor little heart out... ."

The motherly old woman stooped to pat the dog's head, and Binks licked her fingers once to show that he was grateful for what she'd done. But—and this was a big but—she was only a stop-gap. Now—and with another scurry of feet, he was once again jumping round the only one who really mattered. A series of short staccato yelps of joy too great to be controlled; a stumpy tail wagging so fast that the eye could scarcely follow it; a dog... .

"I believe, Mrs. Green," said Vane quietly, "that quite a number of people in England have lately been considering whether it wouldn't be a good thing to kill off the dogs... ."

"Kill off the dogs, sir!" Mrs. Green's tone was full of shrill amazement. "Kill Binks? I'd like to see anyone try." ... Vane had a momentary vision of his stalwart old landlady armed with a poker and a carving knife, but he did not smile.

"So would I, Mrs. Green... . So would I... ." And with a short laugh he took the key from her and went upstairs.

The room into which he went first was such as one would have expected to find in the abode of a young bachelor. Into the frame of the mirror over the fireplace a score of ancient invitations were stuck. Some heavy silver photo frames stood on the mantel-piece, while in the corner a bag of golf clubs and two or three pairs of boxing gloves gave an indication of their owner's tastes. The room was spotlessly clean, and with the sun shining cheerfully in at the window it seemed impossible to believe that it had been empty for six months. A few good prints—chiefly sporting—adorned the walls; and the books in the heavy oak revolving bookcase which stood beside one of the big leather chairs were of the type generally described as light... .

For a time Vane stood by the mantelpiece thoughtfully staring out of the window; while Binks, delirious with joy, explored each well-remembered corner, and blew heavily down the old accustomed cracks in the floor. Suddenly with a wild scurry, he fled after his principal joy—the one that never tired. He had seen Vane throw it into the corner, and now he trotted sedately towards this wonderful master of his, who had so miraculously returned, with his enemy in his mouth. He lay down at Vane's feet; evidently the game was about to begin.

The enemy was an indiarubber dog which emitted a mournful whistling noise through a hole in its tummy. It was really intended for the use of the very young in their baths—to enable them to squirt a jet of water into the nurse's eye; but it worried Binks badly. The harder he bit, the harder it whistled. It seemed impossible to kill the damn thing... .

For a while he bit the whistling atrocity to his heart's content; then with it still between his fore paws he looked up into Vane's face. Surely his master had not forgotten the rules of the game. Really—it was a little steep if it was so. But Vane, as far as Binks could see, was looking at one of the photographs on the mantelpiece with a slight smile on his face. One or two mournful whistles produced no apparent result. So Binks decided it was time for desperate measures. He stood up; and, with his head on one side, he contemplated his hated adversary, prone on the carpet. Then he gave a short sharp bark—just as a reminder... .

It was quite sufficient, and Vane apologised handsomely. "Beg your pardon, old man," he remarked. "For the moment I was thinking of trivialities." He moved his foot backwards and forwards close to the indiarubber dog, and Binks, with his ears pricked up, and his head turning slightly as he followed the movement of his master's foot, waited. Shortly, he knew that this hereditary enemy of his would fly to one side of the room or the other. The great question was—which? It would hit the wall, and rebound on to the floor, where it would be seized, and borne back with blood curdling growls for the process to be repeated ... The game, it may be said, was not governed by any foolish time limit... .

Suddenly the swinging leg feinted towards the left, and Binks dashed in that direction. Curse it—he was stung again. His adversary flew to the right, and was comfortably settled on the floor before Binks appeared on the scene. However, his tail was still up, as he brought it back, and he gave it an extra furious bite, just to show that he would tolerate no uppishness on account of this preliminary defeat... . Vane laughed. "You funny old man," he said. He stopped and picked up the toy, replacing it on the mantelpiece. "That ends the game for to-day, Binks, for I've got to go out. Would you like to come, too?"

The brown eyes looked adoringly up into his. Binks failed to see why the first game after such a long time should be so short; but—his not to reason why on such matters. Besides his master was talking and Binks liked to have his opinion asked.

Once again Vane's eyes went back to the photograph he had been studying. It was one of Margaret—taken years ago… . And as he looked at it, a pair of grey eyes, with the glint of a mocking smile in them, seemed to make the photo a little hazy.

"Come on, old man. We're going to Balham. And I need you to support me."

Culman Terrace was not a prepossessing spectacle. A long straight road ran between two rows of small and dreary houses. Each house was exactly the same, with its tiny little plot of garden between the front door and the gate. In some of the plots there were indications that the owner was fond of gardening; here a few sweet peas curled lovingly up the sticks put in for them —there some tulips showed signs of nightly attention. But in most the plot was plain and drab as the house—a dead thing; a thing without a soul. Individuality, laughter—aye, life itself—seemed crushed in that endless road, with its interminable rows of houses.

As Vane walked slowly up it looking for No. 14, the sun was shining. For the moment it seemed clothed in some semblance of life; almost as if it was stirring from a long sleep, and muttering to itself that love and the glories of love were abroad to-day… . And then the sun went behind a cloud, and everything was grey and dead once more.

Vane pictured it to himself on damp dark mornings in the winter—on evenings when the days were shortening, and the gas lamps shone through the gloom. He saw the doors opening, and each one disgorging some black coated, pallid man, who passed through the gate, and then with quick nervous steps walked towards the station. The 8.30 was their train; though in some very rare cases the 9.3 was early enough… . But as a rule the 9.3 crowd did not live in Culman Terrace. Just a few only, who had come there young and eager, and had died there. True, they caught the 9.3, but they were dead. And the pretty laughing girls who had married them when the lamp was burning with the divine fire of hope, had watched them die … hopelessly, helplessly… . Love will stand most things; but the drab monotony of the successful failure —the two hundred pound a year man who has to keep up appearances—tries it very high… .

Some of them turned into shrews and nagged; some of them ran to fat and didn't care; but most of them just sank quietly and imperceptibly into the dreariness and smallness of their surroundings. At rare intervals there flashed across their horizon something of the great teeming world outside; they went to a bargain sale, perhaps, and saw the King drive past—or they went to the movies and for a space lived in the Land of Make Believe.... But the coils of Culman Terrace had them fast, and the excitement was only momentary—the relapse the more complete. And, dear Heavens, with what high ideals they had all started.... It struck Vane as he walked slowly along the road that here, on each side of him, lay the Big Tragedy—bigger far than in the vilest slum. For in the slum they had never known or thought of anything better....

Odd curtains were pulled aside as he walked, and he felt conscious of people staring at him. He pictured them getting up from their chairs, and peering at him curiously, wondering where he was going—what he was doing—who he was.... It was the afternoon's excitement—a wounded officer passing the house.

A familiar singing noise behind him made him look round and whistle. Long experience left no doubt as to what was happening, and when he saw Binks on his toes, circling round a gate on which a cat was spitting angrily, he called "Binks" sharply once, and walked on again. It was the greatest strain Binks was ever called on to face, but after a moment of indecision he obeyed as usual. Cats were his passion; but ever since he had carried the Colonel's wife's prize Persian on to parade and deposited it at Vane's feet he was discreet in the matter. The infuriated pursuit by the lady in question on to the parade ground, armed with an umbrella in one hand and a poker in the other, had not tended towards steadiness in the ranks. In fact, something like alarm and despondency had been caused amongst all concerned—especially Binks....

"Lord! old man," muttered his master, "here we are." Vane turned in at the gate of No. 14 and rang the bell. There was an unpleasant sinking feeling in the pit of his stomach and he nervously dried his left hand on his handkerchief.

"Pray Heaven she doesn't cry," he said to himself fervently, and at that moment the door opened. A pale, grave-eyed woman in black confronted him, and after a moment or two she smiled very slightly and held out her hand. Vane took it awkwardly.

"It is good of you to take the trouble to come, Captain Vane," she said in a singularly sweet voice. "Won't you come inside?"

He followed her into the small drawing-room and sat down. It was scrupulously clean, and it was more than that—it was homely.... It was the room of a woman who loved beautiful things, and who had with perfect taste banished every single object which might jar on the fastidious mind. It struck

Vane that it was probably a unique room in Culman Terrace; he felt certain that the rest of the house was in keeping... .

"What a charming room," he said involuntarily, and it was only when she looked at him with a little lift of her eyebrows that he realised she might regard the remark as impertinent. Why shouldn't the room be charming? ...

But Mrs. Vernon quickly removed his embarrassment. "It's always been a passion of mine—my house," she said quietly. "And now—more than ever... . It's a duty, even, though a pleasant one—— After all, whatever may go on outside, whatever wretchedness worries one—it's something to have a real sanctuary to come to. I want the children to feel that—so much. I want them to love the beautiful things in life," she went on passionately, "even though they live in these surroundings." She stared out of the window for a moment, and then she turned with a sudden quick movement to Vane. "But, forgive me. I don't know why I should inflict my ideas on you. Will you tell me about Philip?"

It was the moment he had been dreading, and yet, now that it had come, he found it easier than he had expected. There was something about this quiet, steadfast woman which told him that she would not make a scene. And so, gently and quietly, with his eyes fixed on the empty fireplace, he told her the story. There are thousands of similar stories which could be told in the world to-day, but the pathos of each one is not diminished by that. It was the story of the ordinary man who died that others might live. He did not die in the limelight; he just died and was buried and his name, in due course appeared in the casualty list... .

Not that Vane put it that way. He painted his picture with the touch of glamour; he spoke of a charge, of Vernon cheering his men on, of success. Into the peaceful drawing-room he introduced the atmosphere of glory— unwittingly, perhaps, he fell back on the popular conception of war. And the woman, who hung on every word, silent and tearless, thrilled with the pride of it. Her man, running at the head of others—charging—dying at the moment of victory... . It would be something to tell her two boys, when their turn came to face the battle of life; something which would nerve them to the success which her man would have won except for... .

Vane's voice died away. He had finished his story, he had painted his picture. No suspicion had he given that a stray bit of shell had torn Vernon to bits long after the tumult and the shouting had ceased. After all, he was dead ... it was the living who counted. No man could have done more. Surely he deserved the white lie which pictured his death more vividly—more grandly... .

"He died in my arms," went on Vane after a little pause, "and his last words were about you." He told her the few simple sentences, repeated to her the words which a man will say when the race is run and the tape is reached. God knows they are commonplace enough—those short disjointed phrases; but God knows also that it is the little things which count, when the heart is breaking... .

And, then, having told her once, perforce he had to tell her again—just the end bit... . With the tears pouring down her cheeks she listened; and though each word stabbed her to the heart afresh—woman-like, she gloried in her pain.

"'God bless you, Nell,' and then he died," she said softly to herself, repeating Vane's last sentence. "Ah! but you made good, my man. I always knew you would some day... ."

It seemed to the man staring into the fireplace that he was very near to holy ground; and suddenly he rose and strode to the window. With eyes that were a trifle dim he saw the beautifully kept little garden—a mass of colour; he saw the name plate, "Sea View," on the gate, glinting bravely in the sun. Something of the hopeless tragedy of that "Some day" was getting him by the throat... . "Made good"—dear Lord! and he thought of his two travelling companions in the morning... .

For perhaps five minutes he stood there silently, and then he turned back into the room. It had come to him quite clearly that Philip Vernon had indeed made good; that the real tragedy would have been his return to "Sea View." By his death he had justified himself; in his life he would have failed... . For he had been branded with the brand of Culman Terrace, and there is no need to say more. He was relieved to see that Mrs. Vernon was quite composed again. He had performed the first part of his mission, and now the second required tackling. And something warned him that he would have to tread very delicately; any suspicion of the word charity would be fatal to success...
.

"About your eldest boy, Mrs. Vernon," he began; "your husband often spoke about him to me. Let me see—what age is he?"

"Jack is fifteen, Captain Vane," she said quietly.

"Fifteen! Couldn't be better. Now I was wondering, Mrs. Vernon, whether you would care in a year or two, to let him come to me. I'm in a very big business in the City, and my boss is always on the look out for bright boys. I know your boy is clever—but so much depends on getting a good start these days. Of course he'd be judged entirely on his merits ... but he'd start with a real good chance of making the best of his talents." He looked quickly at her, and found she was watching him gravely. "It's part of the privilege of the brotherhood of the trenches, Mrs. Vernon, to be allowed to make such an offer... ." He was finding it easier now. "To do anything for your husband's son would be a real pleasure; though, I need hardly say that, beyond giving him the chance, I could offer nothing else. It would be up to him to make good."

For a while Mrs. Vernon was silent, and he flashed a quick look at her. Had he put it well? Had he kept every suspicion of patronage out of his offer?

"Thank you very much, Captain Vane," she said at last, "for your offer. I hope you won't think me ungrateful when I refuse. Four years ago I think I should have accepted it with gratitude; but now ..." She shook her head "A lot of the shams have gone; we see clearer—some of us... . And I tell you that I would not willingly condemn Jack to such a life as his father led—even if I was penniless. Wait—let me finish"—as Vane started to speak—"Of course with you he would have better chances than his father had before him—but the city life would kill him—even as it has killed thousands of others... . I wonder if you can realise the hideous tragedy of the poor clerk. He can't strike for higher wages, like the British working man. He just goes on and on and suffers in silence... . In Jack's case it would be the same... . What—four hundred a year?" She laughed a little scornfully. "It's not much to bring up a family on, Captain Vane... . Four hundred a year, and Acacia Avenue—two streets up... . Acacia Avenue doesn't call on Culman Terrace, you know... ." Again she laughed. "No, Jack isn't made for that sort of life, thank God. He aches for the big spaces in his boyish way, for the lands where there are big things to be done... . And I've encouraged him. There'll be nobody there to sneer if his clothes get frayed and he can't buy any more—because of the children's boots. There'll be no appearances to keep up there. And I'd a thousand times rather that Jack should stand—or fall—in such surroundings, than that he should sink slowly ... here."

She paused for a moment, and then stood up and faced him. "It's emigration, Captain Vane, that I and people like me have got to turn to for our boys. For ourselves—it doesn't much matter; we've had our day, and I don't want you to think the sun never shined on us, for it did... . Just wonderfully at times... ." She gave a quick sigh. "Only now ... things are different... . And up till now, Culman Terrace hasn't considered emigration quite the thing. It's not quite respectable... . Only aristocratic ne'er-do-wells and quite impossibly common men emigrate. It's a confession of failure... . And so we've continued to swell the ranks of the most pitiful class in the country—the gentleman and his family with the small fixed income. The working man regards him with suspicion because he wears a black coat—or, with contempt because he doesn't strike; the Government completely ignores him because they know he's too much a slave to convention to do anything but vote along so-called gentlemanly lines. What do you suppose would be the result if the enormous body of middle class slaves in this country did, one day, combine and refuse to be bled by every other class? We're bled by the people on top for their own advantage; and then we're bled again for the advantage of the dear workman... ." She laughed a little. "Forgive me talking so much; but not for Jack, thank you."

Vane bowed. "Mrs. Vernon, I think you're perfectly right—and I wish you and him the very best of luck." He shook hands gravely and a few moments later he was walking back towards the station with Binks trotting sedately at his heels. In all probability he would never see Mrs. Vernon again; war and its aftermath had brought their paths together for a space, and now they were diverging again. But that short space had been enough to make him feel ashamed and proud. Ashamed of himself for his cynicism and irritability; proud of the woman who, with her faith clear and steadfast, could face the future without faltering. Her man's job had been laid upon her; she would never fail him till the time came for her to join him... . And by then she would have earned her reward—rest... . She will deserve every moment of it... . Surely the Lord of True Values will not grudge it to her... .

And though he had said nothing to her of his thoughts—men when deeply moved are so hopelessly inarticulate—somehow he wished going up in the train that he had. Falteringly, crudely, he might have said something, which would have helped her. If only a man had the power of expressing sympathy without words. He needn't have worried, had he known ... and Binks, who was looking out of the window with interest, could not tell him. Anyway, it was not anything to make a song or dance about—putting a cold wet nose into a hand that hung down from a chair, and letting it rest there—just for a while... . But it was not the first time, and it will not be the last, that the Peace that passeth all understanding has been brought to the human heart by the touch of a dog... . Binks had justified his inclusion in the trip... .

CHAPTER VII

The days that followed passed pleasantly enough. Gradually the jaundice was disappearing, and Vane was becoming normal again. The war seemed very far away from Rumfold; though occasionally a newcomer brought some bit of intimate gossip about Crucifix Alley or Hell Fire Corner, or one of the little places not shown on any map, which mean so much more to the actual fighting man than all the big towns rolled together. Pipes would come out and men would draw together in the smoking-room—while in imagination the green flares would go hissing up again, silhouetted against the velvet of the night. But for the most part the war had ceased to count; tennis and golf, with a visit now and then to London, filled the days.

Vane's arm prevented him playing any game, but the country around was admirably suited for walking, and most afternoons he found himself strolling out past the lodge gates for a ramble. Sometimes one of the other officers accompanied him; but more often he went alone. And on those long lonely walks he found himself obeying Margaret's injunctions, given to him at Paris Plage—"Go and find out... ."

In common with many others who were beginning, almost unconsciously, to think for the first time, he found considerable difficulty in knowing where to start the quest. Vane was no fool, but in days gone by he had accepted a certain order of things as being the only possible order—just as England had been the only possible country. But now it seemed to him that if England was to remain the only possible country an alteration would have to be made in the order. Before, any danger to her supremacy had come from without—now the trouble lay within.

Each day, alongside the war news, he read of strikes and rumours of strikes, and when he came to ask himself the reason why, he was appalled at his own ignorance. Something was wrong somewhere; something which would have to be put right. And the trouble was that it did not seem a matter of great ease to put it right. He felt that the glib phrases about Capital and Labour pulling together, about better relations between employers and men, about standing shoulder to shoulder, failed to hit the point. They were rather like offering a hungry lion a halfpenny bun. They could always be relied on to raise a cheer from a political platform provided the right audience was present; but it seemed doubtful whether even such a far-reaching result as that was quite enough.

At times his natural indolence made him laugh inwardly. "What on earth is the use?" he would mutter, throwing pebbles into the pond below him. "What has to be—has to be." It was a favourite haunt of his—that pond; in the heart of a wood, with a little waterfall trickling over some rounded stones and falling musically into the pond a few feet below. The afternoon sun used to shine through the branches of some great beech trees, and the dense undergrowth around screened him from the observation of any chance passer by walking along the path behind.... "You can't do anything," the mocking voice would continue. "So why worry?"

But the mental jaundice was passing—and the natural belief of man in himself was coming back. Ho felt the gas expert had been right, even though he had died. And so Vane became a reader of books of a type which had not formerly been part of his daily programme. He was groping towards knowledge, and he deliberately sought every help for the way. He tried some of H. G. Wells's to start with.... Previously he had read the "First Men in the Moon," because he'd been told it was exciting; and "Ann Veronica," because he had heard it was immoral. Now he tried some of the others.

He was engaged thus when Joan Devereux found him one afternoon in his favourite haunt. She had stumbled on his hiding place by mistake, and her first instinct was to retire as quickly as she had come. Since their first meeting, their conversation, on the rare occasions they had met at Rumfold Hall, had been confined to the most commonplace remarks, and those always in the presence of someone else. Any possibility of a *tête-à-tête* she had avoided; and the necessary mental effort had naturally caused her to think all the more about him. Now, just as she halted in her tracks and prepared to back out through the undergrowth, Vane looked up at her with his slow lazy smile.

"Discovered!" he remarked scrambling to his feet, and saluting her. "Joan, you have come in the nick of time."

"I would prefer you not to call me Joan," she answered coldly. "And after your abominable rudeness last time we were alone together, I don't want to talk to you at all."

"I suppose I was rather rude," answered Vane reflectively. "Though, if it's any comfort to you to know, I was much ruder to two men going up in the train a few days later...."

"It isn't of the slightest interest to me," she returned, "whom you're rude to, or how you spend your spare time. The habits of an ill-mannered boor are not of great importance, are they?" She turned her back on him, and parted the undergrowth with her hands, preparatory to leaving.

"Don't go." His voice close behind her made her pause. "I need you—officially."

She looked round at him, and despite herself the corners of her lips began to twitch. "You really are the most impossible person," she remarked. "What do you need me for?"

He stepped back to his usual seat, and pointed to a small mossy bank beside him. "Come and sit down there, and let's think... ."

After a moment's hesitation she did as he said.

"It's rather a knotty problem, isn't it?" he continued after a moment. "I might want you to flirt with me in order to avert my suicide in the pond through boredom... ."

"You may want," she retorted.

"But it's in the official programme?"

"You're not on the official list," she flashed back.

"Worse and worse," he murmured. "I begin to despair. However, I won't try you as highly as that. I will just ask you a plain, honest question. And I rely on you to answer me truthfully... . Do you think I should be a more attractive being; do you think I should be more capable of grappling with those great problems which—ah—surround us on all sides, if I could dissect rats—or even mice?" he added thoughtfully after a pause.

The girl looked at him in amazement. "Are you trying to be funny?" she asked at length.

"Heaven forbid!" he said fervently. "I was never more serious in my life. But, in that book,"—he pointed to one lying between them—"everybody, who is anybody dissects rodents."

She picked up the book and gazed at the title. "But this is the book everybody's talking about," she said.

"I am nothing if not fashionable," returned Vane.

"And do they dissect rats in it?"

"Don't misunderstand me, and take too gloomy a view of the situation," said Vane reassuringly. "They do other things besides... . Brilliant things, all most brilliantly written about; clever things, all most cleverly told. But whenever there's a sort of gap to be filled up, a *mauvais quart d'heure* after luncheon, the hero runs off and deals with a mouse. And even if he doesn't, you know he could... . And the heroine! It's a fundamental part of all their educations, their extraordinary brilliance seems to rest on it as a foundation."

She looked at him curiously. "I'm not particularly dense," she said after a while, "but I must admit you rather defeat me."

"Joan," answered Vane seriously, and she made no protest this time at the use of her name, "I rather defeat myself. In the old days I never thought at all— but if I ever did I thought straight. Now my mind is running round in circles. I chase after it; think I'm off at last—and then find myself back where I started. That's why I've put up the S.O.S., and am trying to get help." He laid his hand on the book beside him.

"Are you reading all the highbrows?" she asked.

"Most of 'em," he answered. "In the first place they're all so amazingly well written that it's a pleasure to read them for that alone; and, secondly—I'm hoping … still hoping… ." He took out his cigarette case and offered it to her. "I feel that it's I who am wrong—not they—that it's my lack of education that huffs me. I expect it's those damned rats… ."

Joan laughed, and lit a cigarette. "They're all so frightfully clever, Joan," went on Vane blowing out a cloud of smoke. "They seem to me to be discussing the world of men and women around them from the pure cold light of reason… . Brain rules them, and they make brain rule their creations. Instead of stomach—stomach really rules the world, you know." For a while they sat in silence, watching a dragon-fly darting like a streak of light over the pond below them.

"I wouldn't bother if I were you," said the girl after a while. "After all, if one is happy oneself, and tries to make other people happy too, it's bound to help things along a bit, isn't it? It strikes me that whatever people write, or say, everything will go on much the same. Besides—it's so impertinent. You don't want to be reconstructed; nor does anybody else. So why worry?"

"But, my dear girl," said Vane feebly, "don't you think one ought… ."

"No, I don't," she interrupted. "You listen to me for a bit, my friend; and you can take it or leave it, just as you like. It strikes me you're a great deal too occupied about other people, and you don't pay sufficient attention to yourself. You've got to live your own life—not the man's next door. And you'll do most good by living that life, as you want to live it. If you really want to reform other people—well go and do it, and get a thick ear… . It's part of your job. But if you don't want to, there's no earthly use trying to pretend you do; you're merely a hypocrite. There's no good telling me that everybody can be lumped into classes and catered for like so many machines. We're all sorts and conditions, and I suppose you'd say I was one of the supremely selfish sort. In fact, you have said so," she said defiantly.

"All right—we'll leave it at that," she went on before he could speak. "But I'm happy—and I'm sincere. I do the most awful things at times—because I like doing them. I should loathe to be a nurse, and the W.A.A.C. uniform makes me look a fright. I may not realise the horrors over the water; I don't want to. And do you suppose half these women who talk about them so glibly do either? … . Of course they don't; they're just posing. They pretend it's awful and horrible to dance and play the fool; and all the while their teeth are chattering with envy and malice… ."

"We seem," remarked Vane, taking advantage of a temporary lull in the flood, "to have arrived at rather a personal discussion."

"Of course we have," she took him up. "Isn't it I—I—I everywhere? Only a lot of people aren't sufficiently truthful to admit it. It's Number One first all the way through, right from the people up at the top down to the poor brutes in the slums. All the wonderful schemes of reform are for the glory of the schemer first, with the happy recipients amongst the also rans." She paused a moment, and a sudden tender look came into her eyes. "Of course there are exceptions. There's a boy I know—he's a cousin of mine—with weak lungs. Rejected for the Army three times as totally unfit. For the last four years he's been living in a slum off Whitechapel and the people there love him… . He just walks in and planks down a pork chop in the back room; or a bottle of Basa, or something and has a talk to the woman … he's dying … but he's dying happy… . I couldn't do that; no more could you… . We should loathe it, and so we should be fools to attempt it… ."

"I wonder," said Vane slowly… . "I wonder."

"No, you don't," she cried. "You don't wonder… . You know I'm right… . If you loved such a life you'd just do it… . And you'd succeed. The people who fail are the people who do things from a sense of duty."

"What a very dangerous doctrine," smiled Vane.

"Perhaps it is," she answered. "Perhaps in my own way I'm groping too; perhaps," and she laughed a little apologetically, "I've fitted my religion to my life. At any rate it's better than fitting other peoples' lives to one's religion. But it seems to me that God," she hesitated, as if at a loss for words to express herself—"that God—and one's surroundings—make one what one is… . And unless one is very certain that either God or the surroundings are wrong, it's asking for trouble to go on one's own beaten track… . I suppose you think I'm talking out of my turn." She turned and faced him with a slight smile.

"On the contrary," answered Vane, "you have interested me immensely. But you've dodged the one vital question—for me, at any rate. What is the beaten track? Just at present I can't find it?"

"You'll not find it any easier by looking for it too hard," she said thoughtfully.

"I'm certain of that.... It'll come in a flash to you, when you least expect it, and you'll see it as clear as daylight."

For a while they sat in silence, both busy with their own thoughts. Then the girl laughed musically.

"To think of me," she gurgled, "holding forth like this.... Why, I've never done such a thing before that I can remember." Then of a sudden she became serious. The big grey eyes looked steadily, almost curiously, at the face of the man beside her. "I wonder why," she whispered almost below her breath. "You've been most poisonously rude to me, and yet ... and yet here am I talking to you as I've never talked to any other man in my life."

Vane stared at the pool for a few moments before he answered. He was becoming uncomfortably aware that grey eyes with a certain type of chin were attractive—very attractive. But his tone was light when he spoke.

"A quarrel is always a sound foundation." He looked up at her with a smile, but her eyes still held that half speculative look....

"I wonder what you would have thought of me," she continued after a moment, "if you'd met me before the war...."

"Why, that children of fifteen should be in bed by ten," he mocked.

"Yes, but supposing I was what I am now, and you were what you were then —and you weren't filled with all these ideas about duty and futures and things...."

"You would have added another scalp to the collection, I expect," said Vane drily.

They both laughed, then she bent slightly towards him. "Will you forgive me for what I said about—about that woman you were going to see?"

"Why—sure," answered Vane. "I guess you owed me one."

Joan laughed. "We'll wash the first lesson out. Except, of course, for that one thing you said. I mean about—the other.... I'd just hate to forget that there's a wedding coming on, and do anything that would make it awkward for me to be asked to the church...."

"You little devil, Joan," said Vane softly, "you little devil."

She laughed lightly and sprang to her feet. "I must be going," she said. "At least three Colonials are waiting for my ministrations." She stood looking down at him.... "Are you going to walk back with me, or to resume your study of rodents?"

Vane slipped the book in his pocket. "I'm afraid," he remarked, "that I should not be able to bring that undivided attention to bear on the subject which is so essential for my education. Besides—perhaps you'll have a few minutes to spare after you have dealt with the Colonials... ." He parted the branches for her.

"My dear man," she retorted, "You've had far more than your fair official share already... ." She scrambled on to the path and Vane fell into step beside her. "And don't forget that you've only just been forgiven... ."

"Which makes it all the more essential for me to have continual evidence of the fact," retorted Vane.

"It strikes me," she looked at him suddenly, "that you're not quite as serious as you make out. You've got all the makings of a very pretty frivoller in you anyway."

"I bow to your superior judgment," said Vane gravely. "But I've been commissioned to—er—go and find myself, so to speak, by one who must be obeyed. And in the intervals between periods of cold asceticism when I deal with the highbrows, and other periods when I tackle subjects of national importance first hand, I feel that I shall want relaxation... ."

"And so you think you'd like me to fill the role of comic relief," she said sweetly. "Thanks a thousand times for the charming compliment."

"It doesn't sound very flattering put that way, I must admit," conceded Vane with a grin. "And yet the pleasures of life fill a very important part. I want to find myself in them too... ."

"I'm glad to see traces of comparative sanity returning," she said, as they turned into the Lodge Gates. "Do you think it's safe to trust yourself to such an abandoned character as I am? What would She who must be obeyed say?"

She looked at him mockingly, and involuntarily Vane frowned slightly. At the moment he felt singularly unwilling to be reminded of Margaret. And he was far too old a stager not to realise that he was heading directly for waters which, though they ran amongst charming scenery, contained quite a number of hidden rocks.

She saw the sudden frown, and laughed very gently. "Poor young man," she murmured; "poor serious young man. Dare you risk it?"

Then Vane laughed too. They had come to the lawn, and her three Colonial patients were approaching. "Put that way," he said, "I feel that it is my bounden duty to take a prolonged course of those pleasures."

"Splendid," she cried, and her eyes were dancing merrily. "Come over and lunch to-morrow. You can have Father and Aunt Jane first. You'll like Aunt

Jane, she's as deaf as a post and very bloodthirsty—and then you can begin the course afterwards. One o'clock, and it's about half an hour's walk... ."

With a nod she turned and left him. And if those of her friends who knew Joan Devereux well had seen the look in her eyes as she turned to her three Canadians, they would have hazarded a guess that there was trouble brewing. They would further have hazarded a second guess as to the form it was likely to take. And both guesses would have been right. A young man, remarked Joan to herself, who would be all the better for a fall; a young man who seemed very much too sure of himself. Joan Devereux was quite capable of dealing with such cases as they deserved, and she was a young woman of much experience.

CHAPTER VIII

It was the following morning that Vane received a second letter from Margaret. He had written her once—a letter in which he had made no allusion to their last meeting—and she had answered it. Cases were still pouring in and she was very busy. When she did have a moment to herself she was generally so tired that she lay down and went to sleep. It was the letter of a girl obsessed with her work to the exclusion of all outside things.

Of course he admired her for it—admired her intensely. It was so characteristic of her, and she had such a wonderful character. But—somehow … he had wished for something a little more basely material. And so with this second one. He read it through once at breakfast, and then, with a thoughtful look in his eyes, he took it with him to a chair on the big verandah which ran along the whole of the front of Rumfold Hall. The awning above it had been specially erected for the benefit of the patients and Vane pulled one of the lounge chairs back from the stone balustrade, so that his face was shaded from the sun. It was a favourite spot of his, and now, with Margaret's letter outspread beside him, and his pipe held between his knees, he commenced to fill the bowl. He was becoming fairly quick at the operation, but long after it was well alight he was still staring at the misty line of distant hills. Away, out there, beyond, the thing called war was in full swing—the game was at its height. And the letter beside him had taken him back in spirit… . After a while he picked it up again and commenced to re-read the firm, clear handwriting… .

No. 24, STATIONARY HOSPITAL.

MONDAY.

Derek, dear, I've been moved as you see from No. 13. I'm with the men now, and though I hated going at first—yet, now, I think I almost prefer it. With the officers there must always be a little constraint—at least, I have never been able to get rid of the feeling. Perhaps with more experience it would vanish *je ne sais pas* … but with the men it's never there. They're just children, Derek, just dear helpless kiddies; and so wonderfully grateful for any little thing one does. Never a whimper; never the slightest impatience… . they're just wonderful. One expects it from the officers; but somehow it strikes one with a feeling almost of surprise when one meets it in the men. There's one of them, a boy of eighteen, with both his legs blown off above the knee. He just lies there silently, trying to understand. He never worries or frets—but there's a look in his eyes—a puzzled, questioning look sometimes—which asks as clearly as if he spoke—"Why has this thing happened to *me*?" He comes from a little Devonshire fishing village, he tells me; and until the war he'd never been away from it! Can you imagine the pitiful, chaotic, helplessness in his mind? Oh! doesn't it all seem too insensately brutal? … It's not even as if there was any sport in it; it's all so utterly ugly and bestial… . One feels so helpless, so bewildered, and the look in some of their eyes makes one want to scream, with the horror of it… .

But, old man, the object of this letter is not to inflict on you my ideas on war. It is in a sense a continuation, and a development, of our talk on the beach at Paris Plage. I have been thinking a good deal lately about that conversation, and now that I have almost definitely made up my mind as to what I propose to do myself after the war, I consider it only fair to let you know. I said to you then that perhaps my job might only be to help you to fulfil your own destiny, and nothing which I have decided since alters that in any way. If you still want me after the war—if we find that neither of us has made a mistake—I can still help you, Derek, I hope. But, my dear, it won't be quite a passive help, if you understand what I mean. I've got to be up and doing myself— actively; to be merely any man's echo—his complement—however much I loved him, would not be enough. I've come to that, you see.

And so I've decided—not quite definitely as I said, but almost so—to read for Medicine. I'm a little old, perhaps, though I'm only twenty-four: but these years in France have at any rate not been wasted. The question of money does not come in luckily, and the work attracts me immensely. Somehow I feel that I might be helping to repair a tiny bit of the hideous destruction and mutilation which we're suffering from now.

And that's enough about myself. I want to suggest something to you. You may laugh, old boy—but I'm in earnest. I remember you're telling me once that, when you were up at the 'Varsity, you used to scribble a bit. I didn't pay much attention; in those days one didn't pay attention—ever. But now your words have come back to me once or twice, during the night, when I've been seeing dream pictures in my reading lamp and the ward has been asleep. Have you thought that possibly that is the line along which you might develop? Don't you think it's worth trying, Derek? And then, perhaps—this is my wildest dream, the raving of a fevered brain—the day will come when you and I can stand together and realise that each of us in our own way has made good—has done something to help on—*les autres*. Oh! Derek—it's worth trying, old man—surely it's worth trying. We've just got to do something that's worth while, before we come to the end—if only to balance a little of the hideous mass of worthlessness that's being piled up to-day… .

Don't bother to answer this, as I know you find writing difficult. I hope to be getting some leave soon: we can have a talk then. How goes the arm? *A toi, mon cheri.*

MARGARET.

PS.—There's rather a dear man living fairly close to Rumfold, old Sir James Devereux. His house is Blandford—a magnificent old place; almost if not quite as fine as Rumfold, and the grounds are bigger. His wife died when the son was born, and I rather think there is a daughter, but she was away at a finishing school when I knew them, Go over and call; from what I heard there's a distinct shortage of money—at least of enough to keep the place going.

P.PS.—He's not really old—about only fifty. Say you know Daddy; they used to shoot together.

With something like a sigh Vane laid down the last sheet, and, striking a match, relit his pipe. Then once again his eyes rested on the misty, purple hills. Margaret a successful doctor; himself literary educator of the public taste… . It was so entirely different from any picture he had previously contemplated, on the rare occasions when he had thought about matrimony or the future at all, that it left him gasping. It was perfectly true that he had scribbled a certain amount in years gone by, when he was at the 'Varsity: but not seriously… . An essay or two which he had been told showed distinct ability: a short story, of possible merit but questionable morality, which had been accepted on the spot by a not too particular periodical and had never been paid for—that was the extent of his scribbling. And yet—Margaret might be right… . One never knows till one tries: and Vane grinned to himself as that hoary platitude floated through his mind… . Then his thoughts passed to the other side of the picture. Margaret, dispensing admonition and pills, in her best professional manner, to long queues of the great unwashed. He felt certain that she would prefer that section of the community to any less odoriferous one… . And she'd probably never charge anything, and, if she did, he would have to stand at the door and collect it, probably in penny stamps. Vane's shoulders shook a little as this engaging tableau presented itself… . What about the little hunting box not far from Melton, where, in the dear long ago, he had always pictured himself and his wife wintering? Provided always the mythical She had some money! There would be stabling for six nags, which, with care, meant five days a fortnight for both of them. Also a garage, and a rather jolly squash racquet court. Then a month in Switzerland, coming back towards the end of January to finish the season off. A small house of course in Town—some country house cricket: and then a bit of shooting... . One needn't always go to Switzerland either in the winter; Cairo is very pleasant, and so is Nice... . It was an alluring prospect, no less now than formerly; but it meant that Margaret's patients would have to hop around some... . And they'd probably leave her if he stood at the door in a pink coat and a hunting topper collecting postage stamps. They are rather particular over appearances, are the ragged trousered and shredded skirt brigade... .

The thing was grotesque; it was out of the question, Vane told himself irritably. After all, it is possible to push altruism too far, and for Margaret, at her age and with her attractions, to go fooling around with medicine, with the mistaken idea that she was benefiting humanity, was nothing more or leas than damned twaddle. If she wanted to do something why not take up her music seriously. ....

And it was at this point in his deliberations that a sentence vibrated across his memory. It was so clear that it might almost have been spoken in his ear: "If you loved such a life you'd just do it... . And you'd succeed."

Vane folded Margaret's letter, and put it in his pocket. If she really loved the thought of such a life she would just do it... . And she would succeed. As far as he was concerned there would be nothing more to say about it; she had a perfect right to decide for herself. She left him free—that he knew; he could still carry out his hunting box programme in full. Only he would have to play the part alone—or with someone else... . Someone else. Abruptly he rose from his chair, and found himself face to face with Lady Patterdale....

"Good morning, Captain Vane," she remarked affably. "'Ad a good night?"

"Splendid, thank you, Lady Patterdale."

"Ain't the news splendid? Marshal Foch seems to be fair making the 'Uns 'um."

Vane laughed. "Yes, they seem to be sitting up and taking notice, don't they?"

"Sir John is marking it all up in the 'All on the map, with flags," continued the worthy old woman. "I can't make 'ead or tail of it all myself—but my 'usband likes to 'ave everything up to date. 'E can't form any real opinion on the strategy, he says, unless he knows where everybody is."

Vane preserved a discreet silence.

"But as I tells 'im," rambled on Lady Patterdale, "it doesn't seem to me to be of much account where the poor fellows are. You may move a pin from 'ere to there, and feel all pleased and joyful about it—but you wouldn't feel so 'appy if you was the pin."

Vane laughed outright. "You've got a way of putting things, Lady Patterdale, which hits the nail on the head each time."

"Ah! you may laugh, Captain Vane. You may think I'm a silly old woman who doesn't know what she's talking about. But I've got eyes in my 'ead; and I'm not quite a fool. I've seen young men go out to France laughing and cheerful; and I've seen 'em come back. They laugh just as much—perhaps a bit more; they seem just as cheerful—but if you love 'em as I do you come to something which wasn't never there before. They've been one of the pins. Lots of us 'ave been one of the pins, Captain Vane; though we ain't been to France you can lose other things besides your life in this world."

She nodded her head at him solemnly and waddled on, while Vane stood for a moment looking after her. Assuredly this common old woman possessed in her some spark of the understanding which is almost Divine.... . And Vane, with a quick flash of insight, saw the proud planting of the pin on Rumfold Hall—a strategic advance, but the casualty list had never been published... .

He strolled along the veranda and into the hall. Sir John with a very small audience—mostly newcomers—around him was holding forth on the new developments in France and Vane paused for a moment to listen.

"You mark my words, me boys," he was saying, "this is the big thing. I put my trust in Foch: he's the fellow who's got my money on him. No nonsense about Foch. Of course it's going to be costly, but you can't have omelettes without breaking eggs. An old proverb, me boys—but a true one."

"More than true, Sir John," remarked Vane quietly. "And one that from time immemorial has proved an immense comfort to the egg."

He went on up to his room. It was too early yet to start for Blandford, but Vane was in no mood for his own thoughts. They had reached a stage, indeed, whence he preferred not to follow them further. Doubtless by the time Margaret returned on leave, the beaten track would have revealed itself; until then—*cui bono*? ... .

He looked at his watch, and it occurred to him that he would just have comfortable time to pay a visit to old John before starting on his walk through the woods. From Robert he had found out where the old man was living in the village, and, a few minutes later, he was strolling down the drive towards his house. He found the little garden, just as perfectly kept as had been the one at the Lodge: the white muslin curtains in the front rooms were just as spotless. And old John himself was watering a row of sweet peas as he came to the little gate... .

"Ah! Mr. Vane, sir," he remarked, putting down his can and hobbling forward.

"I'm honoured to see you, sir." Then as he saw the three stars on Vane's sleeve, he corrected himself. "Captain Vane, sir, I should have said... ."

"I don't think we're likely to fall out over that, John," laughed Vane. "One never knows what anybody is these days. You're a Colonel one minute, and a subaltern the next."

Old John nodded his head thoughtfully. "That's true, sir—very true. One doesn't seem to know where one is at all. The world seems topsy-turvy. Things have changed, sir—and I'm thinking the missus and I are getting too old to keep pace with them. Take young Blake, sir—down the village, the grocer's son. Leastways, when I says grocer, the old man keeps a sort of general shop. Now the boy, sir, is a Captain... . I mis'remember what regiment—but he's a Captain."

"And very likely a devilish good one too, John," said Vane smiling.

"He is, sir. I've seen reports on him—at schools and courses and the like—which say he's a fine officer. But what's going to happen afterwards, sir, that's what I want to know? Is young Bob Blake going to put on his white apron again, and hand the old woman her bit of butter and sugar over the counter? What about that, sir?"

"I wish to Heaven I could tell you, John," said Vane. "Bob Blake isn't the only one, you know."

"Them as is sound, sir," went on the old man, "won't be affected by it. They won't have their heads turned by having mixed with the gentry as their equals —like. And the real gentry won't think no more nor no less of them when they goes back to their proper station... . But there'll be some as will want to stop on in a place where they don't rightly belong. And it'll make a world of unhappiness, sir, for all concerned... ."

Unconsciously the old man's eyes strayed in the direction of Rumfold Hall, and he sighed.

"You can't alter the ways of the Lord, sir," continued old John. "We read in the Book that He made them richer and poorer, and some of one class, and some of another. As long as everybody remembers which class he's in, he'll get what happiness he deserves... ."

Vane did not feel inclined to dispute this from the point of view of Holy Writ. The trouble is that it takes a stronger and more level head than is possessed by every boy of twenty to understand that a khaki uniform unlocks doors on which a suit of evening clothes bought off the peg and a made up tie fail to produce any impression. If only he realises that those doors are not worth the trouble of trying to unlock, all will be well for him; if he doesn't, he will be the sufferer.... Which is doubtless utterly wrong, but such is the Law and the Prophets.

"I reckons there are troublous times ahead of us, sir," went on the old man. "More troublous than any we are going through now—though them's bad enough, in all conscience. Why, only the other evening, I was down at the Fiddlers' Arms, for a glass of what they do call beer—'tis dreadful stuff, sir, that there Government beer.... ." Old John sighed mournfully at the thought of what had been. "I was sitting in there, as I says, when in comes some young feller from Grant's garage, up the road. Dressed classy he was—trying to ape his betters—with a yellow forefinger from smoking them damned stinking fags—and one of them stuck behind his ear.

"'Hullo, gaffer,'" he says, 'how's the turnips?'

"'Looking worse in France than they do in England,' says I. 'Have you been to see?'

"That hit him, sir, that did," chuckled old John. "He fair squirmed for a moment, while the others laughed. 'Don't you know I'm on work of national importance?' he says. 'I'm exempted.'

"'The only work of national importance you're ever likely to do, my lad,' says I, 'won't be done till you're dead. And not then if you're buried proper.'

"'What do you mean?' he asks.

"'You might help the turnips you're so anxious about,' says I, 'if they used you as manure.'" Old John, completely overcome by the remembrance of this shaft, laughed uproariously.

"You should have seen his face, sir," he went on when he had partially recovered. "He got redder and redder, and then he suddenly says, 'e says, 'Weren't you the lodge keeper up at Rumfold Hall?'

"'I was,' I answered quiet like, because I thought young Master Impudence was getting on dangerous ground.

"'One of the poor wretched slaves,' he sneers, 'of a bloated aristocrat.... . We're going to alter all that,' he goes on, and then for a few minutes I let him talk. He and his precious friends were going to see that all that wretched oppression ceased, and then he finished up by calling me a slave again, and sneering at his Lordship."

Old John spat reflectively. "Well, sir, I stopped him then. In my presence no man may sneer at his Lordship—certainly not a callow pup like him. His Lordship is a fine man and a good man, and I was his servant." The old man spoke with a simple dignity that impressed Vane. "I stopped him, sir," he continued, "and then I told him what I thought of him. I said to him, I said, 'Young man, I've listened to your damned nonsense for five minutes—now you listen to me. When you—with your face all covered with pimples, and your skin all muddy and sallow—start talking as you've been talking, there's only one thing should be done. Your mother should take your trousers down and smack you with a hair brush; though likely you'd cry with fright before she started. I was his Lordship's servant for forty-two years, and I'm prouder of that fact than anyone is likely to be over anything you do in your life. And if his Lordship came in at that door now, he'd meet me as a man meets a man. Whereas you—you'd run round him sniffing like the lickspittle you are—and if he didn't tread on you, you'd go and brag to all your other pimply friends that you'd been talking to an Earl... .'"

"Bravo! old John ... bravo!" said Vane quietly. "What did the whelp do?"

"Tried to laugh sarcastic, sir, and then slunk out of the door." The old man lit his pipe with his gnarled, trembling fingers. "It's coming, sir—perhaps not in my time—but it's coming. Big trouble... . All those youngsters with their smattering of edication, and their airs and their conceits and their 'I'm as good as you.'" He fell silent and stared across the road with a troubled look in his eyes. "Yes, sir," he repeated, "there be bad days coming for England— terrible bad—unless folks pull themselves together... ."

"Perhaps the Army may help 'em when it comes back," said Vane.

"May be, sir, may be." Old John shook his head doubtfully. "Perhaps so. Anyways, let's hope so, sir."

"Amen," answered Vane with sudden earnestness. And then for a while they talked of the soldier son who had been killed. With a proud lift to his tired, bent shoulders old John brought out the letter written by his platoon officer, and showed it to the man who had penned a score of similar documents. It was well thumbed and tattered, and if ever Vane had experienced a sense of irritation at the exertion of writing to some dead boy's parents or wife he was amply repaid now. Such a little trouble really; such a wonderful return of gratitude even though it be unknown and unacknowledged... . "You'll see there, sir," said the old man, "what his officer said. I can't see myself without my glasses—but you read it, sir, you read it... . 'A magnificent soldier, an example to the platoon. I should have recommended him for the stripe.' How's that, sir... .? And then there's another bit... . 'Men like him can't be replaced.' Eh! my boy... . Can't be replaced. You couldn't say that, sir, about yon pimply ferret I was telling you about."

"You could not, old John," said Vane. "You could not." He stood up and gave the letter back. "It's a fine letter; a letter any parent might be proud to get about his son."

"Aye," said the old man, "he was a good boy was Bob. None o' this new-fangled nonsense about him." He put the letter carefully in his pocket. "Mother and me, sir, we often just looks at it of an evening. It sort of comforts her.... Somehow it's hard to think of him dead... ." His lips quivered for a moment, and then suddenly he turned fiercely on Vane. "And yet, I tells you, sir, that I'd sooner Bob was dead over yonder—aye—I'd sooner see him lying dead at my feet, than that he should ever have learned such doctrines as be flying about these days."

Thus did Vane leave the old man, and as he walked down the road he saw him still standing by his gate thumping with his stick on the pavement, and shaking his head slowly. It was only when Vane got to the turning that old John picked up his can and continued his interrupted watering.... And it seemed to Vane that he had advanced another step towards finding himself.

CHAPTER IX

Vane, conscious that he was a little early for lunch, idled his way through the woods. He was looking forward, with a pleasure he did not attempt to analyse, to seeing Joan in the setting where she belonged. And if occasionally the thought intruded itself that it might be advisable to take a few mental compass bearings and to ascertain his exact position before going any further, he dismissed them as ridiculous. Such thoughts have been similarly dismissed before.... It was just as Vane was abusing himself heartily for being an ass that he saw her coming towards him through a clearing in the undergrowth. She caught sight of him at the same moment and stopped short with a swift frown.

"I didn't know you knew this path," she said as he came up to her.

"I'm sorry—but I do. You see, I knew Rumfold pretty well in the old days.... Is that the reason of the frown?"

"I wasn't particularly anxious to see you or anybody," she remarked uncompromisingly. "I wanted to try to think something out...."

"Then we are a well met pair," laughed Vane. "I will walk a few paces behind you, and we will meditate."

"Don't be a fool," said Joan still more uncompromisingly. "And anyway you're very early for lunch." She looked at her wrist watch.... "I said one o'clock and it's only half past twelve. The best people don't come before they're asked...."

"I throw myself on the mercy of the court," pleaded Vane solemnly. "I'll sit on this side of the bush and you sit on the other and in a quarter of an hour we will meet unexpectedly with all the usual symptoms of affection and joy...."

The girl was slowly retracing her steps, with Vane just behind her, and suddenly through an opening in the trees Blandford came in sight. It was not the usual view that most people got, because the path through the little copse was not very well known—but from nowhere could the house be seen to better advantage. The sheet of placid, unruffled water with its low red boathouse: the rolling stretch of green sweeping up from it to the house broken only by the one terrace above the tennis lawns; the rose garden, a feast of glorious colour, and then the house itself with its queer turrets and spires and the giant trees beyond it; all combined to make an unforgettable picture.

Joan had stopped and Vane stood silently beside her. She was taking in every detail of the scene, and Vane, glancing at her quickly, surprised a look of almost brooding fierceness in her grey eyes. It was a look of protection, of ownership, of fear, all combined: a look such as a tigress might give if her young were threatened... . And suddenly there recurred to his mind that phrase in Margaret's letter about financial trouble at Blandford. It had not impressed him particularly when he read it; now he found himself wondering... .

"Isn't it glorious?" The girl was speaking very low, as if unconscious that she had a listener. Then she turned on Vane swiftly. "Look at that!" she cried, and her arm swept the whole perfect vista. "Isn't it worth while doing anything— anything at all—to keep that as one's own? That has belonged to us for five hundred years—and now! ... My God! just think of a second Sir John Patterdale—here"—the brooding wild mother look was in her eyes again, and her lips were shut tight.

Vane moved restlessly beside her. He felt that the situation was delicate; that it was only his unexpected and unwelcome arrival on the scene that had made her take him into his confidence. Evidently there was something gravely the matter; equally evidently it was nothing to do with him... .

"I hope there's no chance of such a tragedy as that," he said gravely.

She turned and faced him. "There's every chance," she cried fiercely. "Dad is up against it—I know he is, though he doesn't say much. And this morning ..." She bit her lip, and once more her eyes rested on the old house. "Oh! what's the good of talking?" she went on after a moment. "What has to be— has to be; but, oh! it makes me mad to think of it. What good does it do, what purpose in the scheme of things you may talk about, does it serve to turn out a man, who is beloved for miles around, and put in his place some wretched pork butcher who has made millions selling cat's meat as sausages?"

She faced Vane defiantly, and he wisely remained silent.

"You may call it what you like," she stormed; "but it's practically turning him out. Is it a crime to own land, and a virtue to make a fortune out of your neighbours in trade? Dad has never swindled a soul. He's let his tenants down easy all through the war when they've had difficulties over their rent; he's just idolised by them all. And now he's got to go—unless... ." She paused and her two hands clenched suddenly. Then she continued, and her voice was quite calm. "I know I'm talking rot—so you needn't pay any attention. The great thinkers are all agreed—aren't they?—that the present land system is wrong —and they must know, of course. But I'm not a great thinker, and I can't get beyond the fact that it's not going to increase anybody's happiness—and there are a good many to be considered—if Dad goes, and a pork butcher comes in... . And that's that... ."

"Supposing," said Vane curiously, "it wasn't a pork butcher? Suppose it was someone who—well, let's say whom you wouldn't mind going in to dinner with."

"It would be just the same," she answered after a moment. "Just the same. It's ours, don't you see?—it's *ours*. It's always been ours." And the brooding, animal look had come back into her eyes... .

Then with a laugh she turned to him. "Come on; you've got to make a bow to Aunt Jane. Mind you tell her you've killed a lot of Germans. She'll adore you for ever... ."

She threw off her fit of depression and chatted gaily all the way up to the house.

"I've told Dad you're a very serious young man," she remarked, as they reached the drive; "so you'd better live up to your reputation."

Vane groaned. "Your sins be upon your own head," he remarked. "I've already had one serious dissertation this morning from old John, who used to be lodgekeeper at Rumfold."

"I know him well," cried the girl. "A dear old man... ."

"Who shares your views on the land question," said Vane with a smile.

She stopped and faced him. "Don't you?" she demanded quietly.

"In your own words, Joan—I am a very serious young man; and I am seeking for knowledge."

For a moment she seemed about to reply, and then, with a short laugh, she turned on her heel and walked on. It was just as they were entering the drawing-room that she looked at him over her shoulder. "I hope your search will be successful," she remarked; "and I hope still more that when it is successful you won't commit suicide. To have knowledge, to know to-day what is the truth, would be, I think, the most terrible burden any man could bear. Have you ever thought how tired God must be?"

Before he could answer she was shouting down her aunt's ear-trumpet. And Vane was left wondering at the strange mixture which went to make up Joan Devereux.

* * * * *

Sir James was cordially delighted to see him, especially when he discovered that Vane knew Mr. Trent.

"Where's the little girl?" he asked as they eat down to luncheon. "Margaret was her name, I think."

To his intense annoyance Vane found himself colouring slightly, and at the same moment he became acutely aware that a pair of grey eyes were fixed on him from the other side of the table.

"She is nursing at Etaples, I believe," he answered casually, but a soft gurgle of laughter told him it was useless.

"Captain Vane, Dad, is the soul of discretion," mocked Joan. "I shouldn't be surprised if he wasn't nursed by her... ."

"Devilish nice girl to be nursed by, too, my dear," chuckled her father, "from what I remember of her. What do you think, Vane?" He was mercifully spared the necessity of answering by the intervention of Aunt Jane, who had pursued her own train of thought, blissfully unconscious of any change of conversation.

"How many of the brutes did you say you'd killed, young man?" she boomed at him, at the same time putting her ear-trumpet at the "ready."

"Two for certain," howled Vane; "perhaps three."

She resumed her lunch, and Sir James laughed. "My sister," he remarked, "is full of war... . Rather fuller—like a good many of those who have stayed behind—than you fellows... ."

"It's very much nicer," said Vane with a laugh, "to kill—even a Boche—in imagination than in reality... . Though I've seen many men," he added thoughtfully, "go blood mad."

"Do you remember that description of Kipling's," said Sir James, "of the scrap between the Black Tyrone and the Pathans? Mulvaney was sick, and Ortheris cursed, and Learoyd sang hymns—wasn't it?"

"I've seen them all those ways," said Vane thoughtfully, "and the worst of the lot are the silent ones... . There was one fellow I had who never uttered a word from the time we went over till the finish, and he never—if he could avoid it—struck a man anywhere except in the stomach... . And incidentally he could quote more from the Bible than most Bishops... . In fact, if he ever did speak, so I'm told, when he was fighting it was just to remark, 'And the Lord said'—as he stabbed."

Sir James nodded, and then half-closed his eyes. "One just can't get it," he said. "None of us who haven't been there will ever get it—so I suppose it's not much use trying. But one can't help thinking that if only a few of the people who count over here could go and see, it might make a difference. We might not be having so much trouble... ."

"See the reality and clear away the humbug," said Vane. "Can't be done, Sir James. I know Staff Officers who would willingly give a year's pay to shepherd a personally conducted Cook's party to France of the British working man. They get their legs pulled right and left by everybody out there; and do you wonder?" He laughed shortly. "Tommy's no fool: six pounds a week instead of a shilling a day. And comparisons are odious."

"But couldn't they be taken really into things?" asked his host.

"I can't quite see the party popping the parapet," grinned Vane. "It's not a thing which anyone does for pleasure... ."

It was at that moment that with a loud booming noise Aunt Jane again contributed to the conversation. "I'm afraid you've wasted your time out there, young man."

"She means that two Germans and one doubtful isn't enough," gurgled Joan, as she saw Vane's look of bewilderment. To his relief the old lady did not adjust her trumpet, so he assumed rightly that he would be allowed to suffer her displeasure in silence... .

"Well," said Sir James after a pause. "I suppose there are unsurmountable difficulties in making people understand. But if I had my way I'd take some of these blackguards who are fattening on the country's helplessness and I'd put 'em in the front line trenches... ."

"With a trench mortar bombardment on," supplemented Vane laughing.

"And I'd let 'em stop there and rot," continued Sir James. "It's wicked; it's vile; it's abominable—exploiting their country's danger for their own pockets.... What's going to happen when the war is over, God alone knows."

"Your fish will get cold, Daddy, unless you go on with it," said Joan soothingly.

But Sir James was started on his favourite hobby. It would have taken more than the possibility of cold fish to stem the torrent, and Vane, supported by the most fleeting of winks from Joan, made no attempt to do so. He had heard it all before; the worthy Baronet's views, were such as are delivered daily by the old order in every part of the country. And the thing that perplexed Vane more and more as he listened, and periodically returned a non-committal "Yes" or "No," was where the fallacy lay. These were the views he had been brought up on; they were the views with which, in his heart of hearts, he agreed. And yet he felt dimly that there must be another side to the question: he knew there was another side. Otherwise ... but Sir James, when he got into his stride, did not permit much meditation on the part of his audience.

"Organised labour," he thundered, "has found itself, because we are at war, all powerful. We depend on the organised workers, and they know it. The lives of our men are at stake.... Their brothers, mark you, Vane. What do they care? Not a dam, sir, not a dam. More money, money—that's all they want. They know the State won't dare a lock-out—and they trade on it.... Why don't they conscript 'em, sir?—why don't they put the whole cursed crowd into khaki? Then if they strike send 'em over into the trenches as I said, and let 'em rot there. That would soon bring 'em to their senses...." Sir James attacked his chicken viciously.

"What's going to happen," he went on after a moment, "when we return to peace conditions? The private employer can't pay these inflated wages.... He simply can't do it, and that's an end of it. But now, of necessity it's been a case of surrender—surrender—surrender to any demands the blackguards like to put up. And they've got it each time. Do you suppose they're going to stop?"

"But surely there's such a thing as common sense," interrupted Vane. "Surely the matter can be put in front of them so that they will understand? ... If not, it's a pretty useful confession of ineptitude."

Sir James laughed shortly. "There are several floating round at the moment... . But it isn't quite as easy as all that, my dear fellow. In times of unrest power comes automatically more and more into the hands of the man who can talk; men like Ramage, and others of his kidney. A few meaningless but high flown phrases; a few such parrot cries as 'Down with the Capitalist and the Future is for the Worker,' and you've got even the steadiest man unsettled.... .

Especially if he's one of a crowd; mob psychology is the devil... ." Sir James paused and stared out of the window. "I don't fear for the decent fellow in the long run; it's in the early stages he may get blown... ."

"What are you two men talking about so busily?" Aunt Jane once again presented her trumpet to Vane.

"Labour trouble, Miss Devereux," he roared. "Trouble in the labour market."

The old lady's face set grimly. "My convictions on that are well known," she boomed. "Put them in a row against a wall and shoot them."

"My sister's panacea for all evil," said Sir James with a smile.

"There are others as well as Miss Devereux who would recommend the same thing," said Vane with a short laugh.

"Shoot 'em," rasped the old lady; "shoot 'em, and go on shooting till there are no more left to shoot. I'm sure we'd get along very well without the brutes."

"What's going to stop 'em?" Sir James returned to his former question. "Nothing—until they've tried everything, and found they're wrong. And while they're finding out the simple fact that no employer can pay a guinea for a pound's worth of work the country will crash. We'll have anarchy, Vane —Bolshevism like Russia, unless a miracle saves us... . Financed by the Boche probably into the bargain."

"Dear old Daddy," laughed Joan. "You're such an optimist, aren't you?"

"It's no laughing matter, my dear," snorted her father. "There's a wave of madness over the world ... absolute madness. The more you give into them— the more decently you treat 'em—the more they want... . People talk about the old order changing; what I want to know is what they're going to put in its place? When they've broken up the Empire and reduced England to a fifth-rate Power, they'll probably want the old order back... . It'll be too late to want then."

"I gather, Sir James, that you are not exactly a Socialist," murmured Vane gravely, with a side glance at Joan.

His host rose to the bait. "I—a Socialist—I! Why—why! ..." he spluttered, and then he saw his daughter's face. She was dimpling with laughter, and suddenly Sir James laughed too.

"You nearly had me then, my boy," he cried; "very nearly. But it's on that point, Vane, that I get so wild with these intellectual men—men who should know better. Men like Ramage, and Johnson and all that lot. They know themselves that Socialism is a wild impossibility; they know that equality is out of the question, and yet they preach it to men who have not got their brains. It's a dangerously attractive doctrine; the working man who sees a motor flash past him wouldn't be human if he didn't feel a tinge of envy.... But the Almighty has decreed that it should be so: and it's flying in His Face to try to change it."

Vane looked thoughtfully at his host. "I fancy the Almighty's dictates are less likely to be questioned by the motor car owner than by the working man."

"I agree with you, Vane," returned Sir James at once. "But that doesn't alter the principle of the thing.... By all means improve their conditions ... give them better houses ... stop sweated labour. That is our privilege and our duty. But if they continue on their present line, they'll soon find the difference. Things we did for 'em before, they'll have to whistle for in the future."

"You're getting your money's worth this time, aren't you, Captain Vane?" said Joan demurely.

But Vane only smiled at her gravely and did not answer. Here were the views, crudely expressed, perhaps, of the ordinary landed gentleman. The man who of all others most typically represented feudalism. Benevolent, perhaps—but feudalism.... The old order. "They talk about 'back to the land,'" snorted Sir James suddenly, "as the sovereign cure for all evils. You can take it from me, Vane, that except in a few isolated localities the system of small holdings is utterly uneconomical and unsuccessful. It means ceaseless work, and a mere pittance in return. You know Northern France—well, you've got the small holdings scheme in full blast there. What time do they get up in the morning; what time do they go to bed at night? What do they live on? And from what you know of your own fellow countrymen, do you think any large percentage would tackle such a life? Believe me, these days, none of us want to keep land very much." Sir James frowned slightly. "Unless one has old family traditions.... And even those will have to go by the board—sooner or later... . It doesn't pay, Vane, you can take it from me.... And to split it up into small holdings, and invite men of varying degrees of inefficiency to earn a livelihood on it, won't help matters."

Sir James pushed back his chair and they rose from the table.

"I have victimised you enough, my dear boy," he remarked. "I think Joan had better carry on the good work." She put her arm round his waist, and her father looked down at her lovingly. "What are you going to do with him, old lady?"

"Are you busy, Dad, this afternoon?" she asked.

Sir James nodded, and he seemed to Vane to have grown very old. "The old order is changing—what are they going to put in its place? ..." A sudden fear caught him in its grip. He turned quickly and stared out of the window; at the wonderful bit of England that lay before him. Quiet and smiling in the warm sun, it lay there—a symbol of the thing for which Englishmen have laid down their lives since time started. At that very second men were dying for it—over the water. Was it all to be in vain?

"Yes, girlie," Sir James was speaking. "I've got a lot of business to attend to. That wretched fellow Norton can't pay his rent again...."

"Oh! Dad, he is a bit steep," cried the girl. "That's the third time."

Sir James laughed. "I know, my dear; but things are bad. After all, he has lost one of his sons in Mesopotamia."

"A drunken waster," cried the girl.

"He died, Joan," said her father simply. "No man may do more."

"You're too kind-hearted, Dad," she said, patting his arm, and looking up into his face. "I wouldn't be."

Sir James laughed. "Oh! yes, you would. Besides, I sha'n't have a chance much longer." With a quick sigh, he bent and kissed her. "Run along and take Vane out on the lake. I'll come down later and shout at you from the bank." She watched her father leave the room, and then she turned to Vane.

"Would you care to come on the lake?" she asked, and in her eyes there was a strange, inscrutable look which set him wondering.

"I'd love it," said Vane. He followed her into the open window and together they stepped on to the lawn.

Aunt Jane had already taken her usual position, preparatory to her afternoon nap; but Vane's sudden appearance apparently stirred some train of thought in her mind. As he came up to her she adjusted her trumpet and boomed, "Shoot 'em, young man—shoot 'em until there are none left."

"Why, certainly, Miss Devereux," he shouted. "That's what I think." She nodded her approval at meeting such a kindred spirit, and replaced the foghorn on the ground beside her. He felt that his poor record of dead Huns was forgiven him, and rejoined Joan with a smile.

"How easy it would be, if that was the way," she said quietly. "Dear old Aunt Jane—I remember sitting up with her most of one night, trying to comfort her, when her pug dog went lame on one foot."

Vane laughed, and as they came to a turn in the path, they looked back. The old lady was already dozing gently—at peace with all the world.

CHAPTER X

"If you say one word to me this afternoon which might even be remotely twisted into being serious," said Joan, "I shall upset you in the middle of the lake."

An inspection of the general lines of the boat prevented Vane from taking the threat too seriously; with anything approaching luck a party of four could have crossed the Atlantic in it. Innumerable cushions scattered promiscuously served to make it comfortable, and as the girl spoke Vane from his seat in the stern was helping to push the boat from the boat-house.

"You terrify me, lady," he murmured. "What shall I talk to you about?"

The girl was pulling lazily at the oars, and slowly they drifted out into the sunshine. "So she who must be obeyed is Margaret Trent, is she?"

"The evidence seems a trifle slight," said Vane. "But as I rather gather you're an insistent sort of person, I will plead guilty at once, to save bother."

"You think I generally get my own way, do you?"

"I do," answered Vane. "Don't you?"

The girl ignored the question. "What is she like? I've often heard dad speak about Mr. Trent; and I think she came once to Blandford, when I was away."

"I gather that you were being finished." Vane started filling his pipe. "At least she said so in a letter I got this morning."

Joan looked at him for a moment. "Did you write to her about me?"

"I don't think she even knows you're at home," said Vane shortly, "much less that I've met you."

"Would you mind her knowing?" persisted the girl.

"Why on earth should I?" demanded Vane with a look of blank surprise.

She took a few strokes, and then rested on her oars again. "There are people," she said calmly, "who consider I'm the limit—a nasty, fast hussy... ."

"What appalling affectation on your part," jeered Vane lighting his pipe. "What do you do to keep up your reputation—sell flags in Leicester Square on flag days?" The girl's attention seemed to be concentrated on a patch of reeds where a water-hen was becoming vociferous. "Or do you pursue the line taken up by a woman I met last time I was on leave? She was a Wraf or a Wren or something of that kind, and at the time she was in mufti. But to show

how up to date she was she had assimilated the jargon, so to speak, of the mechanics she worked with. It almost gave me a shock when she said to me in a confidential aside at a mutual friend's house, 'Have you ever sat down to a more perfectly bloody tea?'"

"I think," said Joan with her eyes still fixed on the reeds, "that that is beastly. It's not smart, and it does not attract men …"

"You're perfectly right there," returned Vane, grimly. "However, arising out of that remark, is your whole object in life to attract men?"

"Of course it is. It's the sole object of nine women out of ten. Why ask such absurd questions?"

"I sit rebuked," murmured Vane. "But to return—in what way do your charitable friends consider you the limit?"

"I happen to be natural," said Joan, "and at times that's very dangerous. I'm not the sort of natural, you know, that loves cows and a country life, and gives the chickens their hard-boiled eggs, or whatever they eat, at five in the morning."

"But you like Blandford," said Vane incautiously.

"Blandford!" A passionate look came into her face, as her eyes looking over his head rested on the old house. "Blandford is just part of me. It's different. Besides, the cow man hasn't been called up," she added inconsequently. "He's sixty-three."

"A most tactful proceeding," said Vane, skating away from thin ice.

"I'm natural in another way," she went on after a short silence. "If I want to do a thing—I generally do it. For instance, if I want to go and talk to a man in his rooms, I do so. Why shouldn't I? If I want to dance a skirt dance in a London ballroom, I do it. But some people seem to think it's fast. I made quite a lot of money once dancing at a restaurant with a man, you know—in between the tables. Of course we wore masks, because it might have embarrassed some of the diners to recognise me." The oars had dropped unheeded from her hands, and she leaned forward, looking at Vane with mocking eyes. "I just loved it."

"I'll bet you did," laughed Vane. "What made you give it up?"

"A difference of opinion between myself and some of the male diners, which threatened to become chronic," she returned dreamily. "That's a thing, my seeker after information, which the war hasn't changed, anyway."

For a while he made no answer, but lay back against the cushions, puffing at his pipe. Occasionally she pulled two or three gentle strokes with the oars, but for the most part she sat motionless with her eyes brooding dreamily over the lazy beauty of the water.

"You're a funny mixture, Joan," he said at length. "Devilish funny... ." And as he spoke a fat old carp rose almost under the boat and took an unwary fly. "The sort of mixture, you know, that drives a man insane... ."

She was looking at the widening ripples caused by the fish and she smiled slightly. Then she shrugged her shoulders. "I am what I am... . And just as with that fly, fate comes along suddenly, doesn't it, and pouf ... it's all over! All its little worries settled for ever in a carp's tummy. If only one's own troubles could be settled quite as expeditiously... ."

He looked at her curiously. "It helps sometimes, Joan, to shoot your mouth, as our friends across the water say. I'm here to listen, if it's any comfort... ."

She turned and faced him thoughtfully. "There's something about you, Derek, that I rather like." It was the first time that she had called him by his Christian name, and Vane felt a little pleasurable thrill run through him. But outwardly he gave no sign.

"That is not a bad beginning, then," he said quietly. "If you're energetic enough let's get the boat under that weeping willow. I'm thinking we might tie her up, and there's room for an army corps in the stern here... ."

The boat brushed through the drooping branches, and Vane stepped into the bow to make fast. Then he turned round, and stood for a while watching the girl as she made herself comfortable amongst the cushions... . "There was once upon a time," he prompted, "a man... ."

"Possessed," said Joan, "of great wealth. Gold and silver and precious stones were his for the asking... ."

"It's to be assumed that the fortunate maiden who was destined to become his wife would join in the chorus with average success," commented Vane judicially.

"The assumption is perfectly correct. Is not the leading lady worthy of her hire?" She leaned back in her cushions and looked up at Vane through half-closed eyes. "In the fulness of time," she went on dreamily, "it came to pass that the man possessed of great wealth began to sit up and take notice. 'Behold,' he said to himself, 'I have all that my heart desireth, saving only one thing. My material possessions grow and increase daily, and, as long as people who ought to know better continue to kill each other, even so long will they continue growing.' I don't think I mentioned, did I, that there was a perfectly 'orrible war on round the corner during the period under consideration?"

93

"These little details—though trifling—should not be omitted," remarked Vane severely. "It is the duty of all story tellers to get their atmosphere correct... ." He sat down facing her and started to refill his pipe... . "What was this one thing he lacked?"

"Don't interrupt. It is the duty of all listeners to control their impatience. Only the uninitiated skip."

"I abase myself," murmured Vane. "Proceed, I pray you."

"So the man of great wealth during the rare intervals which he could snatch from amassing more—continued to commune with himself. 'I will look around,' he said to himself, 'and select me a damsel from amongst the daughters of the people. Peradventure, she may be rich—peradventure she may be poor; but since I have enough of the necessary wherewithal to support the entire beauty chorus which appears nightly in the building down the road known as the House of Gaiety—the question of her means is immaterial. Only one thing do I insist upon, that she be passing fair to look upon. Otherwise— nix doing for this child... .'"

Joan stirred restlessly, and her fingers drummed idly on the side of the boat. And Vane—because he was a man, and because the girl so close to him was more than passing lovely—said things under his breath. The parable was rather too plain.

"And behold one night," went on Joan after a while, "this man of great wealth partook of his dried rusk and Vichy water—his digestion was not all it might be—at the house of one of the nobility of his tribe. The giver of the feast had permitted his name to be used on the prospectus of some scheme organised by the man of wealth—thereby inspiring confidence in all who read, and incidentally pouching some of the Bradburys. He further considered it possible that by filling his guest with food and much wine, he might continue the good work on other prospectuses, thereby pouching more Bradburys. In the vulgar language in vogue at the period, however, Vichy water put the lid on that venture with a bang... . But even with champagne it is doubtful whether there would have been much doing, because—well, because—the man of wealth had his attention for the moment occupied elsewhere. To be exact on the other side of the table... ."

"Ah!" said Vane, and his breath came in a sort of sigh. "I'm thinking you had better let me tell this bit. It was just after the slaves had thrown open the doors, and the guests had seated themselves, that the man of great wealth chanced to look up from his rusk. He frequently did look up when consuming these delicacies, otherwise he found they made him excited, and calmness is necessary for the poor digestion. He looked up then, as usual, and suddenly he caught his breath. Over a great silver bowl filled with roses… ."

"Carnations sound better," said Joan.

"Filled with carnations he saw a girl… . They were pink and red those carnations—glorious in the shaded light; and the silver and the glass with which this tribe was wont to feed its face glittered and shone on the polished table. But the man of wealth had silver and glass as good, and he had no eyes for that… . For it had come to him, and he was a man who was used to making up his mind quickly, that he had found the damsel he required. She was dressed—ah! how was she dressed, lady? She was dressed in a sort of grey gauzy stuff, and her neck and shoulders gleamed white—gloriously white. A great mass of brown hair which shimmered as if it was alive; a little oval face, with cheeks that seemed as if the sun had kissed them. A mouth quite small, with lips that parted in a mocking smile; a nose—well, just a nose. But crowning everything—dominating everything—a pair of great grey eyes. What eyes they were! They made the man of wealth bolt his rusk. There was one mouthful he only chewed fifteen times instead of the customary thirty-two. They contained all Heaven, and they contained all Hell; in them lay the glory of a God, the devilment of a Siren, and the peace of a woman … . And just once she looked at him during dinner—the look of a stranger—cool and self-possessed. Just casually she wondered whether it was worth while to buy money at the cost of a rusk diet; then she turned to the man next her… . Let's see—he was a warrior, snatching a spell of rest from the scrap round the corner. And she didn't even hear the man of great wealth choke as the half-chewed rusk went down wallop."

The girl looked at Vane for a moment. "But you are really rather a dear," she remarked thoughtfully.

"It's your turn now," said Vane shortly.

"The donor of the feast," she resumed at once, "was going a mucker. The possession of extra Bradburys, coupled with a wife who combined a champagne taste with his gin income, had inspired him to give a dance. He hoped that it might help to keep the damn woman quiet for a bit; and, besides everybody was giving dances. It was the thing to do, and warriors fresh from the fierce battle were wont to step lightly on the polished floor. As a matter of historical interest nine out of every ten of the warriors who performed nightly at different houses were fresh from the office stool at the House of War—a large edifice, completely filled with girl scouts and brain-storms… ."

"Beautiful," chuckled Vane; "quite beautiful."

"You see the actual warriors didn't get much of a look in. By the time they got to know anybody they had to go back round the corner again and they got tired of propping up the walls and looking on. Besides what made it even more dangerous for them was that kind-hearted women took compassion on them, and their own empty programmes and introduced themselves. And in the vernacular they were the snags. But all these things were hidden from the man of great wealth... ."

"Contrary to a life-long habit," said Vane, "he remained after dinner and haunted the door. Just every now and then a girl in grey gauzy stuff floated past him—and once, only once, he found himself looking into those big grey eyes when she passed quite close to him going out to get some lemonade. And the rusk did a somersault... ."

"But he didn't haunt the door," gurgled Joan. "He got roped in. He fell an easy victim to the snag parade—and women fainted and men wept when the man of great possessions and the pointed woman took the floor... ."

"Pointed?" murmured Vane.

"All jolts and bumps," explained the girl. "Her knees were like steel castings. I think that if the—if the girl in grey gauzy stuff had realised that the man of wealth had stopped behind for her, she might, out of pity, have given him one dance. But instead all she did was to shake with laughter as she saw him quivering in a corner held fast in the clutch of the human steam engine. She heard the blows he was receiving; they sounded like a hammer hitting wood; and then later she saw him limping painfully from the room—probably in search of some Elliman's embrocation. But, as I say, she didn't realise it... . She only thought him a silly old man... ."

"Old," said Vane slowly... . "How old?"

"About fifty," said the girl vaguely. Then she looked at Vane. "She found out later that he was forty-eight, to be exact."

"Not so very old after all," remarked Vane, pitching a used match into the water, and stuffing down the tobacco in his pipe with unusual care.

"It was towards the end of the dance," she resumed, "that the man of great wealth was introduced to the girl in grey, by the donor of the feast. The band had gathered in all the coal-scuttles and pots it could, and was hitting them hard with pokers when the historical meeting took place. You see it was a Jazz band and they always economise by borrowing their instruments in the houses they go to... ."

"And did she dance with him?" asked Vane.

"I don't think he even asked her to," said Joan. "But even as she went off with a boy in the Flying Corps she realised that she was face to face with a problem."

"Quick work," murmured Vane.

"Most of the big problems in life are quick," returned the girl. "You see the man of great possessions was not accustomed to disguising his feelings; and the girl—though she didn't show it—was never far removed from the skeleton in her cupboard."

She fell silent, and for a while they neither of them spoke.

"It developed along the accepted lines, I suppose," remarked Vane at length.

"Everything quite conventional," she answered. "A fortnight later he suggested that she should honour him by accepting his name and wealth. He has repeated the suggestions at frequent intervals since… ."

"Then she didn't say 'Yes' at once," said Vane softly.

"Ah! no," answered the girl. "And as a matter of fact she hasn't said it yet."

"But sometimes o' nights," said Vane, "she lies awake and wonders. And then she gets out of bed, and perhaps the moon is up, shining cold and white on the water that lies in front of her window. And the trees are throwing black shadows, and somewhere in the depths of an old patriarch an owl is hooting mournfully. For a while she stands in front of her open window. The air is warm, and the faint scent of roses comes to her from outside. A great pride wells up in her—a great pride and a great love, for the sleeping glory in front of her belongs to her; to her and her father and her brother." The girl's face was half-turned away, and for a moment Vane watched the lovely profile gravely. "And then," he went on slowly, "with a sigh she sits down in the big arm-chair close to the window, and the black dog comes in and settles on her. In another room in the house she sees her father, worrying, wondering whether anything can be done, or whether the glory that has been theirs for hundreds of years must pass into the hands of a stranger…. And after a while the way out comes into her thoughts, and she stirs restlessly in her chair. Because, though the girl in grey is one of the set in her tribe who dance and feed in many public places, and which has nothing in common with those who sit at home doing good works; yet she possesses one or two strange, old-fashioned ideas, which she will hardly ever admit even to herself. Just sometimes o' night they creep out as she stares through the window, and the weird cries of the wild come softly through the air. 'Somewhere, there is a Prince Charming,' they whisper, and with a sigh she lets herself dream. At last she creeps back to bed—and if she is very, very lucky the dreams go on in her sleep." Vane knocked out his pipe on the side of the boat.

"It's only when morning comes," he went on, and there was a hint of sadness in his voice, "that the strange, old-fashioned ideas creep shyly into the corner. Along with the tea have come some of the new smart ones which makes them feel badly dressed and dull. They feel that they are gauche—and yet they know that they are beautiful—wonderfully beautiful in their own badly dressed way. Timidly they watch from their corner—hoping, hoping... . And then at last they just disappear. They're only dream ideas, you see; I suppose they can't stand daylight and tea with saccharine in it, and reality... . It's as they float towards the window that sometimes they hear the girl talking to herself. 'Don't be a fool,' she says angrily, 'you've got to face facts, my dear. And a possible.' Charming without a bean in the world isn't a fact—it's a farce. It simply can't be done... . And three new very smart ideas in their best glad rags make three long noses at the poor little dowdy fellows as they go fluttering away to try to find another home."

Vane laughed gently, and held out his cigarette case to the girl. And it was as she turned to take one that he saw her eyes were very bright—with the starry brightness of unshed tears. "Sure—but it's nice to talk rot at times, my lady, isn't it?" he murmured. "And, incidentally, I'm thinking I didn't tell the grey girl's story quite right. Because it wasn't herself that she was thinking of most; though," and his eyes twinkled, "I don't think, from my ideas of her, that she is cut out for love in a cottage, with even the most adorable Prince Charming. But it wasn't herself that came first; it was pride and love of home and pride and love of family."

The girl bit her lip and stared at him with a troubled look. "Tell me, oh man of much understanding," she said softly, "what comes next?"

But Vane shook his head with a laugh. "Cross my palm with silver, pretty lady, and the old gipsy will tell your fortune... . I see a girl in grey surrounded by men-servants and maid-servants, and encased in costly furs and sparkling gems. Standing at the door outside is a large and expensive Limousine into which she steps. The door is shut, and the car glides off, threading its way through the London traffic. At last the road becomes clearer, the speed increases, until after an hour's run the car swings in between some old lodge gates. Without a sound it sweeps up the drive, and the girl sees the first glint of the lake through the trees. There is a weeping willow too, and as her eyes rest on it she smiles a little, and then she sighs. The next moment the car is at the front door, and she is in the arms of a man who has come out to meet her. She calls him 'Dad,' and there's a boy just behind him, with his hands in his pockets, who has eyes for nothing except the car. Because it's 'some' car... . She spends the day there, and when she's leaving, the man she calls 'Dad' puts his hand on her arm. He just looks at her—that's all, and she smiles back at him. For there's no worry now on his face, no business trouble to cut lines on his brow. But sometimes—he wonders; and then she just smiles at him, and his doubts vanish. They never put it into words those two, and perhaps it is as well… . A smile is so easy, it conceals so much. Not that there's much to hide on her part. With her eyes wide open she made her choice, and assuredly it had been worth while. Her father was happy; the old house was safe and her husband was kind… . Only as the car glides away from the door, her grey eyes once again rest on a weeping willow. A fat old carp rises with a splash and she sees the ripples widening… . And the smile fades from her lips, because—well, thoughts are capricious things, and the weeping willow and the carp remind her of a certain afternoon, and what a certain foolish weaver of fantasies said to her… once in the long ago. Much has she got—much has she given to others. It may have been worth while—but she has lost the biggest thing in Life. That has passed her by… ."

"The biggest thing in Life," she whispered. "I wonder; oh! I wonder."

"Maybe she would never have found it," he went on, "even if she had not married the man of great possessions. And then, indeed, she could have said with reason—'I sure have made a damn fool of myself.' To throw away the chances of costly furs and sparkling gems; to see *les papillons noirs* fluttering round her father's head in increasing numbers—and not to find the biggest thing in Life after such a sacrifice—yes, that would be too cruel. So, on balance, perhaps she had chosen wisely… ."

"And is that all!" she asked him. "Is there no other course?" She leaned towards him, and her lips were parted slightly. For a moment or two he watched the slow rise and fall of her bosom, and then with a short, hard laugh he turned away.

"You want a lot for your money, my lady," he said, and his voice shook a little. "But I will paint you another picture, before we drift through the branches back to the boat-house and—reality. I see another house—just an ordinary nice comfortable house—four reception, ten bed, h. & c. laid on, with garage. Close to good golf links. A girl in grey is standing in the hall, leaning over a pram in which the jolliest, fattest boy you've ever thought of is sitting and generally bossing the entire show. He is reputed by his nurse, who is old enough to know better, to have just spoken his first consecutive sentence. To the brutal and unimaginative father who is outside with his golf clubs it had sounded like 'Wum—wah!' According to the interpreter it meant that he wanted an egg for tea; and it was being duly entered up in a book which contained spaces for Baby's first tooth, the first time he was sick, when he smashed his first toy—and other milestones in his career… . Ah! but it's a jolly house. There are no crowds of men-servants and maid-servants; there is no priceless Limousine. And the girl just wears a grey silk jersey with a belt, and a grey skirt and grey brogues. And, ye Gods! but she looks topping, as she steps out to join the brutal man outside. Her golf clubs are slung over her shoulder, and together they foot it to the first tee.... He is just scratch, and she.... let's think...."

"Eight would be a good sort of handicap," murmured the girl.

"Eight it is," said Vane. "That means he gives her six strokes, and generally beats her."

"I'll bet he doesn't," cried the girl.

"You must not interrupt the old gipsy, my lady," rebuked Vane, "You see, it doesn't matter to those two which wins—not a little bit, for the most important hole in the course is the tenth. It's a short hole, with the most enormous sand bunker guarding the green on the right. And though for nine holes neither of them has sliced, at the tenth they both do. And if by chance one of them doesn't, that one loses the hole. You see it's the most dreadful bunker, and somehow they've got to get to the bottom of it. Well—it would be quite unfair if only one of them went there—so the non-slicer loses the hole."

The girl's face was dimpling gloriously....

"Then when they've got there—he just takes her in his arms and kisses her; and she kisses him. Just now and then she'll whisper, 'My dear, my dear—but it's good to be alive,' but most times they just kiss. Then they go on and finish their game. Except for that interlude they are really very serious golfers."

"And when they've finished their game—what then?"

"They go back and have tea—a big fat tea with lots of scones and Devonshire cream. And then, after tea, the man goes round to the garage and gets the car. Just a jolly little two-seater that does fifty on the level. The girl gets in and they drive away to where the purple heather merges into the violet of the moors! And it's great. Perhaps they'll come back to dinner, or perhaps they'll have it somewhere and come home when the sun has set and the stars are gleaming above them like a thousand silver lamps. They don't know what they're going to do when they start—and they don't care. They'll just be together, and that's enough.... Of course they're very foolish and inconsequent people..."

"Ah! but they're not," she cried quickly. "They're just the wisest people in the world. Only don't you see that one day after their golf they drive on and on, and suddenly it seemed to the girl in grey that the road was getting familiar? There was an old church she recognised and lots of landmarks. And then suddenly they drive past some lodge gates, and there—in the middle of the road—stands a dreadful man smoking a cigar with a band round it. All the glory has gone from the drive, and the girl feels numb and sick and mad with fury… ."

"But that was bad steering on the man's part," said Vane. "He ought to have avoided that road."

"The girl could never avoid it, Derek," she answered sadly. "Even in the bunker at the tenth she'd be seeing that cigar… ."

"I don't believe it," said Vane.

"I know it," answered the girl.

A sudden hail of "Joan" came ringing over the water, and she gave an answering hail.

"There's Dad," she said. "I suppose we ought to be going… ."

With a sigh Vane rose and stood over her. "Come on," he laughed, holding out his hand to help her up. "And then I'll untie the boat… ."

He swung her up beside him and for a moment they looked into one another's eyes.

"I hope," he said, "that you'll be happy, my dear, so happy." And his voice was very tender… .

They rowed back towards the boat-house, where Sir James was waiting for them.

"Come and have tea, you two," he cried cheerily, and Joan waved her hand at him. Then she looked at Vane.

"It's been a wonderful afternoon of make-believe," she said softly. "I've just loved it… ." Vane said nothing, but just as they were stepping out of the boat he took her arm gently.

"Are you quite certain, lady," he whispered, "that it must be—make-believe? …"

For a while she stood motionless, and then she smiled "Why, of course… . There's your beaten track to find, and there's She who must be obeyed. And there's also… ."

"The cigar with the band round it." Vane's hand dropped to his side. "Perhaps you're right… ."

They strolled together towards Sir James. And it was just before they came within earshot that Vane spoke again. "Would you care to play the game again, grey girl?"

"Why, yes," she said, "I think I would.... I think I would."

CHAPTER XI

During the days that followed his afternoon on the lake at Blandford Vane found himself thinking a good deal more of Joan than augured well for his peace of mind. He had been over to call, and had discovered that she had gone North very suddenly, and it was not certain when she would return. And so he escaped from Aunt Jane as soon as he politely could, and strolled back through the woods, conscious of a sense of acute disappointment.

He went to his customary hiding place by the little waterfall, and, lighting his pipe sat down on the grass.

"My son," he murmured to himself, "you'd better take a pull. Miss Joan Devereux is marrying a millionaire to save the family. You are marrying Margaret Trent—and it were better not to forget those two simple facts...."

He pulled Margaret's letter out of his pocket, and started to read it through again. But after a moment it dropped unheeded on the ground beside him, and he sat motionless, staring at the pool. He did not see the green of the undergrowth; he did not hear a thrush pouring out its little soul from a bush close by. He saw a huddled, shapeless thing sagging into a still smoking crater; he heard the drone of engines dying faintly in the distance and a voice whispering, "The devils ... the vile devils."

And then another picture took its place—the picture of a girl in grey, lying back on a mass of cushions, with a faint mocking light in her eyes, and a smile which hovered now and then round her lips... .

A very wise old frog regarded him for a moment and then croaked derisively. "Go to the devil," said Vane. "Compared with Margaret, what has the other one done in this war that is worth doing?"

"You must be even more damn foolish than most humans," it remarked, "if you try to make yourself think that the way of a man with a maid depends on the doing of things that are worth while." The speaker plopped joyfully into the pool, and Vane savagely beheaded a flower with his stick.

"C-r-rick, C-r-rick," went the old frog, who had come up for a breather, and Vane threw a stone at it. Try as he would he could not check a thought which rioted through his brain, and made his heart pound like a mad thing. Supposing—just supposing... .

"Then why did she go up North so suddenly," jeered the frog. "Without even leaving you a line? She's just been amusing you and herself in her professional capacity."

Vane swore gently and rose to his feet. "You're perfectly right, my friend," he remarked; "perfectly right. She's just an ordinary common or garden flirt, and we'll cut it right out. We will resume our studies, old bean; we will endeavour to find out by what possible method Bolshevism—*vide* her august papa—can be kept from the country. As a precautionary measure, a first-class ticket to Timbuctoo, in case we fail in our modest endeavour, might be a good speculation... ."

For a moment he stood motionless, staring into the cool shadows of the wood, while a curious smile played over his face. And may be, in spite of his derisive critic, who still croaked from the edge of the pool, his thoughts were not entirely centred on his proposed modest endeavour. Then with a short laugh he turned on his heel, and strode back towards Rumfold.

Two days later he found himself once again before a Medical Board. Space, even in convalescent homes, was at a premium, and Vane, to his amazement, found himself granted a month's sick leave, at the expiration of which he was to go before yet another Board. And so having shaken hands with Lady Patterdale and suffered Sir John to explain the war to him for nearly ten minutes, Vane departed for London and Half Moon Street.

He wrote Margaret a long letter in reply to hers telling him of her decision to take up medicine. He explained, what was no more than the truth, that her suggestion had taken him completely by surprise, but that if she considered that she had found her particular job he, for one, would most certainly not attempt to dissuade her. With regard to himself, however, the matter was somewhat different. At present he failed to see any budding literary signs, and his few efforts in the past had not been of the nature which led him to believe that he was likely to prove a formidable rival to Galsworthy or Arnold Bennett... .

"I'm reading 'em all, Margaret—the whole blessed lot. And it seems to me that with the world as it is at present, bread-and-butter is wanted, not caviare... . But probably the mistake is entirely mine. There seems to me to be a spirit of revolt in the air, which gives one most furiously to think. Everybody distrusts everybody else; everybody wants to change—and they don't know what they want to change to. There doesn't seem to be any single connected idea as to what is wanted—or how to get it. The only thing on which everyone seems agreed is More Money and Less Work... . Surely to Heaven there must be a way out; some simple way out. We didn't have this sort of thing over the water. We were pals over there; but here every single soul loathes every other single soul like poison... . Can it be that only by going back to the primitive, as we had to do in France, can one find happiness? The idea is preposterous... . And, yet, now that I'm here and have been here these months, I'm longing to come back. I'm sick of it. Looking at this country with what I call my French eyes—it nauseates me. It seems so utterly petty... . What the devil are we fighting for? It's going to be a splendid state of affairs, isn't it, if the immediate result of beating the Boche is anarchy over here? ... . And one feels that it oughtn't to be so; one feels that it's Gilbertian to the pitch of frenzied lunacy. You've seen those boys in hospital; I've seen 'em in the line—and they've struck me, as they have you, as God's elect... . Then why, WHY, WHY, in the name of all that is marvellous, is this state of affairs existing over here? ... .

"I went to lunch with Sir James Devereux before I left Rumfold. A nice old man, but money, or rather the lack of it, is simply rattling its bones in the family cupboard... ."

Vane laid down his pen as he came to this point, and began to trace patterns idly on the blotting paper. After a while he turned to the sheet again.

"His daughter seems very nice—also his sister, who is stone deaf. One screams at her through a megaphone. He, of course, rants and raves at what he calls the lack of patriotism shown by the working man. Fears an organised strike—financed by enemy money—if not during, at any rate after, the war. The country at a standstill—anarchy, Bolshevism. 'Pon my soul, I can't help thinking he's right. As soon as men, even the steadiest, have felt the power of striking—what will stop them? ... And as he says, they've had the most enormous concessions. By Jove! lady—it sure does make me sick and tired...
.

"However, in pursuance of your orders delivered verbally on the beach at Paris Plage, I am persevering in my endeavours to find the beaten track. I am lunching to-day with Nancy Smallwood, who has a new craze. You remember at one time it used to be keeping parrots—and then she went through a phase of distributing orchids through the slums of Whitechapel, to improve the recipients' aesthetic sense. She only gave that up, I have always understood, when she took to wearing black underclothes!

"I met her yesterday in Bond Street, and she tackled me at once.

"'You must lunch to-morrow ... Savoy ... 1.15 ... Meet Mr. Ramage, Labour leader ... Intensely interesting... .'

"You know how she talks, like a hen clucking. 'Coming, man... . Has already arrived, in fact... . One must make friends with the mammon of unrighteousness these days... . Life may depend on it... . He's such a dear, too... . Certain he'll never let these dreadful men kill me... . But I always give him the very best lunch I can... . In case, you know... . Good-bye.'

"I feel that she will sort of put down each course on the credit side of the ledger, and hope that, if the total proves sufficiently imposing, she may escape with the loss of an arm when the crash comes. She'll probably send the receipted bills to Ramage by special messenger.... I'm rather interested to meet the man. Sir James was particularly virulent over what he called the intellectuals.... .

"Well, dear, I must go. Don't do too much and overtire yourself.... ." He strolled out of the smoking-room and posted the letter. Then, refusing the offer of a passing taxi, he turned along Pall Mall on his way to the Savoy.

As Vane had said in his letter, Nancy Smallwood had a new craze. She passed from one to another with a bewildering rapidity which tried her friends very highly. The last one of which Vane had any knowledge was when she insisted on keeping a hen and feeding it with a special preparation of her own to increase its laying capacity. This necessitated it being kept in the drawing-room, as otherwise she forgot all about it; and Vane had a vivid recollection of a large and incredibly stout bird with a watery and furtive eye ensconced on cushions near the piano.

But that was years ago, and now the mammon of unrighteousness, as she called it, apparently held sway. He wondered idly as he walked along what manner of man Ramage would prove to be. Everyone whom he had ever met called down curses on the man's head, but as far as he could remember he had never heard him described. Nor did he recollect ever having seen a photograph of him. "Probably dressed in corduroy," he reflected, "and eats peas with his knife. Damn clever thing to do too; I mustn't forget to congratulate him if he does.... ."

He turned in at the courtyard of the hotel, glancing round for Nancy Smallwood. He saw her almost at once, looking a little worried. Incidentally she always did look worried, with that sort of helpless pathetic air with which very small women compel very big men to go to an infinity of trouble over things which bore them to extinction.

"My dear man," she cried as he came up to her. "Mr. Ramage hasn't come yet.... And he's always so punctual.... ."

"Then let us have a cocktail, Nancy, to keep the cold out till he does." He hailed a passing waiter. "Tell me, what sort of a fellow is he? I'm rather curious about him."

"My dear," she answered, "he's the most fascinating man in the world." She clasped her hands together and gazed at Vane impressively. "So wonderfully clever ... so quiet ... so ... so ... gentlemanly. I am so glad you could come. You would never think for a moment when you saw him that he sympathised

106

with all these dreadful Bolsheviks and Soviets and things; and that he disapproved of money and property and everything that makes life worth living... . Sometimes he simply terrifies me, Derek." She sipped her cocktail plaintively. "But I feel it's my duty to make a fuss of him and feed him and that sort of thing, for all our sakes. It may make him postpone the Revolution... ."

Vane suppressed a smile, and lit a cigarette gravely. "They'll probably give you a vote of thanks in Parliament, Nancy, to say nothing of an O.B.E... . Incidentally does the fellow eat all right?"

With a gesture of horrified protest, Nancy Smallwood sat back in her chair. "My dear Derek," she murmured... . "Far, far better than you and I do. I always mash my bread sauce up with the vegetables if no one's looking, and I'm certain he never would. He's most respectable... ."

"My God!" said Vane, "as bad as that! I was hoping he'd eat peas with his knife."

She looked towards the door and suddenly stood up. "Here he is, coming down the stairs now... ." She held out her hand to him as he came up. "I was afraid you weren't going to come, Mr. Ramage."

"Am I late?" he answered, glancing at his watch. "A thousand apologies, Mrs. Smallwood... . A committee meeting... ."

He turned towards Vane and she introduced the two men, who followed her into the restaurant. And in his first quick glance Vane was conscious of a certain disappointment, and a distinct feeling of surprise.

Far from being clad in corduroy, Ramage had on a very respectable morning coat. In fact, it struck him that Nancy Smallwood's remark exactly described him. He looked *most* respectable—not to say dull. By no stretch of imagination could Vane imagine him as the leader of a great cause. He might have been a country lawyer, or a general practitioner, or any of those eminently worthy things with which utility rather than brilliance is generally associated. He recalled what he had read in the papers—paragraphs describing meetings at which Mr. Ramage had taken a prominent part, and his general recollection of most of them seemed to be summed up in the one sentence ... "the meeting then broke up in disorder, Mr. Ramage escaping with difficulty through a window at the back." Somehow he could not see this decorous gentleman opposite escaping through windows under a barrage of bad eggs. He failed to fill the part completely. As a cashier in a local bank gravely informing a customer that his account was overdrawn—yes; but as a fighter, as a man who counted for something in the teeming world around— why no... . Not as far as appearance went, at any rate. And at that moment the eyes of the two men met for an instant across the table.... .

It seemed to Vane almost as if he had received a blow—so sudden was the check to his mental rambling. For the eyes of the man opposite, deep set and gleaming, were the eyes of greatness, and they triumphed so completely over their indifferent setting that Vane marvelled at his previous obtuseness. Martyrs have had such eyes, and the great pioneers of the world—men who have deemed everything well lost for a cause, be that cause right or wrong. And almost as if he were standing there in the flesh, there came to him a vision of Sir James raving furiously against this man.

He watched him with a slightly puzzled frown for a moment. This was the man who was deliberately leading the masses towards discontent and revolt; this was the man of intellect who was deliberately using his gift to try to ruin the country.... . So Sir James had said; so Vane had always understood. And his frown grew more puzzled.

Suddenly Ramage turned and spoke to him. A faint smile hovered for a second around his lips, as if he had noticed the frown and interpreted its cause aright.

"Things seem to be going very well over the water, Captain Vane."

"Very well," said Vane abruptly. "I think we've got those arch swine beaten at last—without the help of a negotiated peace."

For a moment the deep-set eyes gleamed, and then, once more, a faint smile hovered on his face. "Of which much maligned substitute for war you doubtless regard me as one of the High Priests?"

"Such is the general opinion, Mr. Ramage."

"And you think," returned the other after a moment, "that the idea was so completely wrong as to have justified the holders of the opposite view expending—what, another two ... three million lives?" ...

"I am afraid," answered Vane a little curtly, "that I'm in no position to balance any such account. The issues involved are a little above my form. All I do know is, that our dead would have turned in their graves had we not completed their work.... .'

"I wonder?" said the other slowly. "It always seems to me that the dead are saddled with very blood-thirsty opinions.... . One sometimes thinks, when one is in a particularly foolish mood, that the dead might have learned a little common sense.... . Very optimistic, but still.... ."

"If they have learned anything," answered Vane gravely, "our dead over the water—they have learned the sublime lesson of pulling together. It seems a pity, Mr. Ramage, that a few of 'em can't come back again and preach the sermon here in England."

"Wouldn't it be too wonderful?" chirruped their hostess. "Think of going to St. Paul's and being preached to by a ghost... ." For the past minute she had been shooting little bird-like glances at a neighbouring table, and now she leaned forward impressively. "There are some people over there, Mr. Ramage, and I'm sure they recognise you." This was better, far better, than feeding a hen in the drawing-room.

He turned to her with a faintly amused smile. "How very annoying for you! I am so sorry... . Shall I go away, and then you can discuss my sins in a loud voice with Captain Vane?"

Nancy Smallwood shook an admonishing finger at him, and sighed pathetically. "Do go on talking, you two. I do so love to hear about these things, and I'm so stupid myself... ."

"For Heaven's sake, Nancy," laughed Vane, "don't put me amongst the highbrows. I'm groping ... crumbs from rich man's table sort of business."

"Groping?" Ramage glanced at him across the table.

"Yes," said Vane taking the bull by the horns. "Wondering why the devil we fought if the result is going to be anarchy in England. Over there everybody seems to be pals; here... . Great Scott!" He shrugged his shoulders. After a while he went on—"Over there we got rid of class hatred; may I ask you, Mr. Ramage, without meaning in any way to be offensive, why you're doing your utmost to stir it up over here?"

The other put down his knife and fork and stared at Vane thoughtfully. "Because," he remarked in a curiously deep voice, "that way lies the salvation of the world... ."

"The machine-gun at the street corner," answered Vane cynically, "is certainly the way to salvation for quite a number."

Ramage took no notice of the interruption. "If labour had controlled Europe in 1914, do you suppose we should have had a war? As it was, a few men were capable of ordering millions to their death. Can you seriously contend that such a state of affairs was not absolutely rotten?"

"But are you going to alter it by fanning class hatred?" demanded Vane going back to his old point.

"Not if it can be avoided. But—the issue lies in the hands of the present ruling class... ."

Vane raised his eyebrows. "I have generally understood that it was

Labour who was bringing things to a head."

"It rather depends on the way you look at it, doesn't it? If I possess a thing which by right is yours, and you demand the return of it, which of us two is really responsible for the subsequent fight?"

"And what does the present ruling class possess which Labour considers should be returned to it?" asked Vane curiously.

"The bond note of slavery," returned the other. "If the present rulers will tear up that bond—willingly and freely—there will be no fight.... If not...." He shrugged his shoulders. "Labour may be forcing that issue, Captain Vane; but it will be the other man who is responsible if the fight comes.... Labour demands fair treatment—not as a concession, but as a right—and Labour has felt its power. It will get that treatment—peacefully, if possible; but if not"— and a light blazed in his eyes—"it will get it by force."

"And the referee as to what is just is Labour itself," said Vane slowly; "in spite of the fact that it's the other man who is running the financial risk and paying the piper. It sounds wonderfully fair, doesn't it? Surely some rights must go with property—whether it's land or a coal mine, or a bucket shop.... Surely the owner must have the principal say in calling the tune." For a few moments he stared at the man opposite him, and then he went on again, with increasing earnestness—with almost a note of appeal in his voice. "I want to get at your point of view, Mr. Ramage—I want to understand you.... And I don't. There are thousands of men like me who have been through this war— who have seen the glory underneath the dirt—who want to understand too. We hoped—we still hope—that a new England would grow out of it; but somehow...." Vane laughed shortly, and took out his cigarette case.

"And we are going to get that new England for which you have fought," burst out the other triumphantly. Then with a slight smile he looked at Vane. "We must not forget our surroundings—I see a waiter regarding me suspiciously. Thanks—no; I don't smoke." He traced a pattern idly on the cloth for a moment, and then looked up quickly. "I would like you to try to understand," he said. "Because, as I said, the whole question of possible anarchy as opposed to a constitutional change lies in your hands and the hands of your class."

Vane gave a short, incredulous laugh, and shook his head.

"In your hands," repeated the other gravely. "You see, Captain Vane, we approach this matter from a fundamentally different point of view. You look around you, and you see men striking here and striking there. And you say 'Look at the swine; striking again!' But there's one thing that you fail to grasp, I think. Underneath all these strikes and violent upheavals, bursting into flame in all sorts of unexpected places—there is the volcano of a vital conflict between two fundamental ideas. Though the men hardly realise it themselves, it's there, that conflict, all the time.... And we, who see a little further than the mob, know that it's there, and that sooner or later that conflict will end in victory for one side or the other. Which side, my friend? Yours *or* ours.... Or both. Yours *and* ours.... England's." He paused for a moment as the waiter handed him the coffee. Then he went on—"To the master-class generally there is a certain order of things, and they can imagine nothing else. They employ workers—they pay them, or they 'chuck' them, as they like. They hold over them absolute power. They are kind in many cases; they help and look after their employees. But they are the masters—and the others are the men. That is the only form of society they can conceive of. Any mitigation of conditions is simply a change within the old order. That is one point of view.... Now for the other." He turned with a smile to his hostess. "I hope I'm not boring you...."

"Why, I'm thrilled to death," she cried, hurriedly collecting her thoughts from an adjacent hat. "Do go on."

"The other point of view is this. We do not wish for mitigation of conditions in a system which we consider wrong. We want the entire system swept away.... We want the entire propertied class removed. We deny that there are any inherent rights which go with the possession of property; and even if there are, we claim that the rights of the masses far outweigh the property rights of the small minority of owners...."

"In other words," said Vane briefly, "you claim for the masses the right to commit robbery on a large scale."

"For just so long as that view of robbery holds, Captain Vane, for just so long will there fail to be any real co-operation between you and us. For just so long as you are convinced that your vested right is the true one, and that ours is false—for just so long will the final settlement by quiet methods be postponed. But if you make it too long the final settlement will not come by quiet means."

"Your proposal, then, is that we should commit suicide with a good grace?" remarked Vane. "Really, Mr. Ramage, it won't do.... I, personally, if I owned property, would go into the last ditch in defence of what was mine." Into his mind there flashed Joan's words.... "It's ours. I tell you, ours," and he smiled grimly. "Why, in the name of fortune, I should give what I possess to a crowd of scally wags who haven't made good, is more than I can fathom...."

"It is hardly likely to go as far as that," said the other with a smile. "But the time is coming when we shall have a Labour Government—a Government which at heart is Socialistic. And their first move will be to nationalise all the big industries.... How far will property meet them and help them? Will they fight—or will they co-operate? ... It's up to property to decide...."

"Because you will have forced the issue," said Vane; "an issue which, I maintain, you have no right to force. Robbery is robbery, just the same whether its sanctioned by an Act of Parliament, or whether it's performed by a man holding a gun at your head.... Why, in God's name, Mr. Ramage, can't we pull together for the side? ..."

"With you as the leaders—the kind employers?"

"With those men as the leaders who have shown that they can lead," said Vane doggedly. "They will come to the top in the future as they have in the past...."

"By all manner of means," cried Ramage. "Leaders—brains—will always rise to the top; will always be rewarded more highly than mere manual labour.... They will occupy more remunerative positions under the State.... But the fruits of labour will only be for those who do the work—be it with their hands or be it with their heads. The profiteer must go; the private owner must go with his dole here and his dole there, generally forced from him as the result of a strike. I would be the last to say that there are not thousands of good employers—but there are also thousands of bad ones, and now labour refuses to run the risk any more."

"And what about depreciation—fresh plant? Where's the capital coming from?"

"Why, the State. It requires very little imagination to see how easy it would be to put away a certain sum each year for that.... A question of how much you charge the final purchaser.... And the profiteer goes out of the picture.... That's what we're aiming at; that is what is coming.... No more men like the gentleman sitting three tables away—just behind you; no more of the Baxters fattening on sweated labour." His deep-set eyes were gleaming at the vision he saw, and Vane felt a sense of futility.

"Even assuming your view is right, Mr. Ramage," he remarked slowly, "do you really think that you, and the few like you, will ever hold the mob? ... You may make your new England, but you'll make it over rivers of blood, unless we all of us—you, as well as we—see through the glass a little less darkly than we do now...."

"Every great movement has its price," returned the other, staring at him gravely.

"Price!" Vane's laugh was short and bitter. "Have you ever seen a battalion, Mr. Ramage, that has been caught under machine-gun fire?"

"And have *you*, Captain Vane, ever seen the hovels in which some of our workers live?"

"And you really think that by exchanging private ownership for a soulless bureaucracy you find salvation?" said Vane shortly. "You're rather optimistic, aren't you, on the subject of Government departments? ..."

"I'm not thinking of this Government, Captain Vane," he remarked quietly. He looked at his watch and rose. "I'm glad to have met you," he said holding out his hand. "It's the vested interest that is at the root of the whole evil—that stands between the old order and the new. Therefore the vested interest must go." ... He turned to his hostess. "I'm sorry to run away like this, Mrs. Smallwood, but—I'm a busy man... ."

She rose at once; nothing would have induced her to forgo walking through the restaurant with him. Later she would describe the progress to her intimates in her usual staccato utterances, like a goat hopping from crag to crag.

"My dear... . So thrilling... . He means wholesale murder... . Told us so... . And there was a man close by, watching him all the time... . A Government spy probably... . Do you think I shall be arrested? ... If only he allows Bill and me to escape when it comes... . The revolution, I mean... . I think Monte is the place... . But one never knows... . Probably the croupiers will be armed with pistols, or something dreadful... . Except that if it's the labouring classes who are rising, we ought to shoot the croupiers... . It is so difficult to know what to do."

Vane turned to follow her, as she threaded her way between the tables, and at that moment he saw Joan. The grey eyes were fixed on him mockingly, and he felt as if everyone in the room must hear the sudden thumping of his heart. With a murmured apology to his hostess, he left her and crossed to Joan's table.

"This is an unexpected surprise," she remarked as he came up.

"Do you know Mr. Baxter—Captain Vane... ."

Vane looked curiously at the man who had invoked his late companion's wrath. Then his glance fell on the bottle of Vichy in front of the millionaire, and his jaw tightened.

"You left Blandford very unexpectedly, Miss Devereux," he said politely.

113

"Yes—I had to go North suddenly." She looked at him with a smile. "You see—I was frightened... ."

"Frightened... ." murmured Vane.

"A friend of mine—a very great friend of mine—a girl, was in danger of making a fool of herself." Her eyes were fixed on the band, and his heart began to thump again.

"I trust the catastrophe was averted," he remarked.

"One never knows in these cases, does one?" she answered. He saw the trace of a smile hover on her lips; then she turned to her companion. "Captain Vane was one of the convalescents at Rumfold Hall," she explained.

Mr. Baxter grunted. "Going over again soon?" he asked in a grating voice.

"I'm on leave at present," said Vane briefly.

"Well, if you'll forgive my saying so," continued Baxter in his harsh voice, "your luncheon companion to-day is a gentleman you want to be careful with... ."

Vane raised his eyebrows. "You are more than kind," he murmured. "But I think... ."

Mr. Baxter waved his hand. "I mean no offence," he said. "But that man Ramage is one of the men who are going to ruin this country...."

"Funnily enough, Mr. Baxter, he seems to be of the opinion that you are one of the men who have already done so."

The millionaire, in no wise offended, roared with laughter. Then he became serious again. "The old catchwords," he grated. "Bloated capitalist—sweated labour, growing fat on the bodies and souls of those we employ... . Rot, sir; twaddle, sir. There's no business such as mine would last for one moment if I didn't look after my workpeople. Pure selfishness on my part, I admit. If I had my way I'd sack the lot and instal machines. But I can't... . And if I could, do you suppose I'd neglect my machine... . Save a shilling for lubricating oil and do a hundred pounds' worth of damage? Don't you believe it, Captain Vane... . But, I'll be damned if I'll be dictated to by the man I pay... . I pay them a fair wage and they know it. And if I have any of this rot of sympathetic strikes after the war, I'll shut everything down for good and let 'em starve... ." He looked at Joan... . "I wouldn't be sorry to have a long rest," he continued thoughtfully.

"Captain Vane is a seeker after truth," she remarked. "It must be most valuable," she turned to Vane, "to hear two such opinions as his and Mr. Ramage's so close together." Her eyes were dancing merrily.

114

"Most valuable," returned Vane. "And one is so struck with the pugilistic attitude adopted by both parties.... It seems so extraordinarily helpful to the smooth running of the country afterwards." He had no occasion to like Baxter from any point of view—but apart altogether from Joan, he felt that if there was any justification in his late luncheon companion's views, men such as Baxter supplied it.

With a movement almost of distaste he turned to Joan. "I was sorry that we didn't have another game before I left Rumfold," he said lightly.

"It was so very even that last one," she returned, and Vane's knuckles showed white on the table.

"My recollection is that you won fairly easily," he murmured.

"Excuse me a moment, will you?" said Mr. Baxter to Joan. "There's a man over there I must speak to...." He rose and crossed the restaurant. Joan watched him as he moved between the tables; then she looked at Vane. "Your recollections are all wrong," she said softly. The grey eyes held no hint of mockery in them now, they were sweetly serious, and once again Vane gripped the table hard. His head was beginning to swim and he felt that he would shortly make a profound fool of himself.

"Do you think you're being quite kind, grey girl," he said in a low voice which he strove to keep calm.

For a few moments she played with the spoon on her coffee cup, and suddenly with a great rush of pure joy, which well-nigh choked him, Vane saw that her hand was trembling.

"Are *you*?" He scarcely heard the whispered words above the noise around.

"I don't care whether I am or not." His voice was low and exultant. He looked round, and saw that Baxter was threading his way back towards them. "This afternoon, Joan, tea in my rooms." He spoke swiftly and insistently. "You've just got to meet Binks...."

And then, before she could answer, he was gone....

CHAPTER XII

Vane walked along Piccadilly a prey to conflicting emotions. Dominant amongst them was a wild elation at what he had seen in Joan's eyes, but a very good second was the uncomfortable remembrance of Margaret. What did he propose to do?

He was not a cad, and the game he was playing struck him rather forcibly as being uncompromisingly near the caddish. Did he, or did he not, mean to make love to the girl he had just left at the Savoy? And if he did, to what end?

A crowd of lunchers coming out of Prince's checked him for a moment or two, and forced him into the arms of an officer and a girl who were standing, apparently waiting for a taxi. Almost unconsciously he took stock of them, even as he apologised... .

The girl, a pretty little thing, but utterly mediocre and uninteresting, was clinging to the officer's arm, a second lieutenant in the Tank Corps.

"Do you think we ought to take a taxi, Bill? Let's go on a 'bus... ."

"No damn fear," returned Bill. "Let's blow the lot while we're about it. I'm going back to-morrow... ."

Then Vane pushed past them, with that brief snapshot of a pair of lives photographed on his brain. And it would have effaced itself as quickly as it had come, but for the very new wedding ring he had seen on the girl's left hand—so new that to conceal it with a glove was simply not to be thought of.

Money—money—money; was there no getting away from it?

"Its value will not be measured by material things. It will leave nothing. And yet it will have everything, and whatever one takes from it, it will still have, so rich will it be... ." And as the words of Oscar Wilde came to his mind Vane laughed aloud.

"This is London, my lad," he soliloquised. "London in the twentieth century. We've a very nice war on where a man may develop his personality; fairy tales are out of date."

He strolled on past the Ritz—his mind still busy with the problem. Joan wanted to marry money; Joan had to marry money. At least he had gathered so. He had asked Margaret to marry him; she had said that in time she would —if he still wanted her. At least he had gathered so. Those were the major issues.

The minor and more important one—because minor ones have a way of influencing the big fellows out of all proportion to their size—was that he had asked Joan to tea.

He sighed heavily and turned up Half Moon Street. Whatever happened afterwards he had his duty as a host to consider first. He decided to go in and talk to the worthy Mrs. Green, and see if by any chance that stalwart pillar would be able to provide a tea worthy of the occasion. Mrs. Green had a way with her, which seemed to sweep through such bureaucratic absurdities as ration cards and food restrictions. Also, and perhaps it was more to the point, she had a sister in Devonshire who kept cows.

"Mrs. Green," called Vane, "come up and confer with me on a matter of great importance... ."

With a wild rush Binks emerged from below as if shot from a catapult—to be followed by Mrs. Green wiping her hands on her apron.

"A most important affair, Mrs. Green," continued Vane, when he had let himself into his rooms, and pacified Binks temporarily with the squeaky indiarubber dog. "Only you can save the situation... ."

Mrs. Green intimated by a magnificent gesture that she was fully prepared to save any situation.

"I have visitors for tea, or rather, to be correct—a visitor. A lady to comfort me—or perhaps torment me—as only your sex can." His eyes suddenly rested on Margaret's photo, and he stopped with a frown. Mrs. Green's motherly face beamed with satisfaction. Here was a Romance with a capital R, which was as dear to her kindly heart as a Mary Pickford film.

"I'm sure I hope you'll be very happy, sir," she said.

"So do I, Mrs. Green—though I've a shrewd suspicion, I shall be profoundly miserable." He resolutely turned his back on the photo. "I'm playing a little game this afternoon, most motherly of women. Incidentally it's been played before—but it never loses its charm or—its danger... ." He gave a short laugh. "My first card is your tea. Toast, Mrs. Green, covered with butter supplied by your sister in Devonshire. Hot toast in your priceless muffin dish —running over with butter: and wortleberry jam... . Can you do this great thing for me?"

Mrs. Green nodded her head. "The butter only came this morning, Mr. Vane, sir. And I've got three pounds of wortleberry jam left... ."

"Three pounds should be enough," said Vane after due deliberation.

"And then I've got a saffron cake," went on the worthy woman. "Fresh made

117

before it was sent on by my sister... ."

"Say no more, Mrs. Green. We win—hands down—all along the line. Do you realise that fair women and brave men who venture out to tea in London to-day have to pay half a crown for a small dog biscuit?" Vane rubbed his hands together. "After your tea, and possibly during it—I shall play my second card —Binks. Now I appeal to you—Could any girl with a particle of natural feeling consent to go on living away from Binks?"

The Accursed Thing emitted a mournful hoot, as Binks, hearing his name spoken, raised his head and looked up at his master. His tail thumped the floor feverishly, and his great brown eyes glowed with a mute inquiry. "To walk, or not to walk"—that was the question. The answer was apparently in the negative, for the moment at any rate, and he again returned to the attack.

"You see my guile, Mrs. Green," said Vane. "Softened by toast, floating in Devonshire butter and covered with wortleberry jam; mellowed by saffron cake—Binks will complete the conquest. Then will come the crucial moment. No one, not even she, can part me from my dog. To have Binks—she must have me... . What do you think of it—as a game only, you know?"

Mrs. Green laughed. "I surely do hope you're successful, my dear," she said, and she laid a motherly hand on his arm. In moments of extreme feeling she sometimes reverted to the language of her fathers, with its soft West Country burr... . "When Green come courtin' me, he just tuk me in tu his arms, and give me a great fat little kiss... ."

"And, by Jove, Mrs. Green, he was a damn lucky fellow to be able to do it," cried Vane, taking the kindly old hand in both his own. "If I wasn't afraid of him coming for me with a broomstick, I'd do the same myself...."

She shook a reproving finger at him from the door, and her face was wreathed in smiles. "You ring when you want the tea, Mr. Vane, sir," she said, "and I'll bring it up to you... ."

She closed the door, and Vane heard the stairs creaking protestingly as she descended. And not for the first time did he thank his lucky stars that Fate had put him into such hands when he left Oxford... .

For a while he stood staring at the door with a slight frown, and then he turned to Binks.

"I wonder, young fellow my lad," he muttered. "I wonder if I'm being the most arrant blackguard!"

He wandered restlessly round the room taking odd books from one table and putting them on another, only to replace them in their original positions on the return journey. He tidied up the golf clubs and a bundle of polo sticks, and pitched the boxing gloves under a settee in the corner from which Binks promptly retrieved them. In fact, he behaved as men will behave when they're waiting for the unknown—be it the answer of a woman, or zero hour at six thirty. And at last he seemed to realise the fact... .

"Oh! Hell, Binks," he laughed. "I've got it bad—right where the boxer puts the sleep dope... . I think I'll just go and wash my hands, old boy; they strike me as being unpleasantly excited... ."

But when he returned Binks was still exhaling vigorously at a hole in the wainscot, behind which he fancied he had detected a sound. With the chance of a mouse on the horizon he became like Gamaliel, and cared for none of these things... .

A taxi drove up to the door, and Vane threw down the book he was pretending to read, and listened with his heart in his mouth. Even Binks, scenting that things were afoot, ceased to blow, and cocked his head on one side expectantly. Then he growled, a low down, purring growl, which meant that strangers were presuming to approach his domain and that he reserved his judgment... .

"Shut up, you fool," said Vane, as he sprang across the room to the door, which at once decided the question in Binks's mind. Here was evidently an enemy of no mean order who dared to come where angels feared to tread when he was about. He beat Vane by two yards, giving tongue in his most approved style... .

"Down, old man, down," cried Vane, as he opened the door—but Binks had to justify his existence. And so he barked twice at the intruder who stood outside, watching his master with a faint smile. True the second bark seemed in the nature of an apology; but damn it, one must do something....

"You've come," said Vane, and with the sight of her every other thought left his head. "My dear—but it's good of you... ."

"Didn't you expect me?" she asked coming into the room. Still with the same faint smile, she turned to Binks. "Hullo, old fellow," she said. "You sure have got a great head on you." She bent over him, and put her hand on the browny-black patch behind his ears... . Binks growled; he disliked familiarity from people he did not know.

"Look out, Joan," said Vane nervously. "He's a little funny with strangers sometimes."

"Am I a stranger, old chap?" she said, taking off her glove, and letting her hand hang loosely just in front of his nose, with the back towards him. Vane nodded approvingly, though he said nothing; as a keen dog lover it pleased him intensely to see that the girl knew how to make friends with them. And not everyone—even though they know the method to use with a doubtful dog —has the nerve to use it... .

For a moment Binks looked at her appraisingly; then he thrust forward a cold wet nose and sniffed once at the hand in front of him. His mind was made up. Just one short, welcoming lick, and he trotted back to his hole in the wainscot. Important matters seemed to him to have been neglected far too long as it was... .

"Splendid," said Vane quietly. "The other member of the firm is now in love with you as well... ."

She looked at Vane in silence, and suddenly she shivered slightly. "I think," she said, "that we had better talk about rather less dangerous topics... ." She glanced round her, and then went to the window and stood looking out into the bright sunlight. "What topping rooms you've got," she said after a moment.

"They aren't bad, are they?" remarked Vane briefly. "What do you say to some tea? My devoted landlady is preparing a repast which millionaires would squander their fortunes for. Her sister happens to live in Devonshire... ."

"So you were expecting me?" she cried, turning round and facing him.

"I was," answered Vane.

She laughed shortly. "Well—what do you think of dyspepsia and Vichy?"

"I've been trying not to think of him ever since lunch," he answered grimly. She came slowly towards him, and suddenly Vane caught both her hands. "Joan, Joan," he cried, and his voice was a little hoarse, "my dear, you can't... . You just can't... ."

"What great brain was it who said something really crushing about that word 'Can't?'" she said lightly.

"Then you just mustn't." His grip almost hurt her, but she made no effort to take away her hands.

"The trouble, my very dear friend, seems to me to be that—I just must." Gently she disengaged her hands, and at that moment Mrs. Green arrived with the tea.

"The dearest and kindest woman in London," said Vane with a smile to Joan. "Since the days of my callow youth Mrs. Green has watched over me like a mother... ."

"I expect he wanted some watching too, Mrs. Green," cried Joan.

Mrs. Green laughed, and set down the tea. "Show me the young gentleman that doesn't, Miss," she said, "and I'll show you one that's no manner of use to anybody... ."

She arranged the plates and cups and then with a final—"You'll ring if you want more butter, sir"—she left the room.

"Think of it, Joan," said Vane. "Ring if you want more butter! Is it a phrase from a dead language?" He pulled up a chair... . "Will you preside, please, and decant the juice?"

The girl sat down and smiled at him over the teapot. "A big, fat tea," she murmured, "with lots of scones and Devonshire cream... ."

"I thought you suggested talking about rather less dangerous topics," said Vane quietly. Their eyes met, and suddenly Vane leaned forward. "Tell me, grey girl," he said, "did you really mean it when you said the last game was very nearly even?"

For a moment she did not answer, and then she looked at him quite frankly. "Yes," she said; "I really meant it. I tell you quite honestly that I had meant to punish you; I had meant to flirt with you—teach you a lesson—and give you a fall. I thought you wanted it... . And then... ."

"Yes," said Vane eagerly... . "What then?"

"Why—I think I changed my mind," said the girl. "I didn't know you were such a dear... . I'm sorry," she added after a moment.

"But why be sorry?" he cried. "It's just the most wonderful thing in the world. I did deserve it—I've had the fall... . And oh! my dear, to think you're crashed as well... . Or at any rate slid a bit." He corrected himself with a smile.

But there was no answering smile on the girl's face. She just stared out of the window, and then with a sort of explosive violence she turned on Vane. "Why did you do it?" she stormed. "Why ... why ...?" For a while they looked at one another, and then she laughed suddenly. "For Heaven's sake, let's be sensible... . The toast is getting cold, my dear man... ."

"I can't believe it," said Vane gravely. "We've done nothing to deserve such a punishment as that... ."

And so for a while they talked of trivial things—of plays, and books, and people. But every now and then would fall a silence, and their eyes would meet—and hold. Just for a moment or two; just for long enough to make them both realise the futility of the game they were playing. Then they would both speak at once, and contribute some gem of sparkling wit, which would have shamed even the writer of mottoes in crackers... .

A tentative paw on Joan's knee made her look down. Binks—tired of his abortive blasts at an unresponsive hole—desired refreshment, and from time immemorial tea had been the one meal at which he was allowed to beg. He condescended to eat two slices of saffron cake, and then Vane presented the slop basin to Joan.

"He likes his tea," he informed her, "with plenty of milk and sugar. Also you must stir it with your finger to see that it isn't too hot. He'll never forgive you if it burns his nose."

"You really are the most exacting household," laughed Joan, putting the bowl down on the floor.

"We are," said Vane gravely. "I hope you feel equal to coping with us... ."

She was watching Binks as he stood beside her drinking his tea, and gave no sign of having heard his remark.

"You know," he continued after a while, "your introduction to Binks at such an early stage in the proceedings has rather spoilt the masterly programme I had outlined in my mind. First you were to be charmed and softened by Mrs. Green's wonderful tea. Secondly, you were to see Binks; be formally introduced. You were to fall in love with him on sight, so to speak; vow that you could never be parted from such a perfect dog again. And then, thirdly..."

"His appearance is all that I could desire," she interrupted irrelevantly; "but I beg to point out that he is an excessively dirty feeder... ."

Vane stood up and looked at the offender. "You mean the shower of tea drops that goes backwards on to the carpet," he said reflectively. "'Twas ever thus with Binks."

"And the tea leaves adhering to his beard." She pointed an accusing finger at the unrepentant sinner.

"You should have poured it through that sieve affair," said Vane. "Your own manners as a hostess are not all they might be. However, Binks and I are prepared to overlook it for once, and so we will pass on to the thirdly... ."

He handed her the cigarette box, and with a faint smile hovering round her lips, she looked up at him.

"Is your thirdly safe?" she asked.

"Mrs. Green thought it wonderful. A suitable climax to a dramatic situation."

"You've had a rehearsal, have you?"

"Just a preliminary canter to see I hadn't forgotten anything."

"And she approved?"

"She suggested an alternative that, I am rather inclined to think, might be better," he answered. "It's certainly simpler... ."

Again she smiled faintly. "I'm not certain that Mrs. Green's simpler alternative strikes me as being much safer than your thirdly," she murmured. "Incidentally, am I failing again in my obvious duties? It seems to me that Binks sort of expects something... ." Another fusillade of tail thumps greeted the end of the sentence.

"Great Scott!" cried Vane, "I should rather think you were. However, I don't think you could very well have known; it's outside the usual etiquette book." He handed her the indiarubber dog. "A feint towards the window, one towards the door—and then throw."

A quivering, ecstatic body, a short, staccato bark—and Binks had caught his enemy. He bit once; he bit again—and then, a little puzzled, he dropped it. Impossible to conceive that it was really dead at last—and yet, it no longer hooted. Binks looked up at his master for information on the subject, and Vane scratched his head.

"That sure is the devil, old son," he remarked. "Have you killed it for keeps. Bring it here... ." Binks laid it obediently at Vane's feet. "It should squeak," he explained to Joan as he picked it up, "mournfully and hideously."

She came and stood beside him and together they regarded it gravely, while Binks, in a state of feverish anticipation, looked from one to the other.

"Get on with it," he tail-wagged at them furiously; "get on with it, for Heaven's sake! Don't stand there looking at one another... ."

"I think," his master was speaking in a voice that shook, "I think the metal squeak has fallen inside the animal's tummy... ."

"You ought to have been a vet," answered the girl, and her voice was very low. "Give it to me; my finger is smaller."

She took the toy from Vane's hand and bent over it.

"Thank goodness somebody takes an intelligent interest in matters of import," thought Binks—and then with a dull, unsqueaking thud his enemy fell at his feet.

"My dear—my dear!" His master's voice came low and tense and pretence was over. With hungry arms Vane caught the girl to him, and she did not resist. He kissed her eyes, her hair, her lips, while she lay passively against him. Then she wound her arms round his neck, and gave him back kiss for kiss.

At last she pushed him away. "Ah! don't, don't," she whispered. "You make it so hard, Derek—so awfully hard... ."

"Not on your life," he cried exultingly. "It's easy that I've made it, my darling, so awfully easy... ."

Mechanically she patted her hair into shape, and then she stooped and picked up the toy.

"We're forgetting Binks," she said quietly. She managed to get the circular metal whistle out of the inside of the toy, and fixed it in its appointed hole, while Vane, with a glorious joy surging through him, leaned against the mantelpiece and watched her in silence. Not until the squeaking contest was again going at full blast in a corner did he speak.

"That was Mrs. Green's simpler alternative," he said reflectively. "Truly her wisdom is great."

In silence Joan went towards the window. For a while she looked out with unseeing eyes, and then she sank into a big easy chair with her back towards Vane. A thousand conflicting emotions were rioting through her brain; the old battle of heart against head was being waged. She was so acutely alive to his presence just behind her; so vitally conscious of his nearness. Her whole body was crying aloud for the touch of his hands on her again—and then, a vision of Blandford came before her. God! what did it matter—Blandford, or her father, or anything? There was nothing in the world which could make up for —what was it he had called it?—the biggest thing in Life.

Suddenly she felt his hands on her shoulders; she felt them stealing down her arms. She felt herself lifted up towards him, and with a little gasp of utter surrender she turned and looked at him with shining eyes.

"Derek, my darling," she whispered. "Que je t'adore... ."

And then of her own accord, she kissed him on the lips... .

It was Binks's expression, about a quarter of an hour later, which recalled them to earth again. With an air of pained disgust he regarded them stolidly for a few minutes. Then he had a good scratch on both sides of his neck, after which he yawned. He did not actually say "Pooh," but he looked it, and they both laughed.

124

"Dear man," she whispered, "wouldn't it be just too wonderful if it could always be just you and me and Binks? ..."

"And why shouldn't it be, lady?" he answered, and his arm went round her waist. "Why shouldn't it be? We'll just sometimes have to see some horrible outsider, I suppose, and perhaps you or somebody will have to order food every year or so.... But except for that—why, we'll just slip down the stream all on our own, and there won't be a little bit of difficulty about keeping your eyes in the boat, grey girl...."

She smiled—a quick, fleeting smile; and then she sighed.

"Life's hell, Derek—just hell, sometimes. And the little bits of Heaven make the hell worse."

"Life's pretty much what we make it ourselves, dear," said Vane gravely.

"It isn't," she cried fiercely. "We're what life makes us...."

Vane bent over and started pulling one of Binks's ears.

"You hear that, old man," he said. "The lady is a base materialist, while I—your funny old master—am sprouting wings and growing a halo as a visionary." Vane looked sideways at the girl. "He manages to make his own life, Joan. He'd be as happy with me in a garret as he would in a palace.... Probably happier, because he'd mean more to me—fill a bigger part of my life."

Suddenly he stood up and shook both his fists in the air. "Damn it," he cried, "and why can't we cheat 'em, Joan? Cheat all those grinning imps, and seize the Blue Bird and never let it go?"

"Because," she answered slowly, "if you handle the Blue Bird roughly or snatch at it and put it in a cage, it just pines away and dies. And then the imps grin and chuckle worse than ever...."

She rose and put her hands on his shoulders. "It's here now, my dear. I can hear it fluttering so gently near the window.... And that noise from the streets is really the fairy chorus...."

A motor car honked discordantly and Vane grinned.

"That's a stout-hearted little fellow with a good pair of lungs on him." She smiled back at him, and then she pushed him gently backwards and forwards with her hands.

"Of course he's got good lungs," she said. "He toots like that whenever anybody falls in love, and twice when they get married, and three times when...."

125

Vane's breath came in a great gasp, and he pushed her away almost roughly.

"Don't—for God's sake, don't, Joan... ."

"My dear," she cried, catching his arm, "forgive me. The Blue Bird's not gone, Derek—it's still there. Don't frighten it—oh! don't. We won't snatch at it, won't even think of making any plans for caging it—we'll just assume it's going to stop.... I believe it will then.... And afterwards—why what does afterwards matter? Let's be happy while we may, and—perhaps, who knows—we will cheat those grinning imps after all... ."

"Right," cried Vane, catching her hands, "right, right, right. What shall we do, my dear, to celebrate the presence of our blue visitor? ..."

For a moment she thought, and then her eyes lit up. "You're still on leave, aren't you?"

"Even so, lady."

"Then to-morrow we will take a car... ."

"My car," interrupted Vane. "And I've got ten gallons of petrol."

"Glorious. We'll take your car, and will start ever so early, and go to the river. Sonning, I think—to that ripping pub where the roses are. And then we'll go on the river for the whole day, and take Binks, and an invisible cage for the Blue Bird.... We'll take our food, and a bone for Binks and the squeaky dog. Then in the evening we'll have dinner at the White Hart, and Binks shall have a napkin and sit up at table. And then after dinner we'll come home. My dear, but it's going to be Heaven." She was in his arms and her eyes were shining like stars. "There's only one rule. All through the whole day—no one, not even Binks—is allowed to think about the day after."

Vane regarded her with mock gravity. "Not even if we're arrested for joy riding?" he demanded.

"But the mascot will prevent that, silly boy," she cried. "Why would we be taking that cage for otherwise?"

"I see," said Vane. "It's the most idyllic picture I've ever even thought of. There's only one thing. I feel I must speak about it and get it over." He looked so serious that for a moment her face clouded. "Do not forget—I entreat of you, do not forget—your meat coupon." And then with the laughter that civilisation has decreed shall not be heard often, save on the lips of children, a man and a girl forgot everything save themselves. The world of men and matters rolled on and passed them by, and maybe a year of Hell is fair exchange for that brief space... .

CHAPTER XIII

The next morning dawned propitious, and Vane, as he drove his two-seater through the park to Ashley Gardens, sang to himself under his breath. He resolutely shut his eyes to the hurrying streams of khaki and blue and black passing in and out of huts and Government buildings. They simply did not exist; they were an hallucination, and if persisted in might frighten the mascot.

Joan was waiting for him when he drove up at half-past nine, with Binks sitting importantly on the seat beside him.

"Get right in, lady," cried Vane, "and we'll be on to the Land of the Pixies. But, for the love of Mike, don't put anything on Binks's adversary in the hood. He hasn't had his proper morning battle yet, and one squeak will precipitate a catastrophe."

Never had he seen Joan looking so charming. Of course she was in grey—that was in the nature of a certainty on such an occasion, but she might have been in sackcloth for all the attention Vane paid to her clothes. It was her face that held him, with the glow of perfect health on her cheeks, and the soft light of utter happiness in her eyes. She was pretty—always; but with a sudden catch of his breath Vane told himself that this morning she was the loveliest thing he had ever seen.

"I've got the cage, Derek," she said, "and the beautifullest bone for Binks that he's ever thought of... ."

"You dear," answered Vane, and for a moment their eyes met. "You absolute dear... ." Then with a quick change of tone he laughed. "Jump in, grey girl—and avaunt all seriousness. Do you mind having Binks on your lap?"

"Do I mind?" she answered reproachfully. "Did you hear that, Binkie? He's insulting you."

But Binks was claiming his share of the Blue Bird and refused to take offence. He just opened one brown eye and looked at her, and then he went peacefully to sleep again. He rather liked this new acquisition to the family...
.

And so began the great day. They didn't go far from the hotel; just under the old bridge and up a little way towards Sonning lock, where the river forks, and the trees grow down to the water's edge. To every man whose steps lead him on to the Long Trail, there is some spot in this island of ours the vision of which comes back to him when the day's work is done and he lies a-dreaming of Home. To some it may be the hills in the Highlands with the wonderful purple mist over them growing black as the sun sinks lower and lower; to others a little golden-sanded beach with the red sandstone cliffs of Devon rising sheer around it, and the tiny waves rippling softly through the drowsy morning. It is not always thus: sometimes the vision shows them a heaving grey sea hurling itself sullenly on a rock-bound coast; a grey sky, and driving rain which stings their faces as they stand on the cliffs above the little cove, looking out into the lands beyond the water, where the strange roads go down... .

And then to some it may be the roar and bustle of Piccadilly that comes back to haunt them in their exile—the theatre, the music and the lights, the sound of women's skirts; or the rolling Downs of Sussex with the white chalk quarries and great cockchafers booming past them through the dusk.

To each and everyone there is one spot hallowed by special memory, and that spot claims pride of place in day dreams. But when the mind rambles on, and the lumber-room of the past is open—to all who have tasted of its peaceful spell there comes the thought of The River. Spell it with Capitals; there is only one. Whether it be Bourne End with its broad reach and the sailing punts, or the wooded heights by Clieveden; whether it be Boulter's Lock on Ascot Sunday, or the quiet stretch near Goring—there is only one River. Henley, Wargrave, Cookham—it matters not... . They all go to form The River. And it's one of them, or some of them, or all of them that brings that faint smile of reminiscence to the wanderer's face as he stirs the fire with his boot.

It's so wonderful to drift—just once in a while. And those of the River always drift when they worship at her shrine. Only people who make money in tinned goods and things, and are in all respects dreadful, go on the River in launches, which smell and offend people. And they are not of the River... .

"If," said Joan lazily, "you had suggested paddling to Reading, or punting several miles towards Henley, I should have burst into tears. And yet there are some people who deliberately set out to go somewhere... ."

"There are two things which precluded such an insane possibility," he said. "The first is Binks; he likes to run about. And the second is that unless I have a kiss within one second I shall blow up... ."

"Of course you've known Binks longer than me, so I suppose I mustn't object to the order of precedence." She looked at him mockingly, then, with a quick, fierce movement, she took his face between her hands. And an intelligent and bewhiskered old water rat regarded the subsequent proceedings with a tolerant eye.

"More of 'em at it, my dear," he told his spouse, in his fastness under a gnarled tree root. "However, there's no objection to the children having a look if it amuses them." He cast a discriminating eye round the larder, and frowned heavily. "Hell! you don't mean to say that we've got that damned ham bone again," he growled. "However, we ought to pick up something when they've finished the exhibition and get down to their lunch... ." He thoughtfully pulled his left whisker. "And by the way, my love, tell Jane not to go wandering about this afternoon, even if she is in love. There's an abominable dog of the most dangerous description on the warpath. Let me know when those fools stop."

He composed himself for a nap, and the wash of a passing launch which flopped against the punt outside lulled him to sleep... . He was a prosaic old gentleman, that water rat, so his peevishness may be forgiven him. After all, a ham bone is a ham bone and pretty poor at that, and when one has been the father of several hundreds, the romantic side of life pales considerably in the light of the possibilities of lunch.

But up above, in the punt, the fools were busy according to their foolishness, quite unmindful of their disapproving audience. Maybe it is dangerous to try to cheat reality; but success justifies any experiment. And the day was successful beyond their wildest dreams. Binks grubbed about in the bank and incidentally gave the love-sick Jane the fright of her young life; until at last, tired and dirty and happy, he lay down on the grass just above Vane's head, and went on hunting in his dreams... .

As for the two chief fools, the day passed as such days have always passed since Time began. And the absolute happiness which comes with the sudden touch of a hand, the quick, unexpected glance, the long, passionate kiss, is not to be put on paper. They talked a little about aimless, intimate things; they were silent a great deal—those wonderful silences which become possible only with perfect understanding. And gradually the shadows lengthened, and the grey water began to grow darker... . Sometimes from the old bridge came the noise of a passing car, and once an electric canoe went past them in the main stream, with a gramophone playing on board. The sound of the record came to them clearly over the water—the Barcarolle from "Les Contes d'Hoffmann," and they listened until it died faintly away in the distance.

Then at last, with a great sigh Vane stood up and stretched himself. For a long while he looked down at the girl, and it seemed to her that his face was sad. Without a word he untied the punt, and, still in silence, they paddled slowly back towards the hotel.

It was only as they were drifting under the bridge that he spoke, just one short sentence, in a voice which shook a little.

"My dear," he whispered, "I thank you," and very gently he raised her hand to his lips... .

But at dinner he had banished all traces of sadness from his mood. They both bubbled with the spontaneous happiness of two children. Binks, to his intense disgust, had to submit to the indignity of a table napkin tied round his neck, and all the occupants of the hotel thought them mad. Incidentally they were— quite mad, which was just as it should be after such a day. Only when they were leaving did they become sane again for a moment.

"Just one more look at the river, my lady," said Vane to her, "before we start. There's a little path I know of, leading out of the rose garden where one can't be seen, and we've just got to say our good-bye to the wateralone."

He led the way and Joan followed with Binks trotting sedately between them. And then with his arm round her waist, and her head on his shoulder, they stood and watched the black water flowing smoothly by.

"I've stuck to the rule, grey girl." Vane's arm tightened round her; "I've said not a word about the future. But to-morrow I am going to come to you; to-morrow you've got to decide."

He felt her shiver slightly against him, and he bent and kissed her passionately. "There can only be one answer," he whispered fiercely. "There shall only be one answer. We're just made for one another... ."

But it seemed to both of them that the air had become colder... .

"You'll come in, Derek," said Joan as the car drew up in Ashley Gardens. "Come in and have a drink; my aunt would like to see you."

Barely a word had been spoken on the drive home, and as Vane followed her into the flat it struck him that her face seemed a little white.

"Are you feeling cold, dear?" he asked anxiously. "I ought to have taken another rug."

"Not a bit," Joan smiled at him. "Only a little tired... . Even the laziest days are sometimes a little exacting!" She laughed softly. "And you're rather an exacting person, you know... ."

She led the way into the drawing-room, and Vane was duly introduced to Lady Auldfearn.

"There are some letters for you, Joan," said her aunt. "I see there's one from your father. Perhaps he'll say in that whether he intends coming up to town or not... ."

With a murmured apology Joan opened her mail, and Vane stood chatting with the old lady.

"I hope you won't think me rude, Captain Vane," she said after a few commonplaces; "but I have arrived at the age when to remain out of bed for one instant after one wishes to go there strikes me as an act of insanity." She moved towards the door and Vane opened it for her with a laugh. "I hope I shall see you again." She held out her hand, and Vane bent over it.

"It's very good of you, Lady Auldfearn," he answered. "I should like to come and call... ."

"You can ask at the door if Joan is in," she continued. "If she isn't, I sha'n't be at all offended if you go away again."

Vane closed the door behind her, and strolled back towards the fireplace. "A woman of great discernment is your aunt, Joan." He turned towards her, and suddenly stood very still. "What is it, my dear? ... Have you had bad news?"

With a letter crumpled up in her hand she was staring at the floor, and she gave a little, bitter laugh. "Not even one day, Derek; the kindly Fates wouldn't even give us that... ."

She looked at the letter once again, and read part of it, while Vane watched her with a hopeless feeling of impending trouble.

"You'd better read it," she said wearily. "It's from Father." She handed it to him, and then pointed to the place. "That bit there... . 'So I'm sorry to say, little Joan, it's come at last. I've been hoping against hope that I might be able to pull things through, but it simply can't be done. The less will not contain the greater, and my irreducible minimum expenditure is more than my income. Humanly speaking, as far as one can see, there can be no considerable fall in the cost of living and income tax for many years after the war.' ..."

Vane's eyes skimmed on over the short, angular writing, picking up a phrase here and there. "Gordon to be considered... . It means practical penury at Blandford, comparative affluence if we go... .

"If I could lay my hand on a hundred thousand it might pull things through till the country is more or less settled once again; that is if it ever does get settled. If labour goes on as it is at present, I suppose we shall have to be grateful for being allowed to live at all... ."

Vane looked at Joan, who was still staring at the floor in front of her, and almost mechanically he returned her the letter... .

"You've known this was coming, Joan," he said at last... .

"Of course," she answered. "But it doesn't make it any better now it has. One always hopes." She shrugged her shoulders, and looked up at him. "Give me a cigarette, Derek, I don't think I'd have minded quite so much if it hadn't come to-day... ."

He held out the match for her, and then with his elbow on the mantelpiece he stood watching her. She seemed inert, lifeless, and the contrast with the laughing, happy girl at dinner hit him like a blow. If only he could help—do something; but a hundred thousand was an absurdity. His total income was only about fifteen hundred a year. And as if to torment him still more there rose before his mind the cold, confident face of Henry Baxter....

"Joan—does it matter so frightfully much giving up Blandford?"

She looked at him for a moment, with a sort of amazement on her face. "My dear," she said, "I simply can't imagine life without Blandford. It's just part of me... ."

"But when you marry you wouldn't live there yourself," he argued.

She raised her eyebrows. "Pride of place belongs to women as much as to men," she answered simply. "Why, Derek, don't try to pretend that you don't understand that." She gave a little tired laugh. "Besides, it's Dad—and Gordon... ."

"And you'd sacrifice yourself for them," he cried. "Not to keep them from want, don't forget—but to keep them at Blandford!" She made no answer, and after a while he went on. "I said I'd come to-morrow, Joan, and ask you to decide; but this letter alters things a bit, my dear. I guess we've got to have things out now... ."

The girl moved restlessly and rested her head on her hand.

"You've said it once, lady; I want to hear you say it again. 'Do you love me?'"

"Yes; I love you," she said without the slightest hesitation.

"And would you marry me if there was no Blandford?"

"To-morrow," she answered simply, "if you wanted it."

With a sudden ungovernable rush of feeling Vane swept her out of the chair into his arms, and she clung to him panting and breathless.

"My dear," he said exultantly, "do you suppose that after that I'd let you go? Not for fifty Blandfords. Don't you understand, my grey girl? You've got your sense of proportion all wrong. You're mine—and nothing else on God's green earth matters."

So for a while they stood there, while he smoothed her hair with hands that trembled a little and murmured incoherent words of love. And then at last they died away, and he fell silent—while she looked at him with tired eyes. The madness was past, and with almost a groan Vane let his arms fall to his side.

"Dear man," she said, "I want you to go; I can't think when you're with me. I've just got to worry this thing out for myself. I don't want you to come and see me, Derek, until I send for you; I don't want you even to write to me. I don't know how long it will take.... but I'll let you know, as soon as I know myself."

For a while he argued with her—but it was useless. In the bottom of his heart he knew it would be even as he pleaded and stormed. And, because he recognised what lay behind her decision, he loved her all the more for her refusal. There was a certain sweet wistfulness on her face that tore at his heart, and at last he realised that he was failing her, and failing her badly. It was a monstrous thing from one point of view that such a sacrifice should be possible—but it came to Vane with cynical abruptness that life abounds in monstrous things.

And so, very gently, he kissed her. "It shall be as you say, dear," he said gravely. "But try not to make it too long... ."

At the door he stopped and looked back. She was standing as he had left her, staring out into the darkness, and as he paused she turned and looked at him. And her eyes were very bright with unshed tears... .

Mechanically he picked up his hat and gloves, and drove back to his rooms. He helped himself to a whisky and soda of such strength that Binks looked at him with an apprehensive eye, and then he laughed.

"Hell, Binks," he remarked savagely—"just Hell!"

CHAPTER XIV

During the weeks that followed Vane did his best to put Joan out of his mind. He had given her his promise not to write, and as far as in him lay he tried his hardest not to think. A Medical Board passed him fit for light duty, and he joined up at the regimental depot in the cathedral city of Murchester. Once before he had been there, on a course, before he went overseas for the first time, and the night he arrived he could not help contrasting the two occasions. On the first he, and everyone else, had had but one thought—the overmastering desire to get across the water. The glamour of the unknown was calling them—the glory which the ignorant associate with war. Shop was discussed openly and without shame. They were just a band of wild enthusiasts, only longing to make good.

And then they had found what war really was—had sampled the reality of the thing. One by one the band had dwindled, and the gaps had been filled by strangers. Vane was sitting that night in the chair where Jimmy Benton had always sat... . He remembered Jimmy lying across the road near Dickebush staring up at him with sightless eyes. So had they gone, one after another, and now, how many were left? And the ones that had paid the big price—did they think it had been worth while ... now? ... They had been so willing to give their all without counting the cost. With the Englishman's horror of sentimentality or blatant patriotism, they would have regarded with the deepest mistrust anyone who had told them so. But deep down in each man's heart—it was England—his England—that held him, and the glory of it. Did they think their sacrifice had been worth while ... now? Or did they, as they passed by on the night wind, look down at the seething bitterness in the country they had died for, and whisper sadly, "It was in vain—You are pulling to pieces what we fought to keep standing; you have nothing but envy and strife to put in its place... . Have you not found the truth—yet? ..."

Unconsciously, perhaps, but no less certainly for that, Vane was drifting back into the same mood that had swayed him when he left France. If what Ramage had said to him was the truth; if, at the bottom of all the ceaseless bickering around, there was, indeed, a vital conflict between two fundamentally opposite ideas, on the settlement of which depended the final issue—it seemed to him that nothing could avert the catastrophe sooner or later. It was against human nature for any class to commit suicide—least of all the class which for generations had regarded itself and been regarded as the leading one. And yet, unless this thing did happen; unless voluntarily, the men of property agreed to relinquish their private rights, and sink their own interests for the good of the others, Ramage had quite calmly and straightforwardly prophesied force. Apparently the choice lay between suicide and murder... .

It all seemed so hopelessly futile to Vane. He began to feel that only over the water lay Reality; that here, at home, he had discovered a Land of Wild Imaginings... .

Though he refused to admit it to himself, there was another, even more potent, factor to account for his restlessness. Like most Englishmen, however black the outlook, however delirious the Imagining, he had, deep down in his mind, the ingrained conviction that the country would muddle through somehow. But the other factor—the personal factor—Joan, was very different. Try as he would he could not dismiss her from his mind entirely. Again and again the thought of her came back to torment him, and he began to chafe more and more at his forced inaction. Where large numbers of officers are continually passing through a depot, doing light duty while recovering from wounds, there can be nothing much for the majority to do. Twice he had begun a letter to Margaret, to tell her that after all she had been right—that it had been nervous tension—that it wasn't her after all. And twice he had torn it up after the first few lines. It wasn't fair, he pacified his conscience, to worry her when she was so busy. He could break it far more easily by degrees—when he saw her. And so the restlessness grew, and the disinclination to do anything but sit in the mess and read the papers. His arm was still too stiff for tennis, and the majority of the local people bored him to extinction. Occasionally he managed to get ten minutes' work to do that was of some use to somebody; after that his time was his own.

One day he tried his hand at an essay, but he found that the old easy style which had been his principal asset had deserted him. It was stiff and pedantic, and what was worse—bitter; and he tore it up savagely after he had read it through. He tried desperately to recover some of his old time optimism—and he failed. He told himself again and again that it was up to him to see big, to believe in the future, and he cursed himself savagely for not being able to.

There was a woman whom he had met at lunch on one of his periodical visits to London. She was a war widow, and a phrase she had used to him rang in his brain for many days after. It seemed to him to express so wonderfully the right feeling, the feeling which in another form he was groping after.

"It wouldn't do," she had said very simply, "for the Germans to get a 'double casualty.'" It was the sort of remark, he thought, that he would have expected Margaret to make. With all the horror of genteel pauperism staring her in the face, that woman was thinking big, and was keeping her head up. With all the bitterness of loss behind her, she had, that very day, so she told him, been helping another more fortunate one to choose frocks for her husband's next leave... .

Try as he might, he could not rid himself of the mocking question "Cui bono?" What was the use of this individual heroism to the country at large? As far as the woman herself was concerned it kept her human, but to the big community ...? Would even the soldiers when they came back be strong enough, and collected enough, to do any good? And how many of them really thought ...?

Surely there must be some big, and yet very simple, message which the war could teach. Big because the result had been so wonderful; simple because the most stupid had learned it. And if they had learned it over the water, surely they could remember it afterwards... . pass it on to others. It might even be taught in the schools for future generations to profit by.

It was not discipline or so-called militarism; they were merely the necessary adjuncts to a life where unhesitating obedience is the only thing which prevents a catastrophe. It was not even tradition and playing the game, though it seemed to him he was getting nearer the answer. But these were not fundamental things; they were to a certain extent acquired. He wanted something simpler than that—something which came right at the beginning, a message from the bedrock of the world; something which was present in France—something which seemed to be conspicuous by its absence in England.

"We've caught these fellows," he said one evening after dinner to a regular Major whose life had taken him all over the world, "and we've altered 'em. Their brothers are here at home; they themselves were here a short while ago —will be back in the future. They are the same breed; they come from the same stock. What is this thing that has done it? What gospel has been preached to 'em to turn them into the salt of the earth, while at home here the others are unchanged, except for the worse?"

The Major shifted his pipe from one corner of his mouth to the other. "The gospel that was preached two thousand odd years ago," he answered shortly. Vane looked at him curiously. "I admit I hardly expected that answer, Major," he said.

"Didn't you?" returned the other. "Well, I'm not an authority on the subject; and I haven't seen the inside of a church for business purposes since before the South African War. But to my mind, when you've shorn it of its trappings and removed ninety per cent. of its official performers into oblivion, you'll find your answer in what, after all, the Church stands for." He hesitated for a moment, and glanced at Vane, for he was by nature a man not given to speech. "Take a good battalion in France," he continued slowly. "You know as well as I do what's at the bottom of it—good officers. Good leaders… . What makes a good leader? What's the difference between a good officer and a dud? Why, one has sympathy and the other hasn't: one will sacrifice himself, the other won't… . There's your gospel… ." He relapsed into silence, and Vane looked at him thoughtfully.

"Sympathy and sacrifice," he repeated slowly. "Is that your summing up of Christianity?

"Isn't it?" returned the other. "But whether it is or whether it isn't, it's the only thing that will keep any show going. Damn it, man, it's not religion—it's common horse sense." The Major thumped his knee. "What the deuce do you do if you find things are going wrong in your company? You don't snow yourself in with reports in triplicate and bark. You go and see for yourself. Then you go and talk for yourself; and you find that it is either a justifiable grievance which you can put right, or an error or a misunderstanding which you can explain. You get into touch with them… . Sympathy. Sacrifice. Have a drink?" He pressed the bell and sank back exhausted. As has been said, he was not addicted to speech.

Neither of them spoke until the waiter had carried out the order, and then suddenly the Major started again. Like many reserved men, once the barrier was broken down, he could let himself go with the best. And Vane, with his eyes fixed on the quiet face and steady eyes of the elder man, listened in silence.

"I'm a fool," he jerked out. "Every Regular officer is a fool. Numbers of novelists have said so. Of course one bows to their superior knowledge. But what strikes me in my foolishness is this… . You've got to have leaders and you've got to have led, because the Almighty has decreed that none of us have the same amount of ability. Perhaps they think He's a fool too; but even they can't alter that… . If ability varies so must the reward—money; and some will have more than others. Capital and Labour; leader and led; officer and man… . In the old days we thought that the best leader for the Army was the sahib; and with the old army we were right. Tommy … poor, down-trodden Tommy, as the intellectuals used to call him, was deuced particular. He was also mighty quick on the uptake at spotting the manner of man he followed. Now things have changed; but the principle remains. And it answers… . You'll always have an aristocracy of ability who will be the civilian leaders, you'll always have the rank and file who will be led by them. The same rules will hold as you apply in the army… . You'll have good shows and bad shows, according to whether the leader has or has not got sympathy. A good many now should have it; they've learned the lesson over the water. And on their shoulders rests the future… ."

"You put the future on the leaders, too," said Vane a little curiously.

"Why, naturally," returned the other. "What else fits a man to lead?"

"But your broad doctrine of sympathy"—pursued Vane. "Don't you think it's one of those things that sounds very nice in a pulpit, but the practical application is not quite so easy… ."

"Of course it isn't easy," cried the other. "Who the deuce said it was? Is it easy to be a good regimental officer? Sympathy is merely the—the spiritual sense which underlies all the work. And the work is ceaseless if the show is going to be a good one. You know that as well as I do. You take an officer who never talks to his men, practically never sees 'em—treats 'em as automatons to do a job. Never sacrifices his own comfort. What sort of a show are you going to have?"

"Damn bad," said Vane, nodding his head.

"And you take a fellow who talks to 'em, knows 'em well, is a friend to 'em, and explains things—that's the vital point—explains things; listens to what they have to say—even makes some small amendments if he thinks they're right… . A fellow who makes them take a pride in their show… . What then?"

"But could you apply it to civil life?" queried Vane.

"Don't know," returned the other, "because I'm a fool. Everybody says so; so I must be. But it seems to me that if you take a concern, and every week the boss sends for his men, or some chosen representative of theirs, and explains things to 'em, it won't do much harm. Shows 'em how the money is going— what it's being spent on, why he's putting in fresh plant, why his dividends ain't going to be as big this year as they were last—all that sort of thing. Don't play the fool with them… . Dividends may be bigger, and he'll have to stump up… . A good many of the bosses will have to alter their ways, incidentally. No man is going to sweat himself in order that someone else up the road can keep a second motor car, when the man himself hasn't even a donkey cart. You wouldn't yourself—nor would I. Up to a point it's got to be share and share alike. Over the water the men didn't object to the C.O. having a bedroom to himself; but what would they have said if he'd gone on to battalion parade in a waterproof one bad day, while they were uncloaked?"

"Yes, but who is going to decide on that vital question of money?" pursued Vane. "Supposing the men object to the way the boss is spending it… ."

The other thoughtfully filled his pipe. "Of course, there will always be the risk of that," he said. "Seventeen and twenty per cent. dividends will have to cease—I suppose. And after all—not being a Croesus myself I'm not very interested—I'm blowed if I see why man should expect more than a reasonable percentage on his money. I believe the men would willingly agree to that if they were taken into his confidence and sure he wasn't cooking his books.... . But when one reads of ten, herded together in one room, and the company paying enormous dividends, do you wonder they jib? I would. Why shouldn't the surplus profit above a fair dividend be split up amongst the workmen? I'm no trade expert, Vane. Questions of supply and demand, and tariffs and overtime, leave me quite cold. But if you're going to get increased production, and you've got to or you're going to starve, you can't have civil war in the concern. And to ensure that you must have all the cards on the table. The men must understand what they're doing; the boss must explain.

"What made a man understand the fact of dying over the water? What made thousands of peace-loving men go on in the filth and dirt, only to die like rats at the end.... . What made 'em keep their tails up, and their chests out? Why— belief and trust in their leaders. And how was it inculcated? By sympathy— nothing more nor less. God above—if it was possible when the stakes were life and death—can't it be done over here in the future? The men won't strike if only they understand; unless in the understanding they find something they know to be wrong and unjust."

"I was talking to that Labour fellow—Ramage—the other day," said Vane thoughtfully. "According to him State control of everything is the only panacea. And he says it's coming... ."

"Dare say it will," returned the other. "The principle remains the same. With sympathy nine out of ten strikes will be averted altogether. Without it, they won't. The leaders will be in touch with their men; as leaders they will be able to feel the pulse of their men. And when things are going wrong they'll know it; they'll anticipate the trouble.... . Sympathy; the future of the Empire lies in sympathy. And this war has taught many thousands of men the meaning of the word. It has destroyed the individual outlook.... . There, it seems to me, lies the hope of our salvation." He finished his drink and stood up. "If we're going to continue a ceaseless war between leaders and led—it's me for Hong-Kong. And it is only the leaders who can avert it... ."

"Incidentally that's what Ramage said," remarked Vane. "Only he demands complete equality … the abolition of property… ."

The other paused as he got to the door. "Then the man's a fool, and a dangerous fool," he answered gravely. "Night-night… ."

For a long while Vane sat on, staring at the fire. Though only early in October, the night was chilly, and he stretched his legs gratefully to the blaze. After a time he got up and fetched an evening paper. The great push between Cambrai and St. Quentin was going well; behind Ypres the Boche was everywhere on the run. But to Vane gigantic captures in men and guns meant a very different picture. He saw just the one man crawling on his belly through the mouldering bricks and stinking shell-holes of some death-haunted village. He saw the sudden pause—the tense silence as the man stopped motionless, listening with every nerve alert. He felt once again the hideous certainty that he was not alone; that close to, holding his breath, was someone else … then he saw the man turn like a flash and stab viciously; he heard the clatter of falling bricks—the sob of exultation as the Boche writhed in his death agony… . And it might have been the other way round.

Then he saw the other side; the long weary hours of waiting, the filthy weariness of it all—the death and desolation. Endured without a murmur; sticking it always, merry, cheerful, bright—so that the glory of the British soldier should be written on the scroll of the immortals for all eternity.

Was it all to be wasted, thrown away? His jaw set at the thought. Surely— surely that could never be. Let 'em have their League of Nations by all manner of means; but a League of Britain was what these men were fighting for. And to every Britisher who is a Britisher—may God be praised there are millions for whom patriotism has a real meaning—that second League is the only one that counts.

The door opened and Vallance, the Adjutant, came in. "There's a letter for you, old boy, outside in the rack," he remarked. He walked over to the fire to warm his hands. "Bring me a large whisky and a small soda," he said to the waiter, who answered his ring. "Drink, Vane?"

Vane looked up from the envelope he was holding in his hand and shook his head. "No, thanks, old man," he answered. "Not just now… . I think I'll read this letter first." And the Adjutant, who was by nature an unimaginative man, failed to notice that Vane's voice was shaking a little with suppressed excitement.

It was ten minutes before either of them spoke again. Twice Vane had read the letter through, and then he folded it carefully and put it in his pocket.

"Contrary to all service etiquette, old boy," he said, "I am going to approach you on the subject of leave in the mess. I want two or three days. Can it be done?"

Vallance put down his paper, and looked at him.

"Urgent private affairs?" he asked lightly.

"Very urgent," returned Vane grimly.

"I should think it might be managed," he said. "Fire in an application and I'll put it up to-morrow."

"Thanks," said Vane briefly, "I will."

For a moment or two after he had left the room Vallance looked at the closed door. Then he picked the envelope out of the grate, and studied the handwriting.

"Confound these women," he muttered, and consigned it to the flames. He liked to think himself a misogynist, and, incidentally, thoughts of drafts were worrying him.

Up in his own room Vane was poking the fire. His face was stern, and with care and deliberation he pulled up the arm chair to the blaze. Then he took the letter out of this pocket, and proceeded to read it through once again.

MELTON HOUSE, OFFHAM, NEAR LEWES.

MY DEAR,—It's just on midnight, but I feel in the mood for doing what I've been shirking for so long. Don't you know the feeling one gets sometimes when one has put off a thing again and again, and then there suddenly comes an awful spasm and one fairly spreads oneself? … Like putting one's bills away for months on end, and then one day becoming insane and paying the whole lot. I've been putting this off, Derek, for what I'm going to write will hurt you … almost as much as it hurts me. I'm not going to put in any of the usual cant about not thinking too hardly of me; I don't think somehow we are that sort. But I can't marry you. I meant to lead up to that gradually, but the pen sort of slipped—and, anyway you'd have known what was coming.

I can't marry you, old man—although I love you better than I ever thought I'd love anyone. You know the reasons why, so I won't labour them again. They may be right and they may be wrong; I don't know—I've given up trying to think. I suppose one's got to take this world as it is, and not as it might be if we had our own way… . And I can't buy my happiness with Blandford, Derek—I just can't.

I went down there the morning after Our Day—oh! my God! boy, how I loved that time—and I saw Father. He was just broken down with it all; he seemed an old, old man. And after luncheon in the study he told me all about it. I didn't try to follow all the facts and figures—what was the use? I just sat there looking out over Blandford—my home—and I realised that very soon it would be that no longer. I even saw the horrible man smoking his cigar with the band on it in Father's chair.

Derek, my dear—what could I do? I knew that I could save the situation if I wanted to; I knew that it was my happiness and yours, my dear, that would have to be sacrificed to do it. But when the old Dad put his arm round my waist and raised his face to mine—and his dear mouth was all working—I just couldn't bear it.

So I lied to him, Derek. I told him that Mr. Baxter loved me, and that I loved Mr. Baxter. Two lies—for that man merely wants me as a desirable addition to his furniture—and I, why sometimes I think I hate him. But, oh! my dear, if you'd seen my Father's face; seen the dawning of a wonderful hope…. I just couldn't think of anything except him—and so I went on lying, and I didn't falter. Gradually he straightened up; twenty years seemed to slip from him ….

"My dear," he said. "I wouldn't have you unhappy; I wouldn't have you marry any man you didn't love. But if you do love him, little Joan, if you do —why it just means everything…. Baxter's worth millions…."

But it makes one laugh, my Derek, doesn't it? laugh a little bitterly. And then after a while I left him, and went down to the boat-house, and pulled over to our weeping willow. But I couldn't stop there…. I can't try myself too high. I guess I'm a bit weak where you're concerned, boy—a bit weak. And I've got to go through with this. It's my job, and one can't shirk one's job…. Only sometimes it seems that one gets saddled with funny jobs, doesn't one? Try to see my point of view, Derek; try to understand. If it was only me, why, then, my dear, you know what would be the result. I think it would kill me if you ever thought I was marrying Mr. Baxter for money for myself….

And you'll forget me in time, dear lad—at least, I'm afraid you will. That's foolish, isn't it?—foolish and weak; but I couldn't bear you to forget me altogether. Just once or twice you'll think of me, and the Blue Bird that we kept for one day in the roses at Sonning. You'll go to She who must be obeyed and I hope to God I never meet her…. For I'll hate her, loathe her, detest her.

I'm engaged to Mr. Baxter. I've exacted my full price to the uttermost farthing. Blandford is saved, or will be on the day I marry him. We are neither of us under any illusions whatever; the whole thing is on an eminently business footing.... We are to be married almost at once.

And now, dear, I am going to ask you one of the big things. I don't want you to answer this letter; I don't want you to plead with me to change my mind. I daren't let you do it, my man, because, as I said, I'm so pitifully weak where you are concerned. And I don't know what would happen if you were to take me in your arms again. Why, the very thought of it drives me almost mad.... Don't make it harder for me, darling, than it is at present—please, please, don't.

Mr. Baxter is not here now, and I'm just vegetating with the Suttons until the sale takes place—my sale. They were talking about you at dinner to-night, and my heart started pounding until I thought they must have heard it. Do you wonder that I'm frightened of you? Do you wonder that I ask you not to write?

It's one o'clock, my Derek, and I'm cold—and tired, awful tired. I feel as if the soul had departed out of me; as if everything was utterly empty. It is so still and silent outside, and the strange, old-fashioned ideas—do you remember your story?—have been sitting wistfully beside me while I write. Maybe I'll hear them fluttering sadly away as I close down the envelope.

I love you, my darling, I love you.... I don't know why Fate should have decreed that we should have to suffer so, though perhaps you'll say it's my decree, not Fate's. And perhaps you're right; though to me it seems the same thing.

Later on, when I'm a bit more used to things, we might meet.... I can't think of life without ever seeing you again; and anyway, I suppose, we're bound to run across one another. Only just at the moment I can't think of any more exquisite torture than seeing you as another woman's husband....

Good-night, my dear, dear Love, God bless and keep you.

JOAN.

Oh! Boy—what Hell it all is, what utter Hell!

The fire was burning low in the grate as Vane laid the letter down on the table beside him. Bolshevism, strikes, wars—of what account were they all combined, beside the eternal problem of a man and a woman? For a while he sat motionless staring at the dying embers, and then with a short, bitter laugh he rose to his feet.

"It's no go, my lady," he muttered to himself. "Thank Heaven I know the Suttons... ."

CHAPTER XV

Vane stepped into the train at Victoria the following afternoon, and took his seat in the Pullman car. It was a non-stop to Lewes, and a ticket for that place reposed in his pocket. What he was going to do—what excuse he was going to make, he had not yet decided. Although he knew the Suttons very well, he felt that it would look a little strange if he suddenly walked into their house unannounced; and he had been afraid of wiring or telephoning from London in case he should alarm Joan. He felt vaguely that something would turn up which would give him the excuse he needed; but in the meantime his brain was in an incoherent condition. Only one thought rose dominantly above all the others, and it mocked him, and laughed at him, and made him twist and turn restlessly in his seat. Joan was going to marry Baxter…. Joan was going to marry Baxter….

The rattle of the wheels sang it at him; it seemed to fit in with their rhythm, and he crushed the paper he was holding savagely in his hand. By Heaven! she's not…. By Heaven! she's not…. Fiercely and doggedly he answered the taunting challenge, while the train rushed on through the meadows and woods of Sussex. It slowed down for the Wivelsfield curve, and then gathered speed again for the last few miles to Lewes. With gloomy eyes he saw Plumpton race-course flash by, and he recalled the last meeting he had attended there, two years before the war. Then they roared through Cooksbridge and Vane straightened himself in his seat. In just about a minute he would come in sight of Melton House, lying amongst the trees under the South Downs. And Vane was in the condition when a fleeting glance of the house that sheltered Joan was like a drink of water to a thirsty man. It came and went in a second, and with a sigh that was almost a groan he leaned back and stared with unseeing eyes at the high hills which flank the valley of the Ouse, with their great white chalk pits, and rolling grass slopes.

He had determined to go to an hotel for the night, and next day to call at Melton House. During the evening he would have to concoct some sufficiently plausible tale to deceive the Suttons as to the real reason for having come—but sufficient unto the evening was the worry thereof. He walked slowly up the steep hill that led into the High Street, and booked a room at the first inn he came to. Then he went out again, and sauntered round aimlessly.

The town is not full of wild exhilaration, and Vane's previous acquaintance with it had been formed on the two occasions when he had attended race-meetings there. Moreover, it is very full of hills and after a short while Vane returned to his hotel and sat down in the smoking-room. It was unoccupied save for one man who appeared to be of the genus commercial traveller, and Vane sank into a chair by the fire. He picked up an evening paper and tried to read it, but in a very few moments it dropped unheeded to the floor... .

"Know these parts well, sir?" the man opposite him suddenly broke the silence.

"Hardly at all," returned Vane shortly. He was in no mood for conversation.

"Sleepy old town," went on the other; "but having all these German prisoners has waked it up a bit."

Vane sat up suddenly. "Oh! have they got prisoners here?" The excuse he had been looking for seemed to be to hand.

"Lots. They used to have conscientious objectors—but they couldn't stand them... ." He rattled on affably, but Vane paid no heed. He was busy trying to think under what possible pretext he could have been sent down to deal with Boche prisoners. And being a man of discernment it is more than likely he would have evolved something quite good, but for the sudden and unexpected arrival of old Mr. Sutton himself... .

"Good Heavens! What are you doing here, my dear boy?" he cried, striding across the room, and shaking Vane's hand like a pump handle.

"How'd you do, sir," murmured Vane. "I—er—have come down to inquire about these confounded conscientious prisoners—Boche objectors—you know the blighters. Question of standardising their rations, don't you know... . Sort of a committee affair... ."

Vane avoided the eye of the commercial traveller, and steered rapidly for safer ground. "I was thinking of coming out to call on Mrs. Sutton to-morrow."

"To-morrow," snorted the kindly old man. "You'll do nothing of the sort, my boy. You'll come back with me now—this minute. Merciful thing I happened to drop in. Got the car outside and everything. How long is this job, whatever it is—going to take you?"

"Three or four days," said Vane hoping that he was disguising any untoward pleasure at the suggestion.

"And can you do it equally well from Melton?" demanded Mr. Sutton. "I can send you in every morning in the car."

Vane banished the vision of breakers ahead, and decided that he could do the job admirably from Melton.

"Then come right along and put your bag in the car." The old gentleman, with his hand on Vane's arm, rushed him out of the smoking-room, leaving the commercial traveller pondering deeply as to whether he had silently acquiesced in a new variation of the confidence trick... .

"We've got Joan Devereux staying with us," said Mr. Sutton, as the chauffeur piled the rugs over them. "You know her, don't you?"

"We have met," answered Vane briefly.

"Just engaged to that fellow Baxter. Pots of money." The car turned out on to the London road, and the old man rambled on without noticing Vane's abstraction. "Deuced good thing too—between ourselves. Sir James—her father, you know—was in a very queer street... . Land, my boy, is the devil these days. Don't touch it; don't have anything to do with it. You'll burn your fingers if you do... . Of course, Blandford is a beautiful place, and all that, but, 'pon my soul, I'm not certain that he wouldn't have been wiser to sell it. Not certain we all wouldn't be wiser to sell, and go and live in furnished rooms at Margate... . Only if we all did, it would become the thing to do, and we'd soon get turned out of there by successful swindlers. They follow one round, confound 'em—trying to pretend they talk the same language."

"When is Miss Devereux going to be married?" asked Vane as the old man paused for breath.

"Very soon... . Fortnight or three weeks. Quite a quiet affair, you know; Baxter is dead against any big function. Besides, he has to run over to France so often, and so unexpectedly, that it might have to be postponed a day or two at the last moment. Makes it awkward if half London has been asked."

The car swung through the gates and rolled up the drive to the house. The brown tints of autumn were just beginning to show on the trees, and an occasional fall of dead leaves came fluttering down as they passed underneath. Then, all too quickly for Vane, they were at the house, and the chauffeur was holding open the door of the car. Now that he was actually there—now that another minute would bring him face to face with Joan—he had become unaccountably nervous.

He followed Mr. Sutton slowly up the steps, and spent an unnecessarily long time taking off his coat. He felt rather like a boy who had been looking forward intensely to his first party, and is stricken with shyness just as he enters the drawing-room.

"Come in, come in, my boy, and get warm." Mr. Sutton threw open a door. "Mary, my dear, who do you think I found in Lewes? Young Derek Vane— I've brought him along... ."

Vane followed him into the room as he was speaking, and only he noticed that

146

Joan half rose from her chair, and then sank back again, while a wave of colour flooded her cheeks, and then receded, leaving them deathly white. With every pulse in his body hammering, but outwardly quite composed, Vane shook hands with Mrs. Sutton.

"So kind of your husband," he murmured. "He found me propping up the hotel smoking-room, and rescued me from such a dreadful operation... ."

Mrs. Sutton beamed on him. "But it's delightful, Captain Vane. I'm so glad you could come. Let me see—you know Miss Devereux, don'tyou?"

Vane turned to Joan, and for the moment their eyes met. "I think I have that pleasure," he said in a low voice. "I believe I have to congratulate you, Miss Devereux, on your approaching marriage."

He heard Joan give a gasp, and barely caught her whispered answer: "My God! why have you come?"

He turned round and saw that both the old people were occupied for a moment. "Why, just to congratulate you, dear lady ... just to congratulate you." His eyes burned into hers, and his voice was shaking. "Why else, Joan, why else?"

Then Mrs. Sutton began to talk, and the conversation became general.

"It's about these German prisoners; they're giving a bit of trouble," Vane said in answer to her question. "And so we've formed a sort of board to investigate their food and general conditions ... and—er—I am one of the board."

"How very interesting," said the old lady. "Have you been on it for long?"

"No—not long. In fact," said Vane looking fixedly at Joan, "I only got my orders last night... ." With the faintest flicker of a smile he watched the tell-tale colour come and go.

Then she turned on him, and her expression was a little baffling. "And have you any special qualification, Captain Vane, for dealing with such an intricate subject?"

"Intricate?" He raised his eyebrows. "I should have thought it was very simple. Just a matter of common sense, and making ... er ... these men—well —get their sense of proportion."

"You mean making them get your sense of proportion?"

"In some cases there can be only one," said Vane gravely.

"And that one is your own. These—German prisoners you said, didn't you?— these German prisoners may think it their duty to disagree with your views. Doubtless from patriotic motives... ."

"That would be a great pity," said Vane. "It would then be up to me to make them see the error of their ways."

"And if you fail?" asked the girl.

"Somehow I don't think I shall," he answered slowly. "But if I do—the trouble of which I spoke will not diminish. It will increase... ."

"We pander too much to these swine," grumbled Mr. Sutton. "It makes me sick when I hear of the way our boys are treated by the brutes. A damn good flogging twice a day—you'll pardon my language, is what they want."

"Yes—drastic measures can be quite successful at times," said Vane, with a slight smile. "Unfortunately in our present advanced state of civilisation public opinion is against flogging. It prefers violence against the person to be done mentally rather than physically... . And it seems so short-sighted, doesn't it? The latter is transitory, while the other is permanent... ."

Joan rose and looked at him quietly. "How delightful to meet a man who regards anything as permanent these days. I should have thought we were living in an age of ever-changing values... ."

"You're quite wrong, Miss Devereux," said Vane. "Quite, quite wrong. The little things may change—the froth on the top of the pool, which everyone sees and knows about; but the big fundamental things are always the same...
."

"And what are your big fundamental things?" she demanded.

Vane looked at her for a few moments before he answered her lightly. "Things on which there can be no disagreement even though they are my own views. Love and the pleasure of congenial work, and health... . Just think of having to live permanently with anybody whose digestion has gone... ."

"May you never *have* to do it," said the girl quietly. Then she turned and walked towards the door. "I suppose it's about time to dress, isn't it?" She went out of the room and Mr. Sutton advanced on Vane, with his hand upraised, like the villain of a melodrama when on the point of revealing a secret, unaware of the comic relief ensconced in the hollow tree.

"My dear fellow," he whispered hoarsely. "You've said the wrong thing." He peered round earnestly at the door, to make sure Joan had not returned. "Baxter—the man she's going to marry—is a perfect martyr to indigestion. It is the one thorn in the rose. A most suitable match in every other way, but he lives"—and the old gentleman tapped Vane on the shoulder to emphasise this hideous thing—"he lives on rusks and soda-water."

Vane threw the end of his cigarette in the fire and laughed. "There's always a catch somewhere, isn't there, Mr. Sutton? .... I'm afraid I shall have to ask you to excuse my changing; I've only got this khaki with me."

Vane was standing in front of the big open hearth in the hall when Joan came down for dinner. It was the first time he had seen her in an evening dress, and as she came slowly towards him from the foot of the stairs his hands clenched behind his back, and he set his teeth. In her simple black evening frock she was lovely to the point of making any man's senses swim dizzily. And when the man happened to be in love with her, and knew, moreover, that she was in love with him, it was not to be wondered at that he put both hands to his head, with a sudden almost despairing movement.

The girl, as she reached him, saw the gesture, and her eyes grew very soft. Its interpretation was not hard to discover, even if she had not had the grim, fixed look on his face to guide her; and in an instant it swept away the resolve she had made in her room to treat him coldly. In a flash of clear self-analysis just as she reached him, she recognised the futility of any such resolve. It was with that recognition of her weakness that fear came.... All her carefully thought out plans seemed to be crumbling away like a house of cards; all that she wanted was to be in his arms ... to be kissed.... And yet she knew that that way lay folly....

"Why have you come?" she said very low. "It wasn't playing the game after what I wrote you...."

Vane looked at her in silence for a moment and then he laughed. "Are you really going to talk to me, Joan, about such a thing as playing the game?"

She stood beside him with her hands stretched out towards the blazing logs. "You know how utterly weak it makes me—being near you.... You're just trading on it."

"Well," said Vane fiercely, "is there any man who is a man who wouldn't under the circumstances?"

"And yet," she said, turning and facing him gravely, "you know what is at stake for me." Her voice began to quiver. "You're playing with sex .... sex ... . sex, and it's the most powerful weapon in the world. But its effects are the most transitory."

"You lie, Joan, and you know it," Vane gripped her arm. "It's not the most transitory."

"It is," she cried stamping her foot, "it is. Against it on the other side of the balance lie the happiness of my father and brother—Blandford—things that last...."

"But what of your own happiness?" he asked grimly.

"Why do you think I shouldn't be happy?" she cried. "I've told you that it's a purely business arrangement. Henry is very nice and kind, and all that I'll be missing is a few months of the thing they call Love... ."

Vane took his hand from her arm, and let it fall to his side. "I'm afraid I've marked your arm," he said quietly. "I didn't know how hard I was gripping it. There is only one point which I would like to put to you. Has it occurred to you that in the business arrangement which you have outlined so delightfully, it may possibly strike Mr. Baxter—in view of his great possessions—that a son and heir is part of the contract?" As he spoke he raised his eyes to her face.

He saw her whole body stiffen as if she had been struck; he saw her bite her lip with a sudden little gasp, he saw the colour ebb from her cheeks. Then she recovered herself.

"Why, certainly," she said. "I have no doubt that that will be part of the programme. It generally is, I believe, in similar cases."

Vane's voice was very tender as he answered. "My grey girl," he whispered, "it won't do... . It just won't do. If I believed that what you say really expressed what you think, don't you know that I'd leave the house without waiting for dinner? But they don't. You can't look me in the eyes and tell me they do... ."

"I can," she answered defiantly; "that is what I think... ."

"Look me in the eyes, I said," interrupted Vane quietly.

Twice she tried to speak, and twice she failed. Then with a little half-strangled gasp she turned away... . "You brute," she said, and her voice was shaking, "you brute... ."

And as their host came down the stairs to join them, Vane laughed—a short, triumphant laugh... .

Almost at once they went in to dinner; and to Vane the meal seemed to be a succession of unknown dishes, which from time to time partially distracted his attention from the only real thing in the room—the girl sitting opposite him. And yet he flattered himself that neither his host nor hostess noticed anything remarkable about his behaviour. In fact he considered that he was a model of tact and discretion... .

Vane was drunk—drunk as surely as a man goes drunk on wine. He was drunk with excitement; he was mad with the madness of love. At times he felt that he must get up, and go round the table and gather his girl into his arms.

He even went so far as to picture the butler's expression when he did it. Unfortunately, that was just when Mrs. Sutton had concluded a harrowing story of a dead soldier who had left a bedridden wife with thirteen children. Vane had not heard a word of the story, but the butler's face had crossed his mental horizon periodically, and he chose that moment to laugh. It was not a well-timed laugh, but he floundered out of it somehow.... .

And then just as the soup came on—or was it the savoury?—he knew, as surely as he could see her opposite him, that his madness was affecting Joan. Telepathy, the wiseacres may call it, the sympathy of two subconscious minds.... . What matter the pedagogues, what matter the psychological experts? It was love—glorious and wonderful in its very lack of restraint. It was the man calling the woman; it was the woman responding to the man. It was freedom, beauty, madness all rolled into one; it was the only thing in this world that matters. But all the time he was very careful not to give away the great secret. Just once or twice their eyes met, and whenever that happened he made some remark more inordinately witty than usual—or more inordinately foolish. And the girl opposite helped him, and laughed with him, while over the big mahogany table there came leaping her real message—"My dear, I'm yours.... ." It whispered through the flowers in the big cut-glass bowl that formed the centrepiece; it echoed between the massive silver candlesticks with their pink shaded lights. At times it sounded triumphantly from every corner of the room, banishing all the commonplace surroundings with the wonder of its voice; at times it floated softly through the warm, scented air, conjuring up visions of nights on the desert with the Nile lapping softly on the hot sand, and the cries of the waterboys coming faintly through the still air.

But ever and always it was there, dominating everything, so insistent was its reality. As assuredly as if the words had been spoken did they see into one another's hearts that evening at dinner while a worthy old Sussex squire and his wife discussed the war, and housing problems, and the futility of fixing such a price on meat that it paid farmers to put their calves to the cow, instead of selling the milk. After all, the words had been spoken before, and words are of little account. There are times—not often, for artificiality and civilisation are stern taskmasters—but there are times when a man and woman become as Gods and know. What need of words between them then; a mathematician does not require to consult the multiplication table or look up the rules that govern addition and subtraction.

But the condition is dangerous—very dangerous. For the Law of the Universe has decreed that for every Action there is an equal and opposite Reaction. No account may be taken of madness—even though it be Divine. It avails not one jot when the time comes to foot the bill. By that time the madness has passed, like a dream in the night; and cold sanity is the judge before which a man must stand or fall. A few, maybe, there are who cheat the reckoning for a space; but they live in a Fools' Paradise. Sooner or later the bill is presented. It must be—for such is the Law of Things as they Are … . And all that a man may pray for is that he gets good value for his money.

After dinner Joan sang once or twice, and Vane, from the depths of a chair near the fire, watched her through half-closed eyes. His hostess was placidly knitting and the old gentleman was openly and unashamedly asleep. The girl had a small voice, but very sweet and pure; and, after a while Vane rose and went over to the piano. With his elbow resting on it he stood there looking down at her, and once, as their eyes met, her voice faltered a little.

"Ah! when Love comes, his wings are swift,
His ways are full of quick surprise;
'Tis well for those who have the gift
To seize him even as he flies… ."

She sang the simple Indian love song with a sort of wistful tenderness, and it seemed to the man watching her as if she was singing to herself rather than to him. It was as the last note of the refrain trembled and died away that Mr. Sutton awoke with a loud snort and looked round guiltily. Quite satisfied that no one had observed his lapse, he got up and strode over to the piano.

"Delightful, my dear, delightful," he said heartily. "My favourite tune." The number of the old gentleman's favourite tunes heard under similar circumstances was large.

"Come along, my boy," he went on, turning to Vane. "Pool or billiards, and let's see if the old man can't show you a thing or two."

With an inward groan Vane professed himself delighted. "Perhaps Miss Devereux will come and score for us," he murmured.

"Do, my love," said Mrs. Sutton. "And then I'll go to bed."

If Vane remembered little of dinner that evening, he remembered still less about the game of billiards except that he was soundly beaten, to Mr. Sutton's great delight, and that he laughed quite a lot over silly little jokes. Every now and then he stood beside Joan at the scoring board, and touched her arm or her hand; and once, when his host, intent on some shot, had his back towards them, he bent very quickly and kissed her on the lips. And he felt her quiver, and then grow rigid at his touch.

He played execrably, and when he tried to pull himself together to get the game done quicker, he played worse. If only the old man would go to bed, or something, and leave them… . If only he could get a few moments alone with

Joan, just to kiss her, and take her in his arms. But the old man showed no signs of doing anything of the sort. He did not often get a game of billiards; he still less often beat anybody, and he fully intended to make the most of it. Then at last, when the game was finally over, he played half of his shots over again for practice. And Vane, with his cue grasped in both hands, contemplated braining him with the butt.... .

But worse was still to come. Mr. Sutton prided himself on being old fashioned. Early to bed and early to rise, a proverb which Vane had always considered the most detestable in the English language, was one of his host's favourite texts. Especially when applied to other people.... .

"Now, my dear," he said to Joan after he had missed an easy cannon three times, and felt he required a little justification, "off you go to bed. Can't have you missing your beauty sleep so close to your marriage, or I'll have Baxter down on me like a ton of bricks."

Vane turned abruptly to the fire, and it is to be feared that his thoughts were not all they might have been. In fact, he registered a mental vow that if ever he was privileged to meet a murderer, he would shake him warmly by the hand.

"Good night, Captain Vane." Joan was standing beside him, holding out her hand. "I don't think you were playing very well to-night, were you?"

The next moment the door had closed behind her, and Vane turned slowly to answer some question of his host's. And as he turned he laughed softly under his breath. For Joan had not even looked at him as she said "Good night," and though the room was warm, almost to stuffiness, her hand had been as cold as ice.

Vane closed the door of his room, and went thoughtfully over to the fire. He was feeling more or less dazed, like a man who has been through a great strain, and finds for the moment some temporary respite.

He did not profess to account for it; he did not even try to. There had been other days that he had spent with Joan—days when he had been far more physically close to her than he had been that evening. Save for that one brief kiss in the billiard-room he had barely touched her. And yet he felt more vividly alive to her presence than he had ever been before.

Vane was no psychologist, and any way the psychology of sex follows no rules. It makes its own as it goes along. And the one thought which stood out from the jumbled chaos in his brain was a fierce pleasure at having beaten Baxter. The primitive Cave man was very much alive in him that night.... .

Joan was *his*; he knew it, and she knew it—and there was no more to be said.

And with a short, exultant laugh Vane drew up an easy chair to the fire and lit a cigarette. He heard Mr. Sutton pass along the passage and go to his own room; and then gradually the house grew still. Outside the night was silent, and once he rose and went to the window. He stood there for a time staring out into the darkness, with his hands thrust deep in his pockets; then he returned to his chair again. He felt no wish to go to bed; he just wanted to sit and think of his girl.

Three days is a long time when one is at the beginning of it; and in all probability they would give him an extension. Three days with Joan—three whole complete days... .

They would go for a few long glorious tramps over the Downs, where the turf is springy to the foot, and the wind comes straight from the grey Atlantic, and the salt tang of it makes it good to be alive. And then one afternoon when they got home Joan would find a telegram awaiting her to say that coal had been discovered at Blandford, and did she think it would matter having the main shaft opening into the dining-room?

Something like that was bound to happen, and even if it didn't things would be no worse off than they were now. And in the meantime—three days... . For Vane had passed beyond the thinking stage; he was incapable of arguing things out or calling a halt even if he wanted to. It seemed to him that everything was so immeasurably little compared with the one great fact that Joan loved him.

He whistled softly under his breath, and started to unlace his shoes. "We'll cheat 'em yet," he muttered, "some old how." And even as he spoke he stiffened suddenly and stared at the door. On it had come two low faltering knocks... .

For a moment he remained where he was, incapable of movement, while his cigarette, bent in two and torn, fell unheeded in the grate. Every drop of blood in his body seemed to stand still, and then to pound madly on again, as the certainty of who was outside came to him. Then with two great strides he crossed to the door, and opened it... .

"Joan," he whispered, "my dear... ."

She was in a silk dressing-gown, and he could see the lace of her nightdress through the opening at her neck. Without a word she passed by him into the room, and crouched over the fire; while Vane, with his back to the door, stood, watching her with dilated eyes.

"Lock the door." He heard her words come faintly through the roaring in his ears, and mechanically he did as she asked.

Slowly, with short, hesitating steps he came towards the fire, and stood beside her, while his nails cut into the palms of his hands. Then she rose and stood facing him.

"You've won," she said simply. "I've come to you." She swayed into his arms, and so for a long while did they stand, while the man twisted the great masses of hair that hung over her shoulders round and round his fingers. He touched her forehead and her cheeks with hands that shook a little, and suddenly he kissed her fiercely on the lips—so that she gasped, and began to tremble. He could feel her body against him through the thin silk wrap, and he clasped her tighter in his arms as if to warm her.

"My darling," he whispered, "you're cold ... so cold.... Take my dressing gown...."

But the girl only clung to him the more, and the man, being just a man, felt his senses beginning to swim with the wonder of it.

And then of a sudden she pushed him away, and with her hands on the mantelpiece stared into the fire.

Vane's breath came quickly. She looked so utterly desirable with the red glow of the fire lighting up her face, and her hair falling about her. He stretched out his hand and put it on her arm, as if to make sure that it was not a dream, and with the touch of his fingers something seemed to snap. A great wave of colour flooded her face, spreading down to her neck, and she began to shake uncontrollably. He bent over her, whispering in her ear, and suddenly she put both her arms round his neck. And then like a little child who goes to its mother for comfort she laid her head on his shoulder, and the tears came.

He soothed her gently, stroking her hair with his hand, and gradually, as the minutes went by, the raging storm in his mind died down, and gave place to a wonderful peace. All that was best in his nature was called forth by the girl crying so gently in his arms, and with a little flickering smile on his lips he stared at the flames over her head.

The passion had left him; a great sense of protection—man's divine heritage through the ages—had taken its place.

And so after a while he picked her up in his arms and laid her on his bed. He pulled the clothes around her, and taking her hand in his, sat down on a chair by her side.

All through the night he watched beside her, and as he listened to the hall clock striking the hours, gradually the realisation of what he must do came to him.

For he had not beaten Baxter; he had only beaten the girl. Baxter still stood where he was. Baxter still represented the way out for Joan. As a rival—man to man—he failed to count; he might just as well have been Jones or Smith. But as a weapon against the order of things Baxter remained where he was— the winner.

And even as he cursed that order of things, it struck him with a sort of amazed surprise that here he himself was actually up against one of Ramage's vested interests…. If Blandford had been nationalised, the problem would have been so easy….

He moved irritably in his chair. What a muddle the whole thing was—what a muddle. And then with the touch of a woman he bent over the sleeping girl, and wiped away two tears that were glistening on her eyelashes. Poor little girl—poor little Joan….

A sense of overwhelming pity and love for her drowned every other thought. Right or wrong, she was doing what she believed to be her job; and now he had come and made things a thousand times harder for her.

Very gently he withdrew his hand from hers and rose from his chair. He made up the fire again, and then started to pace slowly up and down the room. The drifting period was over; the matter had to be settled now.

He was no fool, and incidentally he knew as much about women as a man may know. He realised exactly why she had come to him that night; as clearly as if she had told him he understood the wild seething thoughts in her mind, the chaos, the sense of futility. And then the sudden irresistible longing to get things settled—to give up fighting—to take hold of happiness or what seemed to her to be happiness at the moment.

And supposing the mood had not broken—supposing the tears had not come…. He stopped in his slow walk, and stared at the sleeping girl thoughtfully…. What would have been the state of affairs by now?

"Sex—sex—sex. The most powerful thing in the world, and the most transitory." Her words before dinner, as they had stood in the hall came back to him, and he took a deep breath. That was the weapon he was using against her; he made no attempt to deceive himself on that score. After all—why not? It was the weapon that had been used since the beginning of things; it was the weapon which would continue to be used till the end. It was Nature's weapon … and yet….

Once again he resumed his walk—six steps one way, turn, six steps back. He moved slowly, his chin sunk on his chest, and his hands twisting restlessly behind his back. Supposing she was right, supposing in a year, or in five, she should turn on him, and say: "Against my better judgment you overruled me. Even though I loved you, even though I still love you—you have made me buy my happiness at too great a price?"

Supposing she should say that—what then? Had he any right to make her run such a risk? Was it fair? Again and again he turned question and answer over in his brain. Of course it was fair—they loved one another; and love is the biggest thing in the universe. But was it only love in his case—was it not overmastering passion as well? Well—what if it was; there are cases where the two cannot be separated—and those cases are more precious than rubies. Against such it were laughable to put the fate of Blandford.... Quite—but whose point of view was that—his or hers?

Vane was essentially a fair man. The average Englishman is made that way— it being the peculiar nature of the brute. If anything—as a referee or a judge— he will give the decision against his own side, which is the reason why England has spread to the ends of the earth, and remained there at the express wish of the Little Peoples. Bias or favouritism are abhorrent to him; as far as in him lies the Englishman weighs the pros and the cons of the case and gives his decision without partiality or prejudice. He may blunder at times, but the blunder is honest and is recognised as such.

And so as Vane walked restlessly up and down his room, every instinct in him revolted at the idea of taking advantage of an emotional crisis such as he knew had been stirred in Joan that evening. It seemed to him to be unfair.

"It's her you've got to consider," he said to himself over and over again. "Only her.... It's she who stands to lose—much more than you."

He felt that he would go right away, clean out of her life—if, by doing so, it would help her. But would it? That was the crux. Was he justified in letting her make this sacrifice? As clearly as if he had seen it written in letters of fire upon the wall, he knew that the issue lay in his hands.

Once again he went to the window and looked out. In the east the first streaks of dawn were showing in the sky, and for a long while he stood staring at them, motionless. How often in France had he watched that same birth of a new day, and wondered what it held in store for him. But over there a man is a fatalist—his part is allotted to him, and he can but tread the beaten path blindly. Whereas here, however much one is the sport of the gods that play, there comes a time when one must play oneself. Incidentally that is the part of the performance which amuses the gods. They plot their fantastic jig-saws; but one of the rules is that the pieces must move themselves. And of their kindness they let the pieces think they control the movement....

Suddenly Vane turned round, and crossed to the girl. He picked her up in his

157

arms, and having silently opened the door he carried her to her room.

Utterly exhausted and worn out, she barely woke up even when he placed her in her own cold bed. Her eyes opened drowsily once, and he bent over and kissed her gently.

"Little Joan," he whispered. "Dear little grey girl."

But she did not hear him. With a tired sigh she had drifted on to sleep again.

CHAPTER XVI

When Joan woke the next morning it was with the consciousness that something had happened. And then the events of the last night flashed over her mind, and for a while she lay very still. The details seemed all hazy and blurred; only the main fact stood out clear and dominant, the fact that she had gone to his room.

After that things got a bit confused. She had a recollection of being carried in his arms, of his bending over her and whispering "Little Joan," of his kissing her—but it all seemed merged in an exquisite dream.

"Oh! my dear," she whispered, while the love-light shone in her grey eyes; "but what a dear you are... ."

By the very nature of things she was incapable of realising the tremendous strain to which she had subjected him; it only seemed to her that there was a new and wonderful secret to share with him. And to the girl, still under the influence of her mood of the night before, the secret forged the final link in the chain. She wondered how she could ever have hesitated; it all seemed so very easy and obvious now.

Baxter, Blandford—what did anything matter? She had gone to Derek; the matter was decided... .

Her maid came into the room, and advanced cautiously to the bed.

"Ah! but Mam'selle es awake," she said. "And ze tea, mon Dieu, but it es quite cold."

"What time is it, Celeste?" asked Joan.

"Nine o'clock, Mam'selle. I have ze dejeuner outside. And a note from M'sieur le Capitaine." She held out an envelope to Joan, and busied herself about the room. "Ah! but he is gentil—M'sieur le Capitaine; young and of a great air." Celeste, it may be stated, viewed Baxter rather like a noisome insect.

"Bring me my breakfast, please."

Joan waited till the maid had left the room before opening the envelope. There was just a line inside, and her eyes grew very tender as she read the words.

"I've got something to say to you, little Joan, which has got to be said in the big spaces. Will you come out with me this morning on to the Downs?"

She read it through half a dozen times and then she turned to Celeste.

"Tell Captain Vane that I will be ready in an hour," she said.

* * * * * *

Vane was standing in the hall when Joan appeared. A faintly tremulous smile was on her lips, but she came steadily up to him and held out both her hands.

"Good morning, my lady," he said gently. "Would you to be liking to know how wonderful you look?"

"Oh! Derek," she whispered. "My dear!"

"Ostensibly you are going into Lewes to shop," he remarked with a grin. "I am dealing with Boche prisoners.... At least that's what I told our worthy host over the kidneys at breakfast...."

She gave a little happy laugh. "And in reality?"

"We're both going to be dropped somewhere, and we're going to tell the car to run away and play, while we walk home over the Downs."

"And my shopping?"

"You couldn't find anything you wanted."

"And your prisoners?"

"Well the only thing about my prisoners that is likely to give the show away is if I turn up at the prison," smiled Vane. "Let us hope Mr. Sutton doesn't know the governor."

And suddenly he added irrelevantly. "Our host was a little surprised that you failed to appear at breakfast, seeing how early he packed you off to bed." He watched the slight quickening of her breath, the faint colour dyeing her cheeks, and suddenly the resolution he had made seemed singularly futile. Then with a big effort he took hold of himself, and for greater safety put both his hands in his pockets. "I think," he remarked quietly, "you'd better go and get ready. The car will be round in a moment...."

Without a word she left him and went upstairs to her room, while Vane strolled to the front door. The car was just coming out of the garage, and he nodded to the chauffeur.

"Glorious day, isn't it?"

"Pity you've got to waste it, sir, over them prisoners," said the man.

"Yes," agreed Vane thoughtfully. "I'll want you to drop me in the town, and then I'll walk back over the Downs.... Splendid day for a walk...." He

160

turned and found Joan beside him. "And lightning performance," he smiled at her. "I won't be a moment."

He slipped on his coat and handed her into the car. "Drop me in the High Street, will you—opposite to the Post Office?" he said to the chauffeur. "I'm expecting a letter."

"I'm afraid," she said, as the car rolled down the drive, "that like most men you're rather prone to overact." With a little, happy laugh she snuggled up to him and slid her hand into his under the rug.

"I shall be walking home, thank you, Thomas," said Joan as she got out of the car, and the man stood waiting for orders.

He touched his cap, and they stood watching the car go down the High Street. Then she turned to Vane.

"You'd better see about your letters," she said demurely. "And then we might go over the Castle. There is a most wonderful collection of oleographic paleographs brought over by the Americans when they discovered England...."

"In one second," threatened Vane, "I shall kiss you. And I don't know that they'd understand it here... ."

"They'd think we were movie actors," she gurgled, falling into step beside him. "Do you know the way?"

"In the days of my unregenerate youth I went to the races here," he answered. "One passes a prison or something. Anyway, does it matter?"

She gave a sigh of utter contentment. "Nothing matters, my man—nothing at all—except that I'm with you. Only I want to get out into the open, with the fresh wind blowing on my face—and I want to sing for the joy of it.... . Do you think if we sang up the town here they'd give me pennies?"

"More probably lock us up as undesirable vagrants," laughed Vane. "It's a county town and they're rather particular. I'm not certain that happiness isn't an offence under the Defence of the Realm Act. Incidentally, I don't think there would be many convictions these days... ."

She stopped for a moment and faced him. "That's not allowed, Derek; it's simply not allowed."

"Your servant craves pardon," he answered gravely, and for a while they walked on in silence.

They passed two ragged children who had collected on their faces more dirt than seemed humanly possible, and nothing would content Joan but that she should present each with a sixpence.

"Poor little devils," and her voice was very soft. "What a life to look forward to, Derek—what a hideous existence... ."

"It's all they've ever been brought up to." He put sixpence into each little grubby paw, and smiled down at the awestruck faces. "Go and spend it all on sweets," he told them, "and be really, wonderfully, happily sick for once in your lives... ."

And then at last they turned a corner, and in front of them stretched the Downs. On their left the grim, frowning prison stood sombre and apparently lifeless, and as Joan passed it she gave a little shudder.

"Oh! Boy," she cried, "isn't it impossible to get away from the suffering and the rottenness—even for a moment?" She shook herself as if to cast off the mood, and stretched out her arms to the open hills. "I'm sorry," she said briefly. "Come into the big spaces and tell me what you want to say... ."

For a while they walked on over the clean-cut turf and the wind from the sea swept through the gorse and the rustling grasses, and kissed them, and passed on.

"There is a hayrick, I see, girl o' mine," said Vane. "Let's go and sit under it. And in defiance of all laws and regulations we will there smoke a cigarette."

They reached the sheltered side of it, and Vane threw down his coat on the ground for her to sit on.

"Aren't you forgetting something?" she whispered, and he drew her into his arms and kissed her. Then he made her sit down, and arranged the coat around her shoulders.

"You come in too," she ordered. "There's plenty of room for both... ."

And so with his arm around her waist, and his cheek touching hers they sat for awhile in silence.

Then suddenly Vane spoke. "Grey girl—I'm going away to-day."

"Going away?" She echoed the words and stared at him incredulously. "But ... but ... I thought... ."

"So did I," he returned quietly. "When I came down here yesterday I had only one thought in my mind—and that was to make you give up Baxter. I wanted it from purely selfish reasons; I wanted it because I wanted you myself... ."

"And don't you now?" Her voice was wondering.

"More—infinitely more—than I did before. But there's one thing I want even more than that—your happiness." He was staring steadily over the great stretch of open country to where Crowborough lay in the purple distance. "When you came to me last night, little Joan, I thought I should suffocate with the happiness of it. It seemed so gloriously trustful of you ... though, I must admit that idea did not come at first. You see I'm only a man; and you're a lovely girl... ." He laughed a little shortly. "I'd made up my mind to drift these next two or three days, and then when you came it seemed to be a direct answer to the problem. I didn't realise just to begin with that you weren't quite capable of thinking things out for yourself... . I didn't care, either. It was you and I—a woman and a man; it was the answer. And then you started to cry—in my arms. The strain had been too much. Gradually as you cried and clung to me, all the tearing overmastering passion went—and just a much bigger love for you came instead of it... . You see, it seemed to me that you, in your weakness last night, had placed the settlement on my shoulders... ."

"It's there now, dear man," she whispered. "I'd just got tired, tired, tired of fighting—— And last night it all seemed so clear." With her breast rising and falling quickly she stared over the hills, and Vane watched her with eyes full of love.

"I know it did—last night," he answered.

"Don't you understand," she went on after a moment, "that a woman wants to have her mind made up for her? She doesn't want arguments and points of view—she wants to be taken into a man's arms, and kissed, and beaten if necessary... . I don't know what was the matter with me last night; I only know that I was lying in bed feeling all dazed and bruised—and then suddenly I saw the way out. To come to you—and get things settled." She turned on him and her face was very tense. "You weren't—you weren't shocked," her voice was very low. "Not disgusted with me."

Vane threw back his head and laughed. "My lady," he said after a moment, "forgive my laughing. But if you could even, in your wildest dreams, imagine the absurdity of such an idea, you'd laugh too... ." Then he grew serious again, and stabbed at the ground with the point of his stick. "Do you suppose, dear, that I wouldn't sooner have taken that way out myself? Do you suppose that the temptation to take that way out isn't beating and hammering at me now? ... That's why I've got to go... ."

"What do you mean?" Her face was half-averted.

"I mean," he answered grimly, "that if I stopped at Melton to-night, I should come to your room. As I think I said before, I'm just a man, and you're a lovely girl—and I adore you. But I adore you sufficiently to run away from a temptation that I know would defeat me... ."

She turned and faced him. "And supposing I want it to defeat you?"

"Ah! don't—don't.... For the love of God—don't!" he cried, getting up and striding away. He stood with his back towards her, while a large variety of separate imps in his brain assured him that he was an unmitigated fool.

"For Heaven's sake!—take what the gods offer you," they sang. "Here in the cold light of day, where there's no question of her being overwrought, she's asking you to settle things for her. Take it, you fool, take it...."

And the god who concerned himself with that particular jig-saw among a hundred others paused for a moment and gave no heed to the ninety-nine. Then he turned over two or three pages to see what was coming, and forthwith lost interest. It is a bad thing to skip—even for a god.

Suddenly Vane felt Joan's hand on his arm, and looking down he found her at his side.

"Don't you understand, dear man?" she said. "I'm frightened of being left to decide ... just frightened to death."

"And don't you understand, dear girl," he answered, "that I'm frightened of deciding for you? If one decides wrong for oneself—well, it's one's own funeral. But if it's for somebody else—and it's their funeral...."

"Even if the other person begs you to do it?"

"Even if the other person begs one to do it," he repeated gravely. "Except that the sexes are reversed, little Joan—something much like this happened not long ago. And the woman told the man to go and make sure.... I guess she was frightened of staking everything on a sudden rush of sex. She was right." He turned to her and caught both her hands in his with a groan. "Oh! my dear —you know what you said to me last night before dinner. Sex—sex—sex; the most powerful weapon in the world—and the most transitory. And I daren't use it—I just daren't any more."

He caught her in his arms and kissed her. "I can't forget that when you decided before—you decided against me. Something has happened since then, Joan.... Last night.... It's another factor in the situation, and I don't quite know how powerful it will prove. It's too near, just at present.... It's out of focus. But clear through everything I know it wouldn't be playing the game to rush you with another—last night...."

He stared over her head, and the wind blew the tendrils of her hair against his cheek. "We've got to get last night into its proper place, grey girl," he went on after a while. "And only you can do it.... As far as I'm concerned—why there's never been any doubt.... It's just for you to decide...."

"But I don't want to decide." Her voice, a little muffled, came from his shoulder. "I want you to decide for me." Then, leaning away from him, she put both her hands on his shoulders. "Take me away, Derek—take me away with you now. Let's go and get married—just you and I and Binks—and go right away from everyone, and be alone." Once again the imps knocked tauntingly, but Vane only smiled gravely and shook his head.

"Where would the difference be, darling?" he asked. "Where would the difference be? I guess it's not a question of with or without benefit of clergy between you and me."

Her hands fell to her side wearily, and she turned away. "I suppose you're doing what you think is right, dear," she said at length. "And I can't take you and drag you to the altar, can I?"

"I'll want no dragging, little Joan, if you're of the same mind in a fortnight's time." Then suddenly he caught both her hands in his. "My dear, my dear!" he cried hoarsely; "don't you see I must give you time to make sure? I must... ."

She shook her head. "I've had too much time already, Derek. I'm frightened of time; I don't want to think... . Oh! boy, boy, don't let me think; just take me, and think for me... ."

But once again Vane smiled gravely, and shook his head. "We can't dodge it like that, my darling—we just can't... ." He bent down to pick up his coat, and the god in charge sent a casual glance in their direction, to see that matters were progressing favourably. And when he saw the little hopeless smile on the girl's face he turned to one of his pals.

"It's too easy," he remarked in a bored voice, and turned his attention to a struggling curate with four children who had married for love... .

And so that afternoon Vane acted according to his lights. Maybe it was wisdom, maybe it was folly, but the point is immaterial, for it was written in the Book of the Things that Happen.

He went, telling his host that he had found fresh orders at the Post Office that morning: and the girl waved her handkerchief at him from her bedroom window as the car went down the drive.

For one brief moment after lunch they had been alone—but she had made no further attempt to keep him. She had just kissed him once, and listened to his words of passionate love with a grave little smile. "Only a fortnight, my darling," he had told her. "But we must give it that. You must be sure." And he had been too much taken up with his own thoughts to notice the weariness in her eyes.

She said nothing to him of the unread letter lying on her dressing-table upstairs, and not till long after he had gone did she pick up the envelope and turn it over and over in her fingers. Then, at last, she opened it.

It was just in the same vein as all the letters her father was writing her at this period. Brimming over with hope and confidence and joy and pleasure; planning fresh beauties for their beloved Blandford—he always associated Joan with himself in the possession of it; scheming how she was to come and stay with him for long visits each year after she was married. It was the letter of a man who had come out of the darkness of worry into the light of safety; and as in all the others, there was the inevitable reference to the black times that were over.

Slowly the dusk came down, the shadows deepened in the great trees outside. The Downs faded into a misty blur, and at length she turned from the window. In the flickering light of the fire she threw herself face downwards on her bed. For an hour she lay there motionless, while the shadows danced merrily around her, and darkness came down outside. Just every now and then a little pitiful moan came from her lips, muffled and inarticulate from the depths of the pillow; and once a great storm of sobs shook her—sobs which drenched the old scented linen with tears. But for the most part she lay in silence with her hands clenched and rigid, and thus did she pass along the way of Pain to her Calvary... .

At six o'clock she rose and bathed her face, and powdered her nose as all normal women must do before facing an unsympathetic world, even if the torments of Hell have got them on the rack. Then with firm steps she went downstairs to the drawing-room, and found it empty. Without faltering she crossed to the piano, and took from the top of a pile of music "The Garden of Kama." She turned to the seventh song of the cycle—

"Ah! when Love comes, his wings are swift,
His ways are full of quick surprise;
'Tis well for those who have the gift
To seize him even as he flies... ."

Her eyes ran over the well-known lines, and she sat down at the piano and sang it through. She sang it as she had never sung before; she sang it as she would never sing it again. For the last note had barely died away, throbbing into silence, when Joan took the score in her hands and tore it across. She tore the pages again, and then she carried the pieces across and threw them into the fire. It was while she was pressing down the remnants with a poker that Mrs. Sutton came into the room and glanced at her in mild surprise.

"It's an old song," said Joan with a clear, ringing laugh. "One I shall never sing again. I'm tired of it... ."

And the god in charge paused for a moment, and wondered if it was worth while... .

CHAPTER XVII

"My hat!" remarked the Adjutant as Vane reported his return to the depot. "Can this thing be true? Giving up leave... ."

Vane grinned, and seated himself on the edge of the table.

"'There are more things, Horatio,'" he quoted genially.

"For the love of Pete—not that hoary motto," groaned the other. "Want a job of work?"

"My hat!" laughed Vane. "Can this thing be true? Work at the depot?"

"Try my job," grunted Vallance. "Of all the bandy-legged crowd of C3 perishers I've ever seen, this crowd fills the bill... . Why one damn fellow who's helping in the cook-house—peeling potatoes—says it gives him pains in the stummick... . Work too hard... . And in civil life he was outside porter in a goods yard." He relapsed into gloomy silence.

"What about this job?" prompted Vane.

The Adjutant lit a cigarette. "I can easily send over a subaltern, if you like," he said; "but you might find it a good trip. It's a draft for the sixth battalion in Ireland; you'll have to cross and hand 'em over in Dublin."

Vane thought for a moment and then nodded.

"I'd like it," he said. "I rather want something to do at the moment... ."

"Right, old boy. Start to-morrow. Come round about ten, and I'll give you the papers."

Vane saluted and left the orderly room. The prospect of the trip pleased him; as he had said, at the moment he wanted something to do. Though it was only the day before that he had left her, the temptation to go back to Joan—or at any rate write to her—was growing in strength. Already he was cursing himself as a fool for having acted as he had; and yet he knew that he had done right. It had to be left for her to decide... .

And if... . Vane shrugged his shoulders at the thought.

Three days later he had safely shepherded his flock across the water, and handed it over to his relief. The trip had been uneventful, save for the extraordinary feat of two of the men who had managed to become incapably drunk on Government beer; and Vane having spent a night in Dublin, and inspected the scene of the Sackville Street fighting with a sort of amazed surprise, prepared to board the S.S. "Connaught" for the return crossing.

Was it not all written in the Book of the Words?

He might have stopped for a day's cubbing—but he did not; he might have crossed the preceding evening—but he had not. He merely went on board the "Connaught," and had an early lunch, which, in all conscience, was a very normal proceeding. There were a few soldiers on board, but for the most part the passengers consisted of civilians, with a heavy percentage of women and children. There were a few expensive-looking gentlemen in fur coats, who retired early to their cabins, and whom Vane decided must be Members of Parliament. The smoking-room was occupied by a party of six young Irishmen, all of them of military age, who announced freely for the benefit of anyone who cared to listen—and it was not easy to avoid doing so—that they were Sinn Feiners. For a while Vane studied them, more to distract his own thoughts than for any interest in their opinions. It struck him that they were the exact counterpart of the new clique of humanity which has sprung up recently on this side of the Irish Sea; advanced thinkers without thought—the products of a little education without the ballast of a brain. Wild, enthusiastic in their desire for change, they know not what they want as the result of the change. Destructive without being constructive, they bemuse themselves with long words, and scorn simplicity. No scheme is too wild or lunatic for them, provided they themselves are in the limelight.... And as for the others— *qu'importe?* ... Self is their God; the ill-digested, half-understood schemes of great thinkers their food; talk their recreation. And they play overtime.... .

He opened the smoking-room door and stepped out on to the deck. For a few moments he stood still watching the water slip by, and drawing in great mouthfuls of fresh air. He felt he wanted to purge himself of the rotten atmosphere he had just left. Then with slow, measured steps he began to pace up and down the deck. The majority of the passengers were sitting muffled up in deck chairs, but, unlike the Boulogne boat, there was plenty of room to walk; and Vane was of the particular brand who always think more easily when they move.

And he wanted to think of Joan. He had not thought of much else since he had left her—but the subject never tired. He could feel her now as she had lain in his arms; he could still smell the soft fragrance of her hair. The wind was singing through the rigging, and suddenly the wonder of her came over him in a great wave and he stared over the grey sea with shining eyes.

After a while he tapped out his pipe, and prepared to fill it again. It was as he stood, with his tobacco pouch open in his hand, that something in the sea attracted his attention. He grew rigid, and stared at it—and at the same moment a frantic ringing of the engine-room bell showed that the officer on the bridge had seen it too. Simultaneously everyone seemed to become aware that something was wrong—and for a brief second almost a panic occurred. The ship was swinging to port, but Vane realised that it was hopeless: the torpedo must get them. And the sea-gulls circling round the boat shrieked discordantly at him…. He took a grip of the rail, and braced himself to meet the shock. Involuntarily he closed his eyes—the devil … it was worse than a crump—you could hear that coming—and this….

"Quick—get it over." He did not know he had spoken … and then it came…. There was a great rending explosion—curiously muffled, Vane thought, compared with a shell. But it seemed so infinitely more powerful and destructive; like the upheaval of some great monster, slow and almost dignified compared with the snapping fury of a smaller beast. It seemed as if the very bowels of the earth had shaken themselves and irrupted.

The ship staggered and shook like a stricken thing, and Vane opened his eyes. Already she was beginning to list a little, and he saw the gaping hole in her side, around which floated an indescribable litter of small objects and bits of wood. The torpedo had hit her forward, but with the headway she still had the vessel drifted on, and the litter of débris came directly underneath Vane. With a sudden narrowing of his eyes, he saw what was left of a girl turning slowly over and over in the still seething water.

Then he turned round and looked at the scene on deck. The crew were going about their job in perfect silence, and amongst the passengers a sort of stunned apathy prevailed. The thing had been so sudden, that most of them as yet hardly realised what had happened.

He saw one man—a funny little, pimply man with spectacles, of the type he would have expected to wring his hands and wail—take off his boots with the utmost composure, and place them neatly side by side on the deck.

Then a large, healthy individual in a fur coat came past him demanding to see the Captain, and protesting angrily when he was told to go to hell.

"It's preposterous, sir," he said to Vane; "absolutely preposterous. I insist on seeing the Captain…."

"Don't be more of a fool than you can help," answered Vane rudely. "It's not the Captain's 'At home' day… ."

And once again it struck him as it had so often struck him in France, what an impossible thing it is to guess beforehand how danger will affect different men. A woman beside him was crying quietly, and endeavouring to soothe a little boy who clung to her with wide-open, frightened eyes… .

"Do you think there's any danger, sir?" She turned to Vane and looked at him imploringly.

"I hope not," he answered reassuringly. "There should be enough boats to go round.... Ah! look—there is the swine."

Rolling a little, and just awash, the conning tower of the submarine showed up out of the sea about half a mile away, and suddenly Vane heard a voice beside him cursing it bitterly and childishly. He turned, to find one of the smoking-room patriots shaking his fist at it, while the weak tears of rage poured down his face. Afterwards, on thinking the experience over, Vane decided that that one spectacle had made it almost worth while.... .

Two boats were pulling away from the ship, which had already begun to settle by the bows, and two more were in the process of being launched, when the Hun lived up to his rightful reputation. There are times when one is nauseated and sickened by the revolting cant of a repentant Germany; by the hypocritical humbug that, at heart, the German is a peace-loving, gentle being who has been led away by those above him. And as Vane watched grimly the path of the second, and so unnecessary torpedo, he felt an overmastering longing that some of the up-holders of the doctrine could be on board.

The "Connaught" was done for; that much was obvious to the veriest land-lubber. And the second torpedo could have but one purpose—the wanton destruction of so many more helpless women. Besides, it revolted his sense of sport; it was like blowing a sitting bird to pieces with a shot gun.... .

He saw it strike amidships; he had a fleeting vision of a screaming, struggling boat load—of curses and shouts, and then he knew no more. There was a roaring in his ears, and he seemed to be travelling through great spaces. Lights danced and flashed before his brain, and suddenly he felt very cold. The noise had ceased, and everything was very still and silent.... . The cold grew more intense, till it seemed to eat into him, and his head grew curiously light. Almost as if it was bursting with some unaccustomed pressure. Then, just as it seemed as if it was the end, and that his skull would literally fly to pieces, relief came with a great rush, and Vane found himself gasping and blowing on the surface of the water. Around him was a mass of débris, and instinctively he struck out for a deck chair that was floating close by. He reached it, and for a long time he clutched it, with only his head out of the water—content to draw great gulps of the air into his panting lungs. Then after a while he raised himself in the water and looked round.

About fifty yards away the "Connaught" was sinking rapidly, and Vane wondered feebly how he had got where he was. People were still struggling and scrambling over her slanting decks, and he watched a man slashing with a knife at the falls of a partially filled boat.

He heard a voice cursing the man for a fool, and wondered who it was who spoke. Then the boat crashed downwards stern first, shooting its load into the water, and the same voice croaked, "I told you so, you bloody fool. I told you so." It was then he realised that the voice was his own... .

Vane closed his eyes, and tried to think. Presumably the wireless messenger had sent out an S.O.S.; presumably, in time, someone would arrive on the scene. Until that happened he must concentrate on saving himself. His head was still swimming from the force of the explosion, and for a long while he lay supporting himself mechanically on the half-submerged chair. Then he felt that he was moving, and opening his eyes he realised that the ship had disappeared. Very soon the suction stopped, and he found himself alone on the grey, sullen water. In the distance, bobbing up and down on the short swell, he could see half a dozen boats; but close at hand there was nothing save the flotsam and wreckage from the ship. The submarine, as far as he could tell, had disappeared; at any rate, he was too low in the water to see her. After a while the ship's boats, too, pulled out of sight, and for the first time Vane began to feel afraid. What if the S.O.S. was not answered? What if only the boats were picked up, and he was never found? ...

An overwhelming panic seized him and he commenced to shout—a puny little noise lost in the vastness around him, and drowned by the shrieking of a countless swarm of gulls, that fought over the prize that had come to them. Then with a great effort he pulled himself together. He must keep his head and save his strength—he must... . Any boat coming up would be attracted to the scene of the disaster by the gulls, he repeated to himself over and over again—and then they would see him.

He took a fresh grip of the chair and swam a few strokes to keep warm. That was the next point that came into his mind—how long could he last before, numbed with the cold, his grip on the chair would relax and he would only have his life-belt to rely on? He must not get cold, he must swim steadily and quietly to keep up his circulation—always keeping near the gulls. He argued it out carefully in his mind, unconsciously talking aloud, and when he had decided what he was going to do he nodded his head in complete agreement. And then he laughed—a strange, croaking laugh and apostrophised a gull which was circling above his head. "How damn funny, old bird," he said still chuckling; "how damn funny... ." The humour of the situation had struck him suddenly. After the long years in France to be drowned like a bally hen inside a coop! ...

Undoubtedly a man clinging to a deck chair did look rather like a hen in a coop—a bedraggled hen, most certainly, very bedraggled. Not at all the sort of hen that should be dished up at the Carlton or the Savoy for dinner. A cheap and nasty hen, Vane decided... .

A splash of water hit him in the mouth and made him splutter and cough. "Pull yourself together, man," he cried fiercely; "for God's sake, pull yourself together!" He realised that his mind had been wandering; he realised that that way lay Death. He started to swim steadily, keeping near the main mass of wreckage, and pushing the chair in front of him. Several times they bumped into things, and once Vane found himself looking through the bars of the back of the chair at something which rolled and sogged in the water. And then it half turned, and he saw it was a woman. Some of her hair, sodden and matted, came through the openings of his chair, and he watched the floating tendrils uncomprehendingly for a while. Dead ... of course, she was dead ... with the water splashing ceaselessly over her face... . At peace; she had chucked her hand in—given up the useless struggle.

What chance was there anyway of a boat coming in time? What a fool he was to go on, when he felt so tired and so cold? ... That woman did not mind—the one lying there in the water so close to him. She was perfectly happy ... while he was numb and exhausted. Why not just lie on the water and go to sleep? ... He would keep the woman company, and he would be happy just like her, instead of having to force his frozen hands to hold that cursed slippery wood... .

And Joan would be happy, because she would have saved Blandford; and Baxter, damn him, he would be happy; and the whole blessed outfit would be happy as well as him when he had just dropped on to sleep... .

He would never have done as a husband for Margaret; the idea was ridiculous. Imagine sitting down and writing a book, while she took the pennies at the door—or did he have to take the pennies? Anyway, this settled the matter, and saved him the trouble of explanation. He loathed explanations; all he wanted was peace and quiet and rest... .

What a farce it all was; man thinking he could struggle against science. Science ruled the universe—aeroplanes, gas, torpedoes. And it served men right for inventing them; they should have been more careful. The smile on the dead German airman's face, as he lay on the ground near Poperinghe, floated before him, and he nodded his head portentously.

"You're right, old bean," he croaked. "The man I want to meet is the fool who doesn't think it's funny ... ."

And then Vane crossed the Valley of the Shadow, as far as a man may cross and yet return. Strange figures crowded around him hemming him in on every side. The Boche whose brains he had blown out near Arras was there with his shattered skull, holding out a hand of greeting—and Baxter, grinning sardonically. Margaret—with a wealth of pity and love shining on her face, and Joan with her grey eyes faintly mocking … . And his tailor with the wart on his nose, and Mrs. Green, and Binks… . They were all there, and then gradually they faded into the great darkness… . Everything was growing still, and peaceful—the rest he wanted had come.

Then suddenly they came back again—the Boche and Baxter and the rest of them—and started pulling him about. He cursed and swore at them, but they paid no heed; and soon the agony he was suffering became almost unbearable. In God's name, why could not they leave him alone? … He raved at them, and sobbed, but it was of no avail. They went on inexorably and the creaking of the oars in the rowlocks of the boat that had picked him up seemed to him to be the creaking of his arms and legs… .

CHAPTER XVIII

When Vane opened his eyes on reality again, he found himself in a strange room. For a few moments he lay very still, groping back into a half-world of grey shadows. He remembered the first torpedo, and then the second one; but after that things seemed confused. A man opened the door, and came over to his bed.

"Feeling better?" he remarked with a smile.

"As far as I can make out at the moment," said Vane, "I'm feeling perfectly well. Where am I, and what happened? …"

"You're in a private hospital not far from Liverpool," answered the man. "You were very nearly drowned in the 'Connaught,' and you've had a nasty knock on the head as well…. Feel at all muzzy now?"

"Not a bit," said Vane, raising himself on his elbow. "I hope they caught the swine."

"There was a rumour three or four days ago that they had."

Vane stared at the speaker. "What did you say?" he remarked at length.

"There was a rumour three or four days ago that the submarine was sunk," repeated the other.

"May I ask how long I've been here?"

"Ten days," answered the doctor. "But I wired to your depot that you were safe, so you needn't worry."

"With regard to the depot," remarked Vane grimly, "you may take it from me that I don't…. Ten days … twelve—fourteen." He was counting on his fingers. "Oh! Hell…."

"They forwarded some letters for you," said the doctor. "I'll get them for you…."

"Thanks," said Vane. "When is the next train to London?"

"In about four days' time as far as you're concerned," laughed the other.

He went out of the room, and Vane lay very still. Fourteen days….
Fourteen days….

The doctor returned and handed him about a dozen letters.

"They've been coming at intervals," he remarked. "I'm going to send you up a cup of bovril in a minute... ."

Vane turned them over rapidly in his hand, and found that there were only two that counted. He looked at the postmarks to get them in the right sequence, and eagerly pulled out the contents of the first. It had been written four days after he left Melton.

"Dear lad, I'm leaving here to-morrow, and am going back to Blandford; but before I go I want to tell you something. A man is not a very good judge of a woman's actions at any time; he's so apt to see them through his own eyes. He reasons, and becomes logical, ... and perhaps he's right. But a woman doesn't want reasons or logic—not if she's in love. She wants to be whirled up breathlessly and carried away, and made to do things; and it doesn't matter whether they're right or wrong—not if she's in love. Maybe you were right, Derek, to go away; but oh! my dear, I would to God you hadn't."

A nurse came in with a cup of bovril, and put it on the table by his bed, and Vane turned to her abruptly.

"Where are my clothes, Nurse?"

"You'll not be wanting clothes yet awhile," she answered with a smile. "I'm coming back shortly to tidy you up," and Vane cursed under his breath as she left the room.

Then he picked up the second letter and opened it. At first he thought it was a blank sheet of paper, and then he saw that there were a few words in the centre of the page. For a moment they danced before his eyes; then he pulled himself together and read them.

"'Tis well for those who have the gift
  To seize him even as he flies... .'

"Oh! you fool—you fool! Why didn't you?"

That was all, and for a long while he lay and stared at the bare wall opposite.

"Why didn't you?" The words mocked him, dancing in great red letters on the pale green distemper, and he shook his feet at them childishly.

"It's not fair," he raved. "It's simply not fair."

And the god in charge took a glance into the room, though to the man in bed it was merely a ray from a watery sun with the little specks of dust dancing and floating in it.

"Of no more account than a bit of dirt," he muttered cynically. "It wasn't my fault... . I never asked to be torpedoed. I only did what I thought was right." He buried his head in his hands with a groan.

The nurse came once more into the room, and eyed him reproachfully. "The bovril is quite cold," she said picking it up. "That's very naughty of you... ."

He looked at her and started to laugh. "I'm a very naughty man, Nurse. But for all that you've got to do something for me. No—take away that awful basin and sponge... . I don't mind if I am dirty... . You've got to go and bring the doctor here, and you've got to get my clothes. And between us, Nurse, we'll cheat 'em yet."

"Cheat whom?" she asked soothingly.

"The blind, malignant imps that control us wretched humans," he answered. "For Heaven's sake! my dear woman, do what I say. I'm not light-headed, believe me."

And the nurse being a stoical and unimaginative lady, it was just as well that, at that moment, the doctor entered the room. For had she murmured in her best bedside manner... . "That's quite all right. Just a nice wash, and then we'll go to sleep," there is but little doubt that a cup of cold bovril would have deluged her ample form. As it was the catastrophe was averted, and Vane turned to the doctor with a sigh of relief.

"May I have a word with you alone, Doctor?" he said. "And, Nurse, would you get my clothes for me?"

"Doctor," he went on as the door closed behind her. "I've got to go—at once."

"My dear fellow," began the other, but Vane silenced him with a wave of his hand.

"I may have had concussion; I may have been nearly drowned. I may be the fool emperor for wanting to get up," he continued quietly. "But it's got to be done. You see, I'm having a bit of a tussle with ..." he paused for a moment as if at a loss for a word, and then added whimsically, "with the Powers that run things. And," savagely, "I'll be damned if they're going to have a walk over... ."

The doctor eyed him gravely for a few moments without replying.

"You oughtn't to get up yet," he said at length.

"But you'll let me," cried Vane.

"There's a good train in two hours," replied the other briefly. "And the result be upon your own head... ."

Vane opened the remainder of his letters on the way up to London. He felt a little dazed and weak, though otherwise perfectly fit, and when he had glanced through them, he stared out of the window at the landscape flashing past. They were passing through the Black Country, and it seemed to him to be in keeping with his thoughts—dour, relentless, grim. The smouldering blast-furnaces, the tall, blackened chimneys, the miles of dingy, squalid houses, all mocked the efforts of their makers to escape.

"You fashioned us," they jeered; "out of your brains we were born, and now you shall serve us evermore.... You cannot—you shall not escape...."

To Vane it was all the voice of Fate. "You cannot—you shall not escape. What is to be—is to be; and your puny efforts will not alter a single letter in the book...."

And yet of his own free will he had left Joan; he had brought it on himself.

"What if I had done as she wished?" he demanded aloud. "What would you have done then, you swine?"

But there is no answer in this world to the Might-have-been; only silence and imagination, which, at times, is very merciless.

He stepped out of the train at Euston and drove straight to his rooms. For the first time in his life he took no notice of Binks, and that worthy, knowing that something was wrong, just sat in his basket and waited. Perhaps later he'd be able to help somehow....

"The young lady who came to tea was round here four or five days ago, Mr. Vane," said Mrs. Green, when she had set a match to the fire.

Vane sat very still. "And what did she want, Mrs. Green?"

"To see you, sir. She said that she had rung up the depot, and the man who answered said you were on leave...."

"He would," said Vane, grimly.

"So she came here," Mrs. Green paused, and watched him with a motherly eye; then she busied herself needlessly over the fire. "I found her with Binks in her arms—and she seemed just miserable. 'Oh! can't you tell me where he is, Mrs. Green?' she said. 'I can't, my dear,' said I, 'for I don't know myself ....' And then she picked up a piece of paper and wrote a few words on it, and sealed it up, and addressed it to you at Murchester...."

"Ah!" said Vane quietly. "She wrote it here, did she?" He laughed a short, bitter laugh. "She was right, Mrs. Green. I had the game in my hands, and I chucked it away." He rose and stared grimly at the houses opposite. "Did she say by any chance where she was staying?"

"Ashley Gardens, she said; and if you came in, I was to let you know."

"Thank you, Mrs. Green." He turned round at length, and took up the telephone book. "You might let me have some tea... ."

The worthy woman bustled out of the room, shaking her head. Like Binks, she knew that something was very wrong; but the consolation of sitting in a basket and waiting for the clouds to roll by was denied her. For the Humans have to plot and contrive and worry, whatever happens... .

"Is that Lady Auldfearn's?" Vane took the telephone off the table. "Oh! Lady Auldfearn speaking? I'm Captain Vane... . Is Miss Devereux stopping with you? Just left yesterday, you say... . Yes—I rather wanted to see her. Going to be where? At the Mainwarings' dance to-night. Thank you. But you don't know where she is at present... ."

He hung up the receiver, and sat back in his chair, with a frown. Then suddenly a thought struck him, and he pulled the letters he had received that morning out of his pocket. He extracted one in Nancy Smallwood's sprawling handwriting, and glanced through it again to make sure.

"Dine 8 o'clock—and go on to Mainwarings' dance afterwards... . Do come, if you can... ."

Vane, placing it on the table in front of him, bowed to it profoundly. "We might," he remarked to Binks, "almost have it framed."

And Binks' quivering tail assented, with a series of thumps against his basket.

"I hope you won't find your dinner partner too dreadful." Nancy Smallwood was shooting little bird-like glances round the room as she greeted Vane that evening. "She has a mission ... or two. Keeps soldiers from drinking too much and getting into bad hands. Personally, anything—*anything* would be better than getting into hers."

"I seem," murmured Vane, "to have fallen on my feet. She isn't that gargantuan woman in purple, is she?"

"My dear boy! That's George's mother. You know my husband. No, there she is—the wizened up one in black... . And she's going on to the Mainwarings' too—so you'll have to dance with her."

At any other time Vane might have extracted some humour from his neighbour, but to-night, in the mood he was, she seemed typical of all that was utterly futile. She jarred his nerves till it was all he could do to reply politely to her ceaseless "We are doing this, and we decided that." To her the war had given an opportunity for self-expression which she had hitherto been denied. Dreadful as she undoubtedly thought it with one side of her nature, with another it made her almost happy. It had enabled her to force herself into the scheme of things; from being a nonentity, she had made herself a person with a mission.... .

True, the doings and the decisions on which she harped continually were for the benefit of the men he had led. But to this woman it was not the men that counted most. They had to fit into the decisions; not the decisions into them...
.

They were inexorable, even as the laws of the Medes and Persians. And who was this wretched woman, to lay down the law? What did she know; what did she understand?

"And so we decided that we must really stop it. People were beginning to complain; and we had one or two—er—regrettable scandals."

With a start Vane woke up from his reverie and realised he had no idea what she was talking about.

"Indeed," he murmured. "Have a salted almond?"

"Don't you think we were right, Captain Vane?" she pursued inexorably. "The men are exposed to so many temptations that the least we can do is to remove those we can."

"But are they exposed to any more now than they were before?" he remarked wearily. "Why not let 'em alone, dear lady, let 'em alone? They deserve it."

At length the ladies rose, and with a sigh of relief Vane sat down next a lawyer whom he knew well.

"You're looking pretty rotten, Derek," he said, looking at Vane critically.

"I've been dining next a woman with a mission," he answered. "And I was nearly drowned in the 'Connaught.'"

The lawyer looked at him keenly. "And the two combined have finished you off."

"Oh! no. I'm reserving my final effort for the third. I'll get that at the Mainwarings'." He lifted his glass and let the ruby light glint through his port. "Why do we struggle, Jimmy? Why, in Heaven's name, does anybody ever do anything but drift? Look at that damned foolishness over the water.... . The most titanic struggle of the world. And look at the result.... . Anarchy, rebellion, strife. What's the use; tell me that, my friend, what's the use? And the little struggles—the personal human struggles—are just as futile... ."

The lawyer thoughtfully lit a cigarette. "It's not only you fellows out there, Derek," he said, "who are feeling that way. We're all of us on the jump, and we're all of us bottling it up. The result is a trial such as we had the other day, with witnesses and judge screaming at each other, and dignity trampled in the mud. Every soul in England read the case—generally twice—before anything else. You could see 'em all in the train—coming up to business—with the sheet on which it was reported carefully taken out of its proper place and put in the centre of the paper so that they could pretend they were reading the war news."

Vane laughed. "We were better than that. We took it, naked and unashamed, in order of seniority. And no one was allowed to read any tit-bit out loud for fear of spoiling it for the next man."

Jimmy Charters laughed shortly. "We're just nervy, and sensationalism helps. It takes one out of one's self for a moment; one forgets."

"And the result is mud flung at someone, some class. No matter whether it's true; no matter whether it's advisable—it's mud. And it sticks alike to the just and the unjust; while the world looks on and sneers; and over the water, the men look on and—die."

George Smallwood was pushing back his chair. "Come on, you fellows. The Cuthberts will advance from their funk-holes." ... He led the way towards the door, and Vane rose.

"Don't pay any attention to what I've been saying, Jimmy." The lawyer was strolling beside him. "It's liver; I'll take a dose of salts in the morning."

Jimmy Charters looked at him in silence for a moment.

"I don't know what the particular worry is at the moment, old man," he said at length, "but don't let go. I'm no sky pilot, but I guess that somewhere up topsides there's a Big Controller Who understands.... Only at times the pattern is a bit hard to follow...."

Vane laughed hardly. "It's likely to be when the fret-saw slips."

Vane strolled into the ballroom and glanced round, but there was no sign of Joan; and then he saw that there was another, smaller, room leading off the principal one where dancing seemed to be in progress also. He walked towards it, and as he came to the door he stopped abruptly and his eyes narrowed. In the middle of it Joan was giving an exhibition dance, supported by a youth in the Flying Corps.

The audience seated round the sides of the room was applauding vociferously, and urging the dancers on to greater efforts. And then suddenly Joan broke away from her partner and danced alone, while Vane leaned against the door with his jaw set in a straight, hard line. Once his eyes travelled round the faces of the men who were looking on, and his fists clenched at his sides.

There was one elderly man in particular, with protruding eyes, who roused in him a perfect fury of rage... .

It was a wild, daring exhibition—a mass of swirling draperies and grey silk stockings. More, it was a wonderful exhibition. She was dancing with a reckless abandon which gradually turned to sheer devilry, and she began to circle the room close to the guests who lined the walls. There were two men in front of Vane, and as she came near the door he pushed forward a little so that he came in full view. For the moment he thought she was going to pass without seeing him, and then their eyes met. She paused and faltered, and then swinging round sank gracefully to the floor in the approved style of curtsey to show she had finished.

The spectators clamoured wildly for an encore, but she rose and came straight up to Vane.

"Where have you been?" she said.

"Unconscious in hospital for ten days," he answered grimly. "I went down in the 'Connaught.' ... May I congratulate you on your delightful performance?"

For a second or two he thought she was going to faint, and instinctively he put out his arm to hold her. Then the colour came back to her face again, and she put her arm through his.

"I want something to eat. Take me, please... . No, no, my dear people, no more," as a throng of guests came round her. "I require food."

Her hand on his arm pushed Vane forward and obediently he led her across the ballroom.

"If there's any champagne get me a glass," she said, sitting down at a table. "And a sandwich... ."

Obediently Vane fetched what she desired; then he sat down opposite her.

"The fortnight is up," he said quietly. "I have come for my answer."

"Did you get my letters?" she asked slowly.

"Both. When I came to this morning. And I wasn't going to be called a fool for nothing, my lady—so I got up and came to look for you. What of the excellent Baxter? Is the date for your wedding fixed?"

She looked at him in silence for a moment, and then she began to laugh. "The ceremony in church takes place on his return from France in a week's time."

"Oh! no, it doesn't," said Vane grimly. "However, we will let that pass. May I ask if your entertainment to-night was indicative of the joy you feel at the prospect?"

She started to laugh again, and there was an ugly sound in it. A woman at the next table was looking at her curiously.

"Stop that, Joan," he said in a low, insistent voice. "For God's sake, pull yourself together... ."

She stopped at once, and only the ceaseless twisting of her handkerchief between her fingers betrayed her.

"I suppose it wouldn't do to go into a fit of high strikes," she said in a voice she strove vainly to keep steady. "The Mainwarings might think it was their champagne—or the early symptoms of 'flu—or unrequited love... . And they are so very respectable aren't they?—the Mainwarings, I mean?"

Vane looked at her gravely. "Don't speak for a bit. I'll get you another glass of champagne... ."

But Joan rose. "I don't want it," she said. "Take me somewhere where we can talk." She laid the tips of her fingers on his arm. "Talk, my friend, for the last time... ."

"I'm damned if it is," he muttered between his clenched teeth.

She made no answer; and in silence he found two chairs in a secluded corner behind a screen.

"So you went down in the 'Connaught,' did you?" Her voice was quite calm.

"I did. Hence my silence."

"And would you have answered my first letter, had you received it?"

Vane thought for a moment before answering. "Perhaps," he said at length. "I wanted you to decide... . But," grimly, "I'd have answered the second before now if I'd had it... ."

"I wrote that in your rooms after I'd come up from Blandford," she remarked, with her eyes still fixed on him.

"So I gathered from Mrs. Green... . My dear, surely you must have known something had happened." He took one of her hands in his, and it lay there lifeless and inert.

"I thought you were being quixotic," she said. "Trying to do the right thing— And I was tired ... my God! but I was tired." She swayed towards him, and in her eyes there was despair. "Why did you let me go, my man—why did you let me go?"

"But I haven't, my lady," he answered in a wondering voice. "To-morrow... ." She put her hand over his mouth with a little half-stifled groan. "Just take me in your arms and kiss me," she whispered.

And it seemed to Vane that his whole soul went out of him as he felt her lips on his.

Then she leaned back in her chair and looked at him gravely. "I wonder if you'll understand. I wonder still more if you'll forgive. Since you wouldn't settle things for me I had to settle them for myself... ."

Vane felt himself growing rigid.

"I settled them for myself," she continued steadily, "or rather they settled me for themselves. I tried to make you see I was afraid, you know ... and you wouldn't."

"What are you driving at?" he said hoarsely.

"I am marrying Henry Baxter in church in about a week; I married him in a registry office the day he left for France."

EPILOGUE

A grey mist was blowing up the valley from Cromarty Firth. It hid the low hills that flanked the little branch railway line, slowly and imperceptibly drifting and eddying through the brown trees on their slopes. Down in London a world had gone mad—but the mist took no heed of such foolishness. Lines of men and women, linked arm-in-arm, were promenading Piccadilly to celebrate the End of the Madness; shrieking parties were driving to Wimbledon, or Limehouse, or up and down Bond Street in overweighted taxis, but the mist rolled on silently and inexorably. It took account of none of these things.

Since the beginning a mist such as this one had drifted up the valley from the open sea; until the end it would continue.... It was part of the Laws of Nature, and the man who watched it coming turned with a little shudder.

In front of him, the moors stretched brown and rugged till they lost themselves in the snow-capped hills. Here and there the bogland showed a darker tint, and at his feet, cupped out in the smooth greystone, lay a sheet of water. It was dark and evil-looking, and every now and then a puff of wind eddied down from the hills and ruffled the smooth surface.

The colours of the moors were sombre and dark; and below the snows far away in the heart of Ross-shire it seemed to the man who watched with brooding eyes that it was as the blackness of night. A deserted dead world, with a cold grey shroud, to hide its nakedness.

He shivered again, and wiped the moisture from his face, while a terrier beside him crept nearer for comfort.

And then came the change. Swiftly, triumphantly, the sun caught the mist and rolled it away. One by one the rugged lines of hills came into being again— one by one they shouted, "We are free, behold us... ."

The first was a delicate brown, and just behind it a little peak of violet loomed up. Away still further the browns grew darker, more rich—the violets became a wondrous purple. And the black underneath the snows seemed to be of the richest velvet.

The pond at the man's feet glinted a turquoise blue; the bogland shone silver in the sunlight. And then, to crown it all, the smooth snow slopes in the distance glowed pink and orange, where before they had been white and cold.

For Life had come to a Land of Death.

Gradually the brooding look on the man's face faded, a gleam of whimsical humour shone in his eyes. He took an old briar out of his pocket and commenced to fill it; and soon the blue smoke was curling lazily upwards into the still air. But he still stood motionless, staring over the moors, his hands deep in the pockets of the old shooting coat he wore.

Suddenly he threw back his head and laughed; then almost unconsciously he stretched out his arms to the setting sun.

"Thank you," he cried, and with a swift whirring of wings two grouse rose near by and shot like brown streaks over the silver tarn. "Sooner or later the mist always goes... ."

He tapped out the ashes of his pipe, and put it back in his pocket. And as he straightened himself up, of a sudden it seemed to the man that the mountains and the moors, the tarn and the bogland approved of the change in him, and, finding him worthy, told him their message.

"The Sun will always triumph," they cried in a mighty chorus. "Sooner or later the mist will always go."

For a space the man stood there, while the sun, sinking lower and lower, bathed the world in glory. Then, he whistled... .

"Your last walk on the moors, Binks, old man, so come on. To-morrow we go back."

And with a terrier scurrying madly through the heather around him, the man strode forward.

Lightning Source UK Ltd.
Milton Keynes UK
UKHW010635240820
368739UK00001B/228